P9-DZZ-406

RAVES FOR
JAMES PATTERSON

"Patterson knows where our deepest fears are buried...
There's no stopping his imagination."
—*New York Times Book Review*

"James Patterson writes his thrillers as if he were building roller coasters." —Associated Press

"No one gets this big without natural storytelling talent—
which is what James Patterson has, in spades."
—Lee Child, #1 *New York Times* bestselling
author of the Jack Reacher series

"James Patterson knows how to sell thrills and suspense
in clear, unwavering prose." —*People*

"Patterson boils a scene down to a single, telling detail, the
element that defines a character or moves a plot along. It's
what fires off the movie projector in the reader's mind."
—Michael Connelly

"James Patterson is the boss. End of."
—Ian Rankin, *New York Times* bestselling
author of the Inspector Rebus series

"James Patterson is the gold standard by which all others are judged."

—Steve Berry, #1 bestselling author
of the Cotton Malone series

"The prolific Patterson seems unstoppable."

—*USA Today*

"Patterson is in a class by himself."

—*Vanity Fair*

CIRCLE OF
DEATH

For a complete list of books, visit JamesPatterson.com.

CIRCLE OF DEATH

JAMES PATTERSON

AND BRIAN SITTS

GRAND
CENTRAL

NEW YORK   BOSTON

The characters and events in this book are fictitious. Any similarity to real persons, living or dead, is coincidental and not intended by the author.

Copyright © 2023 by James Patterson

In association with Conde Nast and Neil McGinness

Hachette Book Group supports the right to free expression and the value of copyright. The purpose of copyright is to encourage writers and artists to produce the creative works that enrich our culture.

The scanning, uploading, and distribution of this book without permission is a theft of the author's intellectual property. If you would like permission to use material from the book (other than for review purposes), please contact permissions@hbgusa.com. Thank you for your support of the author's rights.

Grand Central Publishing
Hachette Book Group
1290 Avenue of the Americas, New York, NY 10104
grandcentralpublishing.com
@grandcentralpub

Originally published in trade paperback and ebook in July 2023
First oversize mass market edition: February 2024

Grand Central Publishing is a division of Hachette Book Group, Inc.
The Grand Central Publishing name and logo is a trademark of Hachette Book Group, Inc.

The publisher is not responsible for websites (or their content) that are not owned by the publisher.

The Hachette Speakers Bureau provides a wide range of authors for speaking events. To find out more, go to hachettespeakersbureau.com or email HachetteSpeakers@hbgusa.com.

Grand Central Publishing books may be purchased in bulk for business, educational, or promotional use. For information, please contact your local bookseller or the Hachette Book Group Special Markets Department at special.markets@hbgusa.com.

ISBNs: 9781538711125 (oversize mass market), 9781538711132 (ebook)

Printed in the United States of America

OPM

10 9 8 7 6 5 4 3 2 1

NEW YORK CITY
2088

ONE

I'M TELLING THE story like it happened just last night. That's how it feels to me. Even with the distance of all these years, parts of it still seem incredible. But it was totally real. All of it.

It was early 1933. New York City was being menaced by an army of bloodsucking killers. I know it sounds strange when I say it out loud, but that's the only way to describe what was going on. They weren't vampires or zombies. Nothing supernatural. They were poverty-stricken young men under the control of a demented doctor. Rodil Mocquino was his name. This guy had taken medical hypnosis to a criminal level. He'd gotten to the point where he could turn ordinary men into murderers, and make them kill on command.

The killers only moved by night, which made them even more horrifying, and they traveled in a pack, which made them even more dangerous. Some people thought they had super-human strength or magical abilities, but it was really just mindless stamina. Nothing could stop them. If you saw the gang from a distance, you had a chance to escape. Maybe. But once they got close, you were dead. Simple as that.

A few years after, somebody wrote a novel about Moc-quino and his killers. It was called *The Voodoo Master*. It was really popular at the time—a bestseller—but they got a lot of stuff wrong. I should know. After all, I'm the real Lamont Cranston, which makes me the real Shadow. And I *lived* it.

Here's the real story.

I was living uptown. Like most nights, my girlfriend, Margo Lane, was staying over. She was my business partner, my confidant, and the person I loved and trusted more than anybody else in the world. Margo was smart and levelheaded. She thought I sometimes went off half-cocked. And she was right. I didn't always think things through.

We'd both been hearing and reading about the maniacal bloodsuckers for weeks, and the NYPD seemed to be powerless against them. The whole city was paralyzed with fear, and the killings just wouldn't stop.

I knew it was time for the Shadow to go into action. I had to find these bloodsuckers and *end* them once and for all. If not me, who? When I heard a report of another killing, I decided to do it. That night. By myself.

Margo and I had a fight about it. She thought I was being reckless again. But pretty soon she realized she couldn't talk me out of going. She hugged me at the door. "Be careful," she said. "I'll be waiting up for you."

"In that case," I said, "I'll be *extra* careful." I kissed her good-bye and headed out into the dark alone. I was trying to keep it light with Margo. I *hoped* I'd be back.

But I knew it wasn't a sure thing.

TWO

THE MOST RECENT victims had been found in a park on the Upper West Side of Manhattan. So why was I heading downtown? Pure instinct. People used to say *"The Shadow knows,"* and sometimes I actually did. At least I made some educated guesses.

I figured that an army of bloodsuckers would need a place to hide and regroup. So I headed for a part of the city with a lot of big, empty buildings.

The waterfront.

In that era, the Lower West Side of Manhattan was filled with docks and warehouses. That's where the big White Star ocean liners came in, and where cargo ships loaded and unloaded. Depending on the season, warehouses would fill up and then go empty. Sometimes companies went bust and spaces would stay vacant for months. Even in normal times, the waterfront was a rough area. Nobody in their right mind would go down there at night. But like I said, I had problems with impulse control.

I was invisible now. At that point in my life, it was the only super power I had. When I reached the waterfront,

I crept along the row of warehouses, trying not to step on a loose plank or a wharf rat. At the end of the row, I saw a huge warehouse with its loading bay partway open. There was a glow from inside, like the flicker from a wood-fired stove. And I could see shapes moving against the back wall. Maybe dock workers on the night shift, I thought at first. But my gut told me it was something else. A chill shot right through me.

As I got closer to the open door, the smell hit me. It was the smell of unwashed humans. Musty. Sour. Sickening. I stepped into the open doorway, and there they were—cadaverous, dull-eyed bloodsuckers. *Dozens* of them! Some were slouched against the wall; others were lying on the floor in some kind of stupor. Their clothes were tattered, and stained with patches of dried blood.

I was pretty good with my fists, but against those odds, I knew that starting a fight would be suicide. For a second, I thought about knocking over the stove, bolting the door, and burning the whole place down with the killers inside. But I worried that the fire would spread to the rest of the waterfront.

So I decided to turn myself into bait.

I made myself visible.

The second I rematerialized, the bloodsuckers rose up and started to come for me. They made low, guttural howls—a sound I'll never forget. I backed out of the doorway and ran. I figured that would trigger some primal pursuit response, and it did. As I headed for the docks, I looked over my shoulder. They came as a pack, lumbering like animals. Their eyes were fixed on me, like I was their favorite prey. So far, so good. My pulse was racing. My plan was working.

I stepped onto one of the main piers. It stretched for two hundred yards into the Hudson River. The pack followed. As long as I held the attention of the few at the head of the crowd, the rest kept following. That was the way they'd been trained—or programmed. They moved like a single organism.

I started running toward the end of the pier, faster and faster. I could hear footsteps pounding on the planks behind me. When I ran out of pier, I did a brave or stupid thing.

I dove off.

As soon as I hit the black water, I doubled back and slipped underneath the pier. I grabbed a piling and watched as the bloodsuckers tumbled off the end. They sank like weighted sacks. I figured they'd be too dazed or demented to swim. A few bubbles rose up. I saw thrashing underneath. Then the water was still. Thank God! My Pied Piper act had worked.

I climbed back onto the dock. I was soaked and exhausted, but relieved. It was over.

Then I heard splashing.

THREE

I LOOKED BACK toward the river. The water was frothing. An arm stretched out from underneath. Then another. And another! As I watched, the damned bloodsuckers rose up, spitting out water and crawling over one another to get back to the dock. They swarmed up the pilings and grabbed the thick metal cleats.

I needed a new plan. Fast.

I ran back toward the warehouses and then took off through the downtown streets. When I reached the 14th Street subway station, I headed down the steps. The station below was empty. I turned around. The filthy, dripping bloodsuckers were coming down the stairs, crowding onto the platform, pressing me toward the edge.

I backed up until my heels were overhanging the lip. Then I turned and jumped down onto the tracks. I ran into the dark tunnel that led out of the station. The mob jumped onto the tracks and came after me. I planted my feet in the middle of a wooden railroad tie between the two main rails. I could hear the howls echoing against the tile. In the tight space, the odor of all those wet bodies hit me like a wave. I grabbed a long metal bar from a service alcove. The creatures surged toward me in a single mass, ready to engulf me. At the last second, I threw the bar like a spear. Not at the mob. At the third rail.

The one carrying six hundred volts of electricity.

The charge ran up the metal bar and jumped to the soaking bloodsuckers, one after the other. I threw myself against the tunnel wall. I could hear the bodies sizzle and explode behind me. When I looked up, I saw blood and brains all over the tunnel.

I climbed out and staggered up the stairs to 14th Street. I walked back uptown, tired and numb. I remember trying to get the howls and the smells and the gore out of my head. I didn't get home until two in the morning, and I could barely make it up the stairs.

When I walked into the bedroom, Margo was waiting.

Just like she promised.

FOUR

AS I WRAP up my story, Maddy gives me a slow clap. Maddy is nineteen—my youngest living descendant. She's sitting on the floor in front of me. To be honest, I expected a little more excitement.

"Pretty good," she says. "I liked the parts with Margo."

"What about the rest?" I ask. "What about *me*?"

"To be honest," says Maddy, "I actually preferred the book. It seemed more believable."

Now I'm really getting annoyed. This used to happen all the time. Fans fell in love with the books and radio shows about the Shadow. But they weren't the real thing. Not even close! Maddy, of all people, should know that by now.

"But the book is not how it happened," I tell her. "I was *there*! I'm the Shadow, remember—the *real* one. Not a character some writers made up!"

Maddy's clearly not impressed. She shrugs. "Maybe they just *told* it better."

CHAPTER 1

MADDY'S A LOT more excited this morning. That's because I'm making my famous banana-nut pancakes. They're a family favorite. And the whole family is here. Maddy and my wife Margo are already sitting at the kitchen table with Maddy's grandmother Jessica, who raised her from a baby. Bando, our Scottish terrier, is crouched at my feet, sniffing the air and pawing my leg. He can't wait for his portion.

"That smells so good!" says Maddy. "I'm *drooling* over here!"

"Be patient," says Margo. "Perfection can't be rushed."

"Remember," says Jessica, "extra nuts in mine."

I'm watching the circles of batter in the hot skillet, waiting for the bubbles to break through the surface, watching for the perfect moment to flip. Patience is key. And Margo is right. It's not my strong suit.

The morning sun is pouring through the windows behind me. The air is filled with the aromas of fresh coffee and sizzling butter and warm bananas. I'm thinking how much I love this room, this house, these people.

We're all living in the mansion I built in the 1930s— back when I started my career as an investigator in New

York. Before Margo and I even met. It was a big house for a bachelor, but I had the money and I liked living in style. And maybe, deep down, I knew that someday I'd be filling this place with a family. I just didn't know it would take more than a century.

Now! The bubbles are popping. I angle my spatula and flip the pancakes one by one. I turn to see the light streaming into the kitchen. Why waste this great weather? I nod to Maddy. "Let's have breakfast on the terrace, okay?"

Maddy grumbles a bit as she picks up the plates and flatware and carries them outside. She's very mature in some ways, but she's also a typical teenager. Cheery one second, grumpy the next.

I think about the changes this house has been through since I built it. About all those years it sat empty after Margo and I nearly died. About those long decades when we were both held in suspended animation—until Maddy found us and brought us back to life. By then the house was in the hands of a world dictator—who turned out to be my old enemy Shiwan Khan. Very dark days.

Khan almost killed us all, right here in this house. *My* house! But we managed to defeat him. Me and Maddy. The girl who turned out to be my great-great-great-great-granddaughter. The girl with powers of her own—powers she's still trying to figure out.

"Hey, chef! Watch the flapjacks!" It's Jessica calling from the terrace.

Dammit! The griddle is starting to smoke. I flip the pancakes just in time. A little dark on top, but still presentable. I really need to focus when I cook. When the pancakes are done on the other side, I grab a pair of oven mitts and carry the whole plateful out to the terrace.

I have to say, even slightly overdone, my pancakes are world-class. I toss one to Bando. He catches it in midair and gobbles it down. The rest of us dig in.

It's a beautiful morning, and a beautiful setting. The terrace overlooks the garden, our own private paradise. Just beyond the bushes and flowers, I can see the bustle of pedestrians and vehicles on Fifth Avenue.

After years of living under Khan's repression, the city is trying to get back to normal. People are starting to trust each other again, instead of worrying about getting rounded up in random police raids or getting murdered en masse, like Khan was planning.

I admit I feel a little guilty living in a thirty-two-room house while so many people are still struggling. I actually resisted moving back here. I thought it might make us too visible to the wrong people. It was Margo who convinced me. She said I'd earned it. I decided she was right. Besides, this isn't just my home. It's my headquarters. And I need it now more than ever.

Maddy pours a river of syrup over her second helping of pancakes. "Not your best," she says, spearing into her stack with a fork. "But still great."

I don't want to spoil the mood by telling the family what I know—what I've learned about the evil brewing on the other side of the globe. First, I need to be sure things are ready on the home front.

"How are the guest rooms?" I ask. We have half a dozen. Almost never used.

"Why?" asks Margo. "Are we expecting company?"

"Yes, we are. Party of five."

Margo raises her eyebrows. First she's heard about it. I still keep a lot to myself.

"Who's coming?" asks Maddy. I can see she's excited by the idea of having some new faces around the house. Maybe some *younger* faces.

"Work associates," I say. "People I trust with my life."

"Sounds like you know them pretty well," says Jessica.

I slice into my pancakes. "Actually, we've never met."

CHAPTER 2

"PLEASE! I'M NOT in *kindergarten*!"

Maddy's right, of course. She's a college freshman, majoring in criminology. And she absolutely *hates* it when I walk her to school. She's made that very clear. Many times. But the City College campus in Harlem just reopened. And there are some pretty rough neighborhoods along the route.

"I'm nineteen, remember?" she says. "And I can throw lightning bolts!"

She's right. I know she's a very capable young woman. But I'm a little overprotective, and I don't apologize for it. I love this girl so much.

"I need the exercise," I tell her. "I'm getting on in years."

"Which is why I'm embarrassed to be *seen* with you!"

After a while, she gives up and stops arguing. She knows that there's no stopping me anyway. I'm just happy to have a little extra time with her. Even when she's doing her best to ignore me.

As we walk north, we see signs of the city coming back from the repressive Khan years. Shops are reopening. People are walking freely. There's new construction everywhere. Things have improved a lot in the past year. But there are still plenty of danger zones. Sometimes one good block is followed by three bad ones. And I've heard about some problems near Maddy's school. That's the real reason why I'm tagging along. *The Shadow knows.*

When we start seeing clusters of other students heading toward the campus, Maddy stops and puts her hand on my arm. "Okay," she says, "I can take it from here. Really."

I decide to do a shape-shift. It's a power I evolved while I was in my long chemical coma. And I have to say, I'm getting pretty good at it. In a second, I'm no longer Lamont Cranston. I'm a doddering old man, white-haired and hunched over.

"Oh for God's sake…" Now Maddy's even *more* embarrassed.

"Pay attention now," I say. "See how harmless and vulnerable I seem?" Even my voice is weaker.

"You *are* harmless and vulnerable," says Maddy. "And you're even older than you look."

CHAPTER 3

WE'RE A BLOCK from campus. Maddy is trying to outpace me. In fact, she's pretending I don't exist. I grab a thin stick of wood from a trash barrel and use it as a cane to push myself along. It always takes a little time to adjust to a new form.

On the outskirts of the campus, there's a low wall shaded by tall bushes. A wooden bench sits back from the sidewalk under some overhanging branches. The bench is occupied by three young men. Not exactly college types. This is the corner I heard about. This is where the trouble is.

The guy sitting in the middle is tall and muscular, with bare arms and a tight-fitting vest. He sits forward and scans his surroundings like a radar dish, looking for threats—and opportunities. His partners lounge back on the bench, legs spread. *Macho*. Arrogant. Like nobody can touch them.

Maddy is a few yards ahead of me. She knows the right thing to do, which is to just keep walking. But the men don't make it easy. I see their eyes tracking her as she gets close.

"Baby, you make my heart stop," says one. He slaps his palm across his chest and pretends to slide off the seat. His buddy starts panting like a dog and strokes his crotch. Classy. The big guy tries to catch Maddy's eye. His right hand taps his pocket. "Whaddaya want, whaddaya need?" he mutters, just loud enough for her to hear. Then again, the same pitch: "Whaddaya want, whaddaya need?" Maddy ignores him. Just keeps going. Smart girl.

I'm catching up to her. My makeshift cane clicks on the sidewalk. Maddy turns around and glares at me. "Stop!" she says, her voice low and quiet. "I'm fine. Don't make a scene, okay?"

Now the two guys on the ends of the bench stand up. They're lean and fit.

One of them is wearing a watch cap. The other has a bald head covered in tattoos.

"We don't have a chance with this lady," says the guy in the cap, joking to his buddy. "Can't you see she already got a boyfriend?"

"Nah, I don't think he's a good match for her," says his friend. "Gimp can barely walk."

Maddy doesn't look at them. Doesn't even acknowledge the taunts. I don't take the insults personally. After all, they're not seeing the real me.

Suddenly, I feel my cane being kicked out from under me. I lurch to one side and catch my balance. The cane clatters on the sidewalk a few feet away.

"See that?" says the guy in the cap. "Old man can't even stand on his own two feet." Both guys are cackling like crows.

Now, for the first time, Maddy turns toward them. "Hey!" she says. "You're making a mistake."

"No mistake, baby," the bald guy says, lifting his T-shirt to expose a chiseled belly.

"I got your attention, didn't I?"

I stoop down and reach for my cane. A heavy boot comes down on top of it, snapping it in half. I look up. It's the guy in the vest. The boss man.

"This is a place of business," he says. "You're distracting my associates." His voice is raspy and threatening.

"He's leaving," says Maddy, calmly. "Right now."

All of a sudden, the guy in the cap grabs Maddy around the waist. He pulls her up tight against him, his nose in her hair, his lips near her ear. "The best idea is you hang with me and forget about this fossil!"

I can feel my blood boiling. It's a really great feeling.

I plant my feet and plow into the boss man's midsection, knocking him off-balance. Then I pick up the two halves of my busted cane, one in each hand. The thugs are surprised at how fast I'm moving. The old fossil. Before they can react, I crack one half of the cane hard against the head of the guy holding Maddy. He rocks backward. She spins away. The third guy comes at me hard. I side-step him and bring the other half of the cane down on the base of his skull. He drops face-first onto the sidewalk.

When I turn around, the big guy is holding an ice pick. He weaves it in front of my face, then thrusts it at my belly. I see a flash and blur. The ice pick is not in his hand anymore. It's in Maddy's. She has the guy on the ground, and the steel point is poking against his throat.

"I changed my mind," says Maddy. "I want drugs. All you've got."

From an early age, Maddy knew she had the power to control the behavior of others. And this guy is in no position to resist anyway. He reaches into his pockets and pulls out small packets of white pills. A bunch of them. Maddy grabs them in her fist and tosses them down a storm drain. Then she stands up and gives the guy a solid kick in the ribs. "Now *go*! If I see any of you back here again, I'll have my doddering old boyfriend murder you."

The thugs struggle to their feet and hustle down the block, looking back over their shoulders as they go, like they can't believe what just happened.

Maddy picks up the two parts of my cane and throws them into the bushes, along with the ice pick. I can see she's annoyed with me. "For once," she says. "Can't you just be *normal*?"

"I made pancakes for breakfast, didn't I?"

"Yes, you did," says Maddy. "And now you made me late for class."

"Admit it," I say. "Wasn't that satisfying? Just a little bit?"

Maddy doesn't even smile. She turns and heads through the campus gate. "Don't get lost on your way home, old-timer."

CHAPTER 4

BY THE TIME I get back to the house, I'm myself again. In my own body. And I'm worn out. Sometimes I forget how much of a drain shape-shifting can be. It really takes a toll, especially in a fight. I have to remind myself that I can only hold another form for short stretches. Just long enough to get the job done. Even my invisibility power is limited now. I used to be able to disappear for hours at a time. Now I can only manage short bursts. I like to pretend that I'm the same Shadow I was in 1937. But I'm not.

When I walk through the front door, Margo is coming down the main staircase. "They're here," she says. "Your mystery guests."

"All of them?"

"Three of them."

"*Which* three?"

"Not sure. I was in the garden when they arrived. Jessica showed them into the library. She said they seemed confused."

"Right. That's not a surprise."

If three are here, that means two are missing. Not good. I need the full team.

I give Margo a kiss on the cheek. "This can't wait. I'll get started." I walk down the long corridor to the library. The pocket doors are open. I walk in and slide them closed behind me. The three visitors are poking around the room, checking out books and bric-a-brac. When they hear the doors shut, they all turn to face me. They look puzzled—and suspicious.

For me, the whole scene takes a few seconds to sink in. I can hardly believe my eyes. It's like going back in time. After all these years, I'm looking at Jericho Druke, Moe Shrevnitz, and Burbank. Actually, their namesakes—the progeny of three of the best associates the Shadow ever had. And I realize that they have no idea who I am.

"Please sit," I tell them. "Welcome."

They all crowd onto the sofa. Jericho occupies a large percentage of the cushion. Like the original Jericho, he's a huge Black man with bulging thighs and broad shoulders. The other two guests take what's left of the real estate on either side of him. Moe is short and pudgy, with a graying crew cut and heavy jowls, like a bulldog. Burbank looks like he just came from teaching a computer class. Slight build. Thinning hair. Wire-frame glasses. Genes are amazing. All three are the spitting images of the men I once knew.

"Your invite," says Jericho. "It didn't say anything about *why* we're here. Or who called this little conference."

He's right. I kept the message brief. I wasn't sure they'd believe me if I told them the truth. And now I have to convince them. I can tell it's going to take a solid sales pitch. So I get started.

"I want you to understand that I searched the world to find you guys. I know your talents. I know your skills. I know your reputations. And I know you can be trusted. I assume you've all introduced yourselves."

"We know who *we* are," says Burbank. "Now who the hell are *you*?"

I knew this was going to be the hard part. I pull over an armchair and set it in front of the sofa. I sit down and look each of them in the eye. Then I rip off the Band-Aid.

"I'm Lamont Cranston."

Jericho scowls. "Bullshit! Lamont Cranston died in 1937."

CHAPTER 5

I CAN SEE that all three of them are ready to walk out. Time for full disclosure.

"Jericho's right," I say. "I *did* die in 1937—temporarily."

Moe leans forward. "What's *that* supposed to mean?"

"I was poisoned by Shiwan Khan. A fatal dose. But I was saved by a medical procedure—an experimental technique that I financed myself. It held me in a state of cryogenic suspension until the toxin dissipated. Later, I was revived."

"How much later?" asks Burbank.

"A hundred and fifty years."

Jericho stands up. "Right. Okay, Sleeping Beauty, that's enough for me."

I'm losing them. But I *can't* lose them. So I plow right ahead.

"I know it sounds impossible. *Listen!* I'm telling you the truth. I knew your ancestors. Your great-great-great-grandfathers. The men who passed their names down to you. They all worked for me—for the Shadow—back in the 1930s. You all grew up hearing the family stories. I *know* you did. You know that Lamont Cranston and the Shadow are one and the same person. *And I'm that person.*"

Moe thinks for a second, then cocks his head. "Nah, you're just some asshole with money to burn." He turns to the others. "We've been pranked, fellas. This is a waste of time."

"Hold on," says Burbank, looking straight at me. "If you're the Shadow, *prove* it."

Of course, I figured it would come to this. But I didn't want to spring it on them too soon. But now it's my only chance of keeping them here.

"All right," I say. "Watch." Then I disappear.

"Holy shit!" Moe practically jumps off the sofa.

Burbank adjusts his glasses. "I'll be damned."

Jericho starts waving his thick arms around. "It's a hologram!" he says. "It's some kind of trick!" I reach out and grab his shoulder from behind. He whips around, fists up, staring into thin air.

The doors open behind me. Perfect timing. It's Margo, carrying a trayful of cold beverages.

"I thought you gentlemen might be thirsty."

I rematerialize and help Margo with the tray. Then I make the intros. "Jericho Druke, Moe Shrevnitz, Burbank—meet my wife, Margo Lane."

"Your *wife*?" says Burbank. "Lamont Cranston got *married*?"

"Hard to believe, right?" says Margo. She holds up her left hand and wiggles her ring. "I was as surprised as anybody."

Jericho plops down in a chair and starts mumbling to himself. "This cannot be real, this cannot be real ..."

Moe steps forward, squinting hard at Margo. He leans in closer. His face lights up. "*Goddamn!* It's true! I recognize you! I've seen pictures. From back then. I don't know how, but—you're *Margo Lane*!"

Margo puts her hand on his arm. "And I haven't aged a day."

CHAPTER 6

ENOUGH WITH GETTING acquainted. I lead the group over to a table with a simple video player. During the Confiscation early in the Khan regime, all mobile phones were disabled, and citizen access to the internet was shut down. The web is still not working, and computer software updates haven't been available in years. So this is what passes for technology in the late twenty-first century—a basic 8K monitor with a slot for a video stick.

I tap the Play button. After a few seconds of static, an image pops on. I wave everybody in closer. "Take a look. This is why you're here."

It's not a well-organized report, just a collection of short video clips, crudely edited and strung together. Some of the images are from handheld cameras, some from body cams. Most of the footage was taken secretly. It wasn't meant to be pretty. It was meant to shock.

It sure as hell shocked me.

The first shots are from somewhere in Southeast Asia. Lush green mountains fill the background. In the foreground, just a few yards from the lens, men with flamethrowers are igniting rows of tall corn plants while villagers stand screaming and crying at the edge of the field. There's no sound, which somehow makes it even more eerie and disturbing. After a jump cut, the flames spread across the field. Black smoke swirls all the way to the horizon.

"What the hell is this?" asks Jericho.

"Keep watching."

After a jerky transition, the next scene shows a large desert oasis surrounded by men on horseback. The men are holding their reins taut, like they're waiting for a signal.

A rider in a black headcloth waves his hand in a circle, unleashing the troops. They sweep through the circle of palms and lush grass at a hard gallop, driving the occupants out into the open. Old men. Young children. Mothers with infants. As the oasis-dwellers run, the horsemen chase them down. Leaning from their saddles, the riders hack with sabers and machetes, leaving separated limbs and mutilated bodies in the white sand.

"Jesus!" Moe is turning pale. Burbank turns away. Jericho is just getting angry.

"What's happening?" he demands. "Who *are* these maniacs?"

"There's more," I say. I've watched the whole video dozens of times. It made me angry, too.

The next scene is grainy, shot at dusk. It shows a ragged line of teenagers, male and female, pale and wasted. Maybe two dozen. They're standing shivering and naked on a stony beach, clearly terrified. A man with an electric prod walks behind them, stunning kids at random and watching them drop to the ground in grotesque spasms.

A young boy with an automatic pistol follows behind him. He steps up to the first victim and...

"That's enough." Margo stops the video. The screen goes black.

Jericho drops down onto a chair. "Looks like two different continents." He looks up at me. "Are you saying it's all connected?"

"That's exactly what I'm saying. What you're seeing is the work of a single tightly organized cabal. It's called the Command. A lot of people risked their lives to get this footage. And a couple more risked their lives getting it to me."

"Who runs the Command?" asks Moe. "Who's behind all this?"

"One man. Identity unknown. He struck first in Java, six months ago. Leveled ten villages in one night. The survivors gave him a name. *Pangrusak Jagad.*"

Burbank and Moe are stumped. But Jericho comes up with the translation.

"Destroyer of Worlds."

Everybody's quiet for a few moments. Including me. I figure they need time to let it all sink in and make it real in their minds. I glance at Margo. She nods. Time to spill the rest.

"These actions seem random," I say. "But there's a pattern. The disorder is moving from east to west. Very calculated. Destroying crops and water supplies. Stirring ethnic conflicts. Inciting genocide. Violence and social disorder at every level. Pretty soon, the sickness will spread across the world. Like a disease."

Burbank blinks behind his thick lenses. He can't even meet my eyes. His hands are trembling. I can tell how disturbed he is by what he's seen. "And what?" he says. "We're supposed to stop it?"

"How?" asks Jericho. "By turning invisible?"

"All due respect," says Moe, "but I think we're a little overmatched."

"Every power has a seam of weakness," I say. "Our job is to find it, and crack it wide open."

The room goes silent again. As I look from Jericho to Burbank to Moe, I'm secretly hoping that I picked the right team. I'm praying that these guys are as strong and competent as their ancestors were. And I'm worried about what the hell happened to the other two I invited.

Without their skills, I wonder if we have a chance at all.

CHAPTER 7

MADDY GOMES SITS at a long wooden table in the City College library, huddled over her notes from her Culture & Crime lecture. Her stomach is growling and her eyes are burning from trying to decipher her handwriting. When she looks up at the clock, it's already 10:00 p.m. Except for a lone librarian posted somewhere on the other side of the building, she's all by herself. Not unusual. She's usually the last one here.

Maddy leans her chair back and raises her arms above her head. She takes a long stretch backward and allows herself a huge yawn. Suddenly, her wrists are grabbed from behind, jerking her off-balance. She hears a female voice, low and intense.

"You're mine now, bitch!"

Maddy pulls free and spins around in her seat. Her assailant stands there grinning. *"Gotcha!"*

Of course it's Deva. Deva Keane. Maddy's classmate and partner in Criminology. Who else would be accosting her in the school library?

"Dammit, Deva, I'm trying to study!"

"Right. I deduced that. From the books and notes and all."

Deva, slim and pretty, reaches over and grabs Maddy's color-coded index cards off the table. She shuffles them like a card sharp and then tosses them into Maddy's backpack. "Study time is over," she says. "Party time... has *begun*!" Deva swings her hips to a beat that only she can hear.

Maddy can tell that her friend has been partying already. The wine on her breath mixes with the citrusy scent of her body wash. She's also made a change of wardrobe, from her shapeless classroom sweats to a shimmery dress that rides halfway up her thighs.

Maddy shakes her head. "You *do* know we have an exam in three days, right? Covering everything from the start of the semester to now?"

"Right," says Deva. "And we both know you'll help me cram like a maniac for the next two nights."

"Lichtman's tests are diabolical."

"You've got her figured out. You've got *everything* figured out."

Maddy isn't so sure about that. Some days, she's not even sure if she picked the right school. Or if she should be in college in the first place. All she knew was that Lamont's big old mansion on Fifth Avenue was starting to feel like a prison. She needed a life of her own. Friends of her own. And she knew Lamont would take care of the tuition.

"Anyway, I can't go clubbing like this." Maddy tugs at the front of her baggy T-shirt. Airtight excuse. Done. Case closed.

"Correct," says Deva. "I can't be seen with you in that." She reaches into the cloth bag over her shoulder. "But in *this*..." She holds up a silk dress as shimmery as her own, and equally short.

"Forget it," says Maddy. "Not my look." T-shirts and jeans are usually as dressed up as she gets.

"C'mon. *Please!* I know a great place." Of course she does. Deva knows *all* the great places. When Maddy sits next to her in class, she can usually spot glitter in her hair from the night before.

"I have to get home," says Maddy.

Deva puts on a dramatic pout. "You can't send me out into the city alone," she whines. "It's dangerous."

"No. *You're* dangerous."

Maddy exhales slowly and stuffs her notebooks and pens into her backpack.

She pauses for a few seconds, then snatches the dress and heads for the restroom to change. "For the record, I'm only coming to protect you from yourself."

CHAPTER 8

DEVA FLASHES TWO passes at the entrance and leads the way downstairs into the club. She turns to Maddy. "My treat," she says. "In exchange for kidnapping you."

The sound and heat roll up the staircase as they descend. When they reach the bottom, Maddy rocks back in disbelief. She realizes that they're standing on the uptown platform of the abandoned 14th Street subway station. The dance floor covers the tracks and extends into the tunnel—the same tunnel where Lamont dispatched the Voodoo Master's bloodsuckers more than a century ago. She's walking in the footsteps of the Shadow.

Maddy rests one hand against the tile wall and closes her eyes, half expecting a grisly flash from the distant past. But all she feels is the vibration of the speakers and the slick condensation rising from a couple hundred bodies. *Live* ones. Within a second, her head clears. Deva spots Maddy's hesitation and shouts above the din. *"Been here before?"*

"Never!" Maddy shouts back. *"But I've heard stories!"*

The bass rumbles through the floor and passes right through Maddy's body. The crowd is young and ecstatic, dancing mostly in darkness, illuminated only by sporadic strobe blasts. The club is more funky than fancy. Maddy feels overdressed.

A bar table along one wall is filled with bottles of cheap beer and booze. A giant garbage bucket full of ice sits to the side. In places like this, admission covers all you can drink. And people drink a lot. The air reeks of sweat and alcohol.

Maddy leans in tight to Deva's ear. Even this close, she still needs to shout. *"Do you know anybody here?"*

Deva shakes her head and shouts back. *"Just you!"* She grabs Maddy by the arm and pulls her into the center of the crowd, creating a tiny space for the two of them. Deva backs off a few inches and starts to move—eyes shut, hips pumping, arms swinging.

Maddy feels the perspiration starting to prickle her scalp and neck as she breathes in the thick atmosphere. At first, it makes her queasy. Then she just surrenders to it. To *all* of it. The noise, the smell, the humidity, the raw human energy. And Deva's pure joy. It's infectious.

Maddy's getting jostled from all sides, but it doesn't matter now. She keeps her eyes on Deva's pulsing silhouette and does her best to mirror her moves. Deva's sparkly dress lights up in the strobe bursts like a series of punchy snapshots.

By the second song, Maddy's hair is damp with sweat, blond strands swinging across her face. Her head is buzzing and her skin is warm and tingly. She's happy she came. Happy to feel like a normal teenager for a few hours. Happy to just melt into the crowd.

As the second song segues into the third, two figures bump their way into the sliver of space between her and Deva. Two guys, lean and glistening, shirts peeled open to expose taut chests. In strobe flashes, they look enough alike to be brothers. Same stringy hair. Same perfect teeth. Same cocky physicality.

Maddy shifts her body to make room, but the men follow her with hip-thrusting moves until she's being pressed from both sides. And not in a good way. The guy on her left places a damp hand on her shoulder, his fingers brushing her neck.

"Let's have a drink!" he shouts.

Maddy pulls his hand away. *"No, thanks!"*

The brush-off doesn't work. He just grinds in closer. Oppressive now. His friend has moved on to Deva, working the same moves. Now they slide in behind the girls, grabbing their hips and moving in tight.

"One drink!" the first guy shouts in Maddy's ear. Maddy sees Deva doing her best to push away from the other one, but the space is too tight for a clean escape.

Maddy shouts again, louder this time. *"Leave us alone!"*

"Don't be so stuck up!" the guy shouts back. There's a nasty edge to his voice now. Maddy realizes that her refusal is not registering.

She looks to the side. Deva has dialed her moves way down, just shifting her weight from one leg to the other as the predator leans over her. Maddy catches his eye, then jerks her head to lure him over. Then she pulls the guy behind her around so that both men are facing her. She smiles and crooks her finger to bring them in close. She leans forward until her head is between the two of them, her lips practically touching their ears.

"Go stick your heads in the ice bin!" she shouts.

The men lean back. Their eyes go dull. They turn and move through the crowd, pushing other dancers aside until they reach the bar area. The huge bin is overflowing with ice water and melting cubes.

Maddy and Deva watch as the two men grab the edge of the bucket and plunge their heads in up to their shoulders. Dancers back off to dodge the splatter. The punks stay under for just a few seconds. Then a massive bouncer yanks them both out by their collars and shoves them up the stairs toward the exit.

Deva wraps her arm around Maddy's shoulders, laughing hard. *"Thank you!"* she shouts. *"You preserved our honor!"*

"Not a problem!" Maddy shouts back. *"I have a way with men!"*

CHAPTER 9

"DAMMIT, WHERE IS she?" I hate it when Maddy's out late. And the Scotch isn't calming me down.

I'm sitting with Margo in the main parlor of the mansion, waiting for the sound of the front door opening. I know the city is safer now than it was before, but it's still a risky place for a young woman—even one as sharp as Maddy. I keep reminding her how much evil still exists in the world. I always tell her to never, *ever* let down her guard.

As usual, Margo tells me to ease up.

"Lamont, she's in college now, not high school. If we try to hold her too close, we'll just end up pushing her away. Be grateful she's still living at home and not in some seamy dorm. Give her some space. Trust her instincts."

"You're right," I say. "Maybe I'm extra paranoid tonight."

"Because of Hawkeye and Tapper?" asks Margo.

She put her finger on the problem. My missing team members. The two who never showed up.

"Exactly. I need them here. And I have no idea where they are."

Their ancestors and namesakes were two of my most trusted associates. Brave. Loyal. Unstoppable. I expected the same from their descendants. They were the hardest two to locate and the hardest to get messages to. Their last known location was Zurich. But now they're totally off the grid.

"Remember," says Margo, "the original Hawkeye and Tapper were both ex-cons."

She's right, of course. Back in the 1930s, Hawkeye and Tapper were tough, hard men, well acquainted with the dark side. Which is exactly why I hired them.

"I *know* they were criminals," I shoot back. "That's what made them so good at fighting crime."

"Well, maybe the bad genes won out in this generation," says Margo. "Maybe these guys aren't coming at all. Maybe they're locked up somewhere. Or maybe they're dead."

I drain my glass. "I appreciate the encouragement."

My other guests are already upstairs in the guest rooms, exhausted from their travel. After just a few hours with them, I can tell that they have a lot in common with their ancestors. Jericho is tough and brilliant. Moe is resourceful and street smart. And Burbank is an electronics savant.

But we're about to go up against somebody called the Destroyer of Worlds. Even when we find his weakness, we'll need all the help we can get.

CHAPTER 10

MADDY WAKES UP at 8:00 a.m., facedown in her pillow. She turns her head slowly and opens one eye to glance at the clock. Christ. Has she really only been home for three hours? She's drained and dehydrated, and her feet feel like two throbbing lumps. The shoes she borrowed from Deva were at least a size too small. She pushes herself up and swings her legs out from under the covers, then waits a second to let her vision settle. She needs food. She needs fluids. She needs caffeine.

As Maddy comes down the main staircase and turns toward the kitchen, she hears a raucous mix of unfamiliar voices. Then she remembers. Oh, shit. Lamont's guests must have arrived. Maddy stops and squeezes her head between her hands.

Why now? After last night, all she wants is a little peace and quiet.

For a second, she thinks about going back to her room and making herself more presentable—maybe something nicer than her gym shorts and ratty sweatshirt. No. Forget it. What they see is what they get. She shuffles her aching feet toward the smell of strong coffee and warm toast.

When Maddy walks through the alcove into the kitchen, the sun is stunningly bright. At first, all she can see around the table are backlit shapes.

"Good morning, beautiful!" says Margo. She squeezes Maddy around the shoulders and plants a kiss on the top of her head. Maddy blinks. *Way* too early to be so chipper.

"Morning, Margo," says Maddy softly, waiting for the rest of the room to come into focus. She sees Lamont standing up, coffee mug in his hand, as the others around the table turn in her direction.

She's hoping there might be somebody her age in the group. But it's not looking good. Everybody around the table is older, much older. Maddy does a quick assessment of the group.

The guest on the right is a Black man who looks like he could bench-press the refrigerator. The guy next to him is short and pudgy and a little pink in the face. The third guy reminds Maddy of one of her college professors. Seems awkward—a little disconnected.

Lamont walks over and pulls her toward the table. "Everybody—this is Maddy." Maddy gives a polite little wave. "Hi, everybody." Margo sticks a mug of coffee in her hand. Thank God. The first sip sharpens her brain, and she starts to evaluate the scenario. For starters, Lamont and Margo *never* have overnight guests. So whoever these guys are, they must be important. And close. Like family. She sees Lamont moving from one chair to the next, making introductions as he goes.

"Maddy, I'd like you to meet Moe Shrevnitz… Jericho Druke…and Burbank."

Maddy doesn't say anything. She just stares at the three visitors. The names are shockingly familiar. She's known these names for just about her whole life. They're the names of three of the Shadow's closest associates.

And she's read all about them in story after story. Jericho Druke, the strongman with brains. Moe Shrevnitz, the Shadow's crafty driver. Burbank, the master of communications. *What the hell is going on here?* Maddy looks around the table, trying to form a question that makes sense.

"You . . . you're all from the 1930s. Does that mean you were . . . ?"

Margo steps up. "No, no," she says. "I know what you're thinking. These gentlemen weren't frozen and thawed like Lamont and me. They're a few generations down. They're *descendants*. Like you."

Maddy sees Jericho sit up straight in his chair. *"Descendant?"* he says. He looks over at Lamont. "Hold on! You mean, this girl is your . . ."

"Right," says Lamont. "Our great-great-great-great-granddaughter."

"See the resemblance?" asks Margo, resting her chin on Maddy's shoulder.

Moe takes another sip of coffee. Burbank starts picking the crust off his toast.

Jericho lets out a slow breath. "Unbelievable."

"Nice to meet you, too," says Maddy.

She leans back against the kitchen counter. The whole gathering seems like a dream—like something that could never, *ever* happen.

It seems impossible.

But if there's one thing she's learned in her brief time with Lamont Cranston and Margo Lane, it's that absolutely *nothing* is impossible.

CHAPTER 11

AFTER BREAKFAST, I ask Maddy to stay behind with me while Margo takes our guests on a walking tour of the Upper East Side. Maddy clears the table as I slide the cooking pans into the sink. I notice that she's being very quiet. Then the patio door slides open. It's Jessica, back with Bando after their morning walk. A daily ritual for these two. As always, Jessica lights up when she sees her only grandchild.

"Maddy! You're awake!" she says. "Did you meet Lamont's friends?"

Maddy sets a pile of plates and flatware down on the counter, then turns and folds her arms. She's clearly peeved. "You guys *could* have tipped me off, you know."

"About what?" I ask.

"About the fact that three characters from the Shadow stories would be showing up for breakfast. Like that's a normal, everyday event."

"I understand, dear," says Jessica. "It takes some getting used to."

Maddy grew up immersed in the Shadow legend. It was an escape for her. A fantasy world. Like every other

Shadow fan, she assumed that the stories were just stories, made up by some pulp-fiction writer. When she discovered that me and Margo were real people—and that she and her grandmother were our descendants—it shook up everything she knew about how the universe works. And right now, I can tell she's really frustrated. Especially with me.

"Look," she says, "you're Lamont Cranston. You've lived with this craziness *forever*! But I'm still getting used to it. And every time I start to think things are getting back to normal, some other freakish event happens. It's a *lot*! That's all I'm saying. I need a little time to adjust. You can't just spring things on me. Especially strange people from the past!"

Jessica cups Maddy's face in her hands. "You seem a little sleep deprived, dear. Have you been studying too hard?"

Maddy sighs. "I'm fine, Grandma." Jessica wraps Maddy in her arms. Maddy melts into her. They've got a connection that's beyond anything I've ever seen. For all those years while Maddy was growing up, Jessica was the only family she had. Margo and I are newcomers in her life. *Late*comers. I know she loves us, but she always says we're from a different world. And we are.

"I love you, Grandma," says Maddy, her face buried in Jessica's sweater.

"Love you, too," says Jessica. "More than anything."

When Jessica and Bando head off down the hall, I ask Maddy to follow me into the library. "Maddy, you're right. I should have brought you into this earlier. I should have told you who was coming, and why they're here."

"Well, now that I know *who*," she says. "Tell me *why*."

I stop and look her in the eye. Might as well get right to the point. "There's a new threat in the world, Maddy. Very serious. It hasn't touched us yet, but it will."

Maddy shakes her head. "What could be more threatening than Shiwan Khan? He was planning to poison the whole damn world before we stopped him! Remember? A year ago. We all almost died in the process!"

"I know. You don't need to remind me. But Khan's threat was to the underclass. He wanted to eliminate the poor to make the world safe for the rich and powerful. The evil I'm talking about is a threat to *everybody*. Rich, poor, and in between. Around the world."

I can see Maddy is still irked. "And why is this something the Shadow has to deal with?" she says. "What about governments? What about *armies*? Why does it always have to be you?"

"This cabal is playing governments and ethnic groups against one another. Nobody trusts anybody else to take charge. And nobody understands how bad this can get."

"So these experts—Jericho, Moe, Burbank—you brought them here to help you?"

"That's right. I need them for the same reason I needed their ancestors. They're people with specific skills. People I can depend on no matter what. People who are loyal only to me."

Maddy sits down on the sofa. "Okay. So who's running this evil cabal? Who are you up against?"

"Not sure who he really is. Right now, all we know is that people call him the Destroyer of Worlds." Just saying it, I realize how unreal it sounds. Maddy stares back at me with her mouth in a little curl.

"*Destroyer of Worlds*. Really? That seems a little… over the top."

That's enough. I'm used to Maddy's moodiness, but I'm in no mood for teenage sass. Not today. I reach down and pull her off the sofa. "Come here." I lead her over to the video player in the corner and press Play.

"What's this?" she asks.

"You'll see."

I watch her face as the images flicker by. After about thirty seconds, she turns pale. After a few seconds more, she turns her head away. I stop the video. "What would *you* call him?"

"I'm sorry," says Maddy softly. "I get it."

I'm not quite sure how to bring up the next topic. Because it involves Maddy directly. And I already know she'll fight it. But before I can start to explain, the room starts to vibrate. A shimmer appears in the corner near the fireplace. Maddy turns, her eyes wide. She glances over at me.

Dammit. Bad timing. My guest is a little early.

CHAPTER 12

THE SLIGHTLY BUILT man materializes next to the fireplace and rests one hand gently on the back of a chair. Amazing! It's been a very long time, but he's just the way I remember him. Old. And timeless. Small boned, gaunt cheeks, big eyes. Wearing a burgundy robe with saffron-yellow trim. He looks totally at ease.

Maddy does not. She spins around, clearly baffled. "Who the hell is *this*?"

I take a deep breath and try to serve it up gently. "Maddy, this…is Dache. He's a Kagyu high priest from Mongolia."

Maddy shifts her feet anxiously, hands at the ready. "He's not dangerous?"

"No. He's a friend. From a long time ago. Ten thousand years."

Maddy blinks. I know she still hasn't adjusted to my true age. Or the fact that I learned my basic skills many centuries ago. It throws her at times—like now.

Dache steps forward and gives Maddy a silent bow.

"Why is he here?" she asks.

I look at Dache, then back at Maddy. "He's your new teacher."

Maddy reacts exactly like I expected. She waves her hands, like she's trying to erase the whole scene. "Nope. No way. I already *have* teachers. Lots of them." She looks at me. "I'm in college, remember? Full course load." Dache stands still and alert, just watching her.

"Dache is worlds beyond that," I tell her. "What he knows, your teachers can't teach. Dache taught *me*."

"Lamont was a superior student," says Dache. "I'm honored that he summoned me to help you."

Maddy is backing away now. I can tell she wants no part of this. "Sorry. No. I'm good." She looks over at Dache. "I apologize for the misunderstanding. Crossed wires, apparently." She flicks her fingers at him. "You can go back to Mongolia now."

Dache nods. His body and clothes begin to shimmer. Then he's gone. I can see relief wash over Maddy's face. She starts to walk out of the room, back toward the kitchen. I call out to her. "Maddy, please..."

Suddenly, Dache is standing in front of her, blocking her path. She takes a step back. "What's going on?" she asks. "Why are you still here?"

Dache's voice is calm and pleasant. "I returned to Mongolia, as you asked. Now I'm back." He leans toward her. "Please. Trust me. You have much to learn."

Maddy shakes her head. "Not happening."

Dache tucks his hands into the arms of his robe and smiles. "You're strong, Madeline. I respect that."

Maddy is flushed. I can see the blood rushing to her face and neck. She jabs a finger at Dache. "Here's a lesson for *you*," she says. "My name is *not* Madeline! Now please leave! *Go!* I don't need this right now!"

"As you say," says Dache. He disappears again. His physical form is totally gone. Then his voice comes out of thin air.

"Training starts tomorrow. *Madeline*."

CHAPTER 13

AT DINNERTIME, I can see that Maddy is still furious. She's silent and sullen, and she hasn't spoken to me all afternoon. I worry that this whole arrangement with Dache got off to a very bad start. Probably my fault. I could have prepped her better. But I've had a lot on my mind. Tonight, I'm hoping that an extended family dinner—with Jericho, Moe, and Burbank included—will improve her mood. I put a lot of faith in Jessica's home cooking.

As everybody sits down around the huge table in the main dining room, I decide to break the ice with a little local drama.

"You know, it happened right here—exactly where we're sitting."

"What did?" asks Moe. He's already helping himself to the wine.

"This is the room—around this same table—where Khan and his ministers made the plan to murder millions of people. The entire lower level of society. Wipe them out entirely all over the world. That was the scheme."

Moe takes another gulp of his merlot. I can see he's not impressed by my history lesson. "Yeah? Well, I guess it didn't work. Khan is gone and we're here. So that's that."

"Should we perform an exorcism?" Jericho jokes. "You know? Erase the bad mojo?"

"My lasagna will take care of that," says Jessica.

She's not kidding. Jessica's lasagna is magical stuff. Meaty, cheesy, and unbelievably delicious. Best I've ever tasted. Bando has already stationed himself under my chair, hoping for some scraps.

Jessica passes the platter. Moe spoons himself a healthy plateful and digs in. With one bite, his face transforms into a vision of pure bliss. "Jesus, that's amazing!"

After a few quick mouthfuls, he looks over at Jessica.

"Okay," he says, "anybody who cooks food this good *has* to be an honest person. So, Jessica—let me ask you, on the level. What's the deal with this family? Is it all true? The frozen body stuff and everything?"

I feel the need to make a correction. "Cryogenic suspension. We weren't actually frozen."

"Lamont and Margo's body processes were slowed, not stopped entirely," says Jessica. "That's how Margo was able to carry a child to term."

"I still *cannot* get my head around that," says Jericho, piling lasagna onto his plate.

Neither can I. The fact that Margo bore a child—*our* child—without knowing it, still seems outrageous. And crushingly sad. It was one of the biggest events in either of our lives. And we missed it. Never even knew it happened. Until Maddy found us in that lab and brought us back to life.

Burbank looks across the table at Margo. "You don't remember anything about giving birth?"

"Nothing," says Margo. "Lamont and I were both in deep chemical comas until Maddy found us. The first time I realized I'd delivered a child was when Maddy uncovered my medical records, five generations later. Bit of a shock."

She says it in a matter-of-fact way, but I know it hurts her, too. The lost memory. The missing years. The hollow space in her life. The child she'd never known.

"But Maddy and I couldn't ask for nicer ancestors," says Jessica with a smile.

Jericho takes a deep sip of wine. "That's beautiful," he says. "A little messed up. But beautiful."

For the whole time, Maddy has been quiet, just pushing food around on her plate. I wonder what the hell she's thinking. I see her look up.

"What's messed up about it?" she says. "Is it really any stranger than other stuff that happened back in the 1930s? Can we talk about the Wasp? Or the Black Falcon? Or the Silver Skull? Your ancestors dealt with all of them. Why is our family history any stranger?"

"She's right," says Burbank. "We've all got plenty of weirdness lurking in our pasts."

Moe looks at Maddy. "How do you know all those names? You're just a kid."

Maddy puts down her fork and leans forward. "Because I'm the biggest Shadow fan who ever lived. Been that way since I was little. I know all the stories, all the radio shows. I know every Shadow enemy who ever lived. Every case the Shadow ever worked on. Every partner he ever had. I probably know your ancestors better than *you* do. And I knew it all long before I found Lamont and Margo."

Margo nods. "It's true. Sometimes she comes up with things that *I'd* forgotten."

Moe dabs his chin with a napkin. "So I guess it was meant to be. All of us here together after all this time. One big crazy family—reunited." He lifts his glass to

Maddy. "And here's to the girl who knows more about the Shadow ... than the Shadow!"

All of a sudden, Bando shoots out from under my chair and starts barking at the window.

When I look up, a huge explosion rocks the room.

CHAPTER 14

A BALL OF fire blasts against the windows, right above where Bando is standing. I grab Margo and Maddy and pull them off their chairs onto the floor. *"Everybody under the table!"*

Another blast hits the window on the other end of the room. My mouth goes dry and my heart is pounding. I was right about this house making us a target! The walls tremble and I can hear the chandelier crystals shaking above us. I do a quick check to make sure we're all accounted for. Jessica is huddled between Burbank and Moe, and Jericho has flattened himself on the floor.

"Stay down, everybody!" I shout. "Stay down!"

Before I can stop him, Jericho starts belly-crawling across the room. Another salvo hits. He huddles under the nearest windowsill. He pops his head up for a second to look outside. The explosions just keep coming.

"Attack drones!" he shouts above the noise. *"Dozens of* 'em!"

I push Maddy and Margo together. "Don't move! Either of you!"

I crawl over to the window, right next to Jericho. I

look up. The night sky is filled with tiny red navigation lights, like a fleet of evil fireflies. They're not predator drones—the high-altitude, silent type. They're smaller, about two feet across, designed to operate close to the ground. They're meant to stir panic and terror. I need to get outside. I need to *do* something. Need to fight back!

Jericho pulls me down just before another strike hits the walls. Bando is running back and forth along the baseboard, barking like crazy. "Bando! *Come!*" yells Jessica. Bando whimpers and runs under the table.

Sparks and flames bounce off outside walls as blast after blast hits the granite.

The noise is deafening.

Then it all just . . . stops.

I wait a few seconds, then peek outside. The drones are gone. Like they were never there. I look around the room. Everybody's intact. The whole place is filled with stone dust, and some of the plaster from the walls has been shaken loose. But that's it. The structure held.

Moe lifts his head. "What the hell was *that?*"

"I'd say somebody knows we're here," says Jericho.

Burbank emerges from under the table and helps Jessica to her feet. He walks slowly to the window and runs his fingers over the cracked, blackened glass. "I don't get it. This is a twentieth-century mansion, not a bomb shelter. How are we not dead?"

"Thank Shiwan Khan," says Margo. She's standing with Maddy on the far side of the table, brushing dust from her dress.

I rest my palm on one of the damaged panes, still hot to the touch. "Margo's right. Khan fortified the whole structure when he lived here. Windows. Walls. Roof. That's what saved us."

"Saved by Khan?" says Moe. "Now *that's* a goddamn first."

CHAPTER 15

IT'S BEEN A long night. I pull the bedroom curtains shut to cover the spidery bullet cracks on the glass. Three hours after the attack, everybody in the house is still on edge, including me. I'm glad the house held up against the assault, but I need to find out who's behind it. I know they'll come back again, stronger next time.

Down the hall, Maddy tucked herself into bed with Bando at her feet. Burbank and Moe decided to bunk together in an inside room—one with no windows. Jericho is sitting outside on the kitchen terrace smoking a cigar and holding one of my twelve-gauge shotguns, keeping watch. I couldn't ask for a more reliable sentry.

Margo is sitting up in bed with a pillow propped behind her. She's being very quiet. I thought she'd want to talk more about what happened. About all the evil we're up against. But she has something else on her mind.

"I hear Maddy has a new teacher," she says.

There's a little edge in her voice. I know that edge. She's reminding me that I made an important family decision without consulting her.

I climb into bed on my side. "I'm sorry. You're right. I should have told you he was coming."

Margo is a lot like Maddy. She gets irritated when people pop up out of nowhere. "So how are they getting along?" she asks. "Maddy and Dache."

"Work in progress. She's not sold yet. But Dache has infinite patience. He did with me."

"Maddy said she's trying to get rid of him."

"Wishful thinking. Dache isn't going anywhere."

Margo slides down and snuggles her head into the pillow. She turns toward me.

"All these new *people*! I remember those times back in the 1930s, when it was just you and me against the world."

I prop myself up on my elbow. "I do, too. And then that damned radio show started publicizing us. *Exposing* us. That's why we needed all the extra help. More undercover operatives. More eyes and ears on the street. The Shadow and Margo Lane couldn't do everything."

"Your *friend and companion*," says Margo. "That's what they called me on the radio show."

"I guess they were trying to be discreet."

"Made me sound like a pet dog."

Margo flicks off the light on the night table. I reach over and push her hair back from her face. That beautiful face.

"They had no idea," I tell her. "They should have said *friend, companion, comrade in arms, esteemed business partner...*"

She slides herself closer. "Don't forget *incredibly sensuous lover*."

"I was about to say that."

She slides her bare foot up along my bare leg and pulls the covers over us. "I'll bet you were."

CHAPTER 16

THE NEXT MORNING. Very early.

Maddy is standing across from Dache on the front lawn of the mansion. Words cannot express how annoyed she is. For one thing, it's barely dawn. Also, Dache appeared in her bedroom to wake her up.

"I could have been naked, you know."

"That would be meaningless to me," says Dache.

With everything that happened last night, Maddy's in no mood for a lesson from a placid monk. "You know we were attacked during dinner, right? Killer drones."

"Yes," says Dache. "And clearly, you survived."

"Just curious," says Maddy. "How come you weren't there to protect us?"

"I'm a teacher," says Dache, "not a fighter."

"Okay. But you see everything. You know everything. Who sent the drones? Tell me!"

"Not my purpose this morning," says Dache. "Let's begin."

Maddy is in bare feet, and the dewy grass tickles her ankles. Dache is standing next to a large marble sphere, about three feet across. It's not clear where it came from.

Maddy's never seen it. But it must weigh a couple hundred pounds. Dache stretches his arms out toward it. As Maddy watches, the giant ball starts to roll back and forth on the grass.

"*This* is your purpose?" says Maddy. "Showing me magic tricks?"

Dache says nothing. He looks totally at peace. He shifts his hands, and the heavy sphere rises slowly up off the grass. It hovers in midair, rotating slowly a few feet off the ground.

Maddy perks up. Okay. This is kind of cool. She takes a few steps forward. "How long did it take you to learn that?"

"Longer than you can imagine," says Dache. With a slow turn of his wrists, he lowers the ball gently back to the ground. "Anything worth learning takes time."

"Too bad," says Maddy. "I have a short attention span."

"So the record shows."

Maddy cocks her head. "*What* record?"

"*Second grade, age seven,*" Dache recites. "*Demonstrates impulsive behavior at play. Difficulty in focusing. Fourth grade, age nine. Intelligent, but scattered. Sometimes fails to complete assigned tasks. Fifth grade, age ten...*"

"You saw my *school* reports?"

"As you say," says Dache, "I see everything." He taps the marble sphere and nods at Maddy. She wrinkles her face.

"What? *Me?* I'm supposed to make that thing move? I have no idea how to do that."

Dache stares at her. "You know more than you think you do, Madeline."

Maddy shakes her head. This is a waste of time. She closes her eyes and raises her arms like a sleepwalker, aiming her fingers loosely toward the sphere. "Abracadabra," she mutters.

"Why are your eyes closed?" asks Dache.

"I'm concentrating. Isn't that the idea?"

"That's the *opposite* of the idea. Relax your thoughts. Tension is counterproductive. It accomplishes nothing."

Maddy blinks. Opens her eyes. Moves her palms sideways. The ball starts to roll slightly to the right. "Holy shit!" She glances at Dache. He nods slightly. She moves her palms in the opposite direction. The ball rolls to the left. Maddy's eyes open wider.

The ball keeps moving. It rolls down a long incline toward a garden bed. Maddy flicks her fingers. Tries to stop it. But the ball just picks up speed. Maddy waves her hands back and forth. No effect. "Hold still, dammit!" she shouts. The ball jumps the border stones and crushes an entire row of chrysanthemums.

Maddy flushes with frustration. "See that? I *told* you this was useless!"

Dache stands, unperturbed, hands tucked into the sleeves of his robe. "Failure is not useless. It is a necessary step."

"Don't fortune cookie me!" says Maddy.

She has a headache now. And she hates feeling embarrassed. She thinks back to the night a year ago when Lamont and Margo first tried to teach her how to turn invisible. It was humiliating. Since then, she's discovered more powers. Like the power to shoot lightning from her fingertips. And she's learned them on her own, without any help from some wizened instructor.

She has no patience for this.

Maddy whips her arm forward. A bolt shoots out and blasts the sphere into a thousand fragments. She turns on her heel and heads back toward the house, raising her middle finger straight into the air.

"Class dismissed!"

CHAPTER 17

MADDY HEADS INTO the mansion through the closest available door, a lower entrance that leads directly into the basement. Without his training toy, she figures maybe Dache will give up and leave her alone. As soon as she passes through the entrance, she hears voices from down the passageway. It's the sound of grown men bickering.

"This could be useful."

"It's a piece of crap!"

"Don't touch that! You'll blow your hand off!"

She recognizes the voices. Burbank. Moe. Jericho. When she rounds the corner into a large underground storage room, there they are, sorting through a pile of equipment and parts on a long metal bench. Maddy pauses in the doorway. "What's going on?" she asks. "Scavenger hunt?"

"Looks like Khan left a lot of shit behind," says Moe. "Lamont told us to salvage anything we think we can use."

As Maddy walks into the room, a chill comes over her. Just breathing the dank air reminds her that this level of the mansion was Khan's hidden domain. One of the underground chambers was a cooler for storing the bodies of his victims. Another was used for testing poison formulas. The wine cellar down the hall was where Khan installed his personal communication center, the same room he tried to destroy with a lightning strike—with Maddy, Margo, and Lamont inside. They were all lucky to escape alive. Maddy hasn't been in the basement since it was repaired.

"This asshole had *everything*," says Jericho, sorting through a carton of antipersonnel mines and grenades.

"Be careful with those, please," says Burbank. He's at the other end of the table, fiddling with the dials on a military-grade radio. So far, he's getting nothing but static.

Maddy steps up and starts picking through the random clutter on the table. Surgical saw blades. Vials of acid. Incendiary bullets. Bits and pieces of pure evil in the wrong hands. She pulls back from the bench and squeezes her eyes shut. She's dizzy for a second, then levels out. The chatter among the others becomes a wordless hum in her head. Comforting. Strangely familiar. She realizes that these guys are exactly what she'd always imagined their ancestors were like. Capable. Eccentric. Obsessive. She can feel why Lamont feels better just having them around. She's starting to feel the same way.

She turns away from the table and opens her eyes. She sees Moe leaning against the back wall, making a cat's cradle with a length of twine. Maddy can tell that he's bored with all the electronics and weaponry. Not really his thing. When she catches his eye, he puts down the string and jerks his head toward the door. "C'mon, Shadow Girl, let's see what else is down here."

Moe turns right out of the storage room and heads down a dimly lit passage. Maddy follows close behind him. After about ten yards, they reach a rusted metal door, half ajar. Moe yanks it open the rest of the way. Behind the door is a metal staircase, leading down. Light glows from below.

"What's down here?" asks Moe.

"No clue," says Maddy. "I didn't even know the basement went down this far."

Moe leads the way. The staircase takes a couple of sharp turns before ending in front of another door, this one gleaming stainless steel.

"Watch out," says Maddy. "It could be booby-trapped."

Moe runs his fingers along the perimeter of the door. He gets down on his hands and knees to peer underneath. "Looks clean."

"If you say so," says Maddy. Not sure why she trusts him, but she does.

Moe touches the metal handle lever and presses it down. Maddy expects it to be locked. But it's not. It swings smoothly on heavy hinges, triggering a bank of lights that illuminate the space inside.

Moe peeks in and starts grinning from ear to ear. "Now we're *talking*!" Maddy follows him through the door. They're standing in an underground room carved out of the bedrock beneath the mansion's foundation. The air smells of rubber and motor oil. Parked in the middle of the huge space is an array of massive vehicles.

"Holy crap!" says Maddy. "This must be Shiwan Khan's motor pool."

Maddy and Moe walk slowly down the row. Three massive personnel carriers. Two vans with one-way windows. A modified Humvee. A PA truck with roof-mounted speakers. All with brutish military designs. Sturdy. Functional. Intimidating.

"Interesting collection," says Moe.

"If you like flat black and camo," says Maddy.

When they reach the far end of the garage, Moe stops

short. "Sweet God." Maddy peeks over his shoulder. Sitting near the wall under a separate bank of bright lights is a massive armor-plated limousine with a midnight-blue finish. Moe steps up and runs his hand reverently along the side panel. He gives a soft whistle of appreciation. Maddy gets another chill, this one more intense.

"Khan's personal ride," she says softly.

Moe turns to her with a broad smile. "Not anymore!"

CHAPTER 18

I POUR MYSELF a cup of coffee and then fill another cup on the counter. Morning light shines through the cracked kitchen window. Margo is at the stove, scrambling eggs. Jessica is already sitting at the table in slippers and her favorite housecoat. I watch her closely as I hand her the coffee. No shakes. No trembles. She's rock steady.

"Are you sure you're okay?" I ask.

"Why wouldn't I be?"

"He means after last night," says Margo.

"Those little buzz bombs?" Jessica waves her hand like shooing a fly. "I've seen worse."

I glance at Margo. She just smiles and shakes her head. Maddy's grandmother is one tough character. The truth is, I can't *imagine* what she must have seen in her sixty-six years. I know for sure that she saw the civilized world descend into chaos and cruelty under the Khan regime. I know she raised Maddy on her own in a tiny one-bedroom walkup—and taught her how to survive in a very dangerous world.

Then, a year ago, she had to deal with the shock of having me and Margo show up in their lives out of nowhere. Jessica was arrested, imprisoned, and nearly killed in our battle against Khan. But none of those things seem to affect her. She just put them in the past and moved on. Right now, she's more peeved by something she sees out of the kitchen window.

"Look at that!" she says, pointing into the distance. "Mindless!"

I lean over to see what she's looking at. It's a huge construction crane poking into the sky on the far side of Manhattan.

"I can't believe they're actually going through with it!" says Jessica.

Now I understand what has her so irritated. It's not the first time we've heard about it. She's looking toward a huge site on the East River where the 2088 World's Fair is under construction. Jessica does not approve of the project, to put it mildly.

Margo sets a platter of scrambled eggs on the table. "If you ask me, the city could use a little distraction," she says.

"Waste of time and resources," says Jessica, taking a small helping of eggs. "People are still trying to get back on their feet. There's no cell service, for God's sake. The power grid is spotty. This is no time for an overgrown circus!"

Margo looks at me across the table. We both know there's no point in arguing.

Suddenly, I sense movement in front of the house. I hear the sound of a car horn from the driveway. Is it possible my missing operatives have finally shown up? I jump out of my chair and head through the front hall.

Better late than never!

CHAPTER 19

I RUN THROUGH the foyer and open the front door.

"How 'bout a spin, boss?"

It's Moe, standing by the driver's-side door of a sleek midnight-blue limo. Not exactly what I was hoping for. Unless he's got Hawkeye and Tapper hidden in the trunk.

I step onto the driveway and take a good look at the vehicle. "Khan's car? Where did you get this?"

Moe flashes a big grin. "Maddy and I found it in the subbasement. Quite the little dealership he had down there."

Moe is practically bouncing in front of the car's open door. I can tell he's dying to test it out. Why not? I know exactly where I want to go.

I turn and call back through the doorway, "Margo! I'm going out!"

"Be careful!" she shouts back. Like always.

I walk around to the other side and climb into the front passenger seat. The interior is all hand-tooled wood, soft leather, and sleek electronics. The car is a custom-made hybrid—electric engine with a small gasoline reserve.

But gasoline is notoriously hard to come by these days. Black market only.

"Don't worry," says Moe. "Plenty of juice in the battery."

The limo makes a satisfying hum as Moe rolls down the driveway toward Fifth Avenue. "Where to, boss?"

I cannot believe how much he sounds like the Moe Shrevnitz I worked with back in the 1930s—the one who bugged his cab to let me listen in on his passengers' conversations. One of the best natural detectives I ever met.

"Head crosstown," I tell him. "I want to check out the fair."

"What fair?" Moe asks. I guess Margo didn't cover it on their tour of the neighborhood.

"A World's Fair," I tell him. "Like back in the old days. I think the city fathers are trying to pretend things are back to normal. Head east."

"You got it, boss."

As we ease out onto the street, I can see people staring at the limo, then turning away and ducking into doorways, terrified. Moe sees it, too. "Jesus. Is my driving that bad?"

Then it hits me. "It's not you, Moe. People recognize the car." To people who lived through the years when Khan ruled the world from New York, the vehicle we're in represented danger, intimidation, and death—not two buddies out for a joy ride.

"Lower your window," I tell Moe. I do the same. "Now wave. Nice and friendly."

I watch the expressions on pedestrians change from fear to puzzlement. That's okay. Better than scaring the hell out of them.

As we drive toward the river, we pass through a patchwork of Upper East Side neighborhoods. Some are recovering nicely; others are still run-down or burned out. For every shop and store that's reopened, several are still boarded up. The city is moving in the right direction, but slowly.

It's only a five-minute ride to the World's Fair site—a ten-acre parcel extending out over the East River. The old FDR Drive runs like a six-lane ribbon underneath, but rising water levels have put it mostly underwater. Moe pulls up in front of a chain-link fence. The site is humming with last-minute construction. Several buildings and exhibits are still shrouded in scaffolding and canvas, but the main pavilion is unveiled and complete, looming like a giant spaceship near the front entrance. A huge lighted crawl runs around the peak. GRAND OPENING NEXT WEEK! it says. Ambitious, from the look of things.

With a patchy communication grid, the city has had to rely on posters, flyers, and word of mouth to circulate the news about the fair. And as everybody in the city has been hearing, the main pavilion is not the most impressive part of the site. Not by a long shot. The fair's signature attraction sits on a huge platform overhanging the river. I guess you'd call it a Ferris wheel. Except there's no wheel. The seats are floating in midair in a circle that rises about fifty stories high. Supported by *nothing*.

Moe leans over and squints through my side window. "How the hell ... ?"

"Neodymium magnets," I tell him. "And a little luck."

I can tell right away that Moe is in Jessica's camp. "What a bunch of claptrap," he says. "What do people need with a World's Fair when the world is going to hell?"

Fair question. And here's my answer:

"That's when they need it most."

CHAPTER 20

AS WE EXIT the fair site and drive north, we hit a string of really bad blocks. Abandoned buildings. Empty lots. Stray dogs. Sad and depressing. In this corner of town, it's like the Khan years never ended.

Moe pulls to a stop at a red light. Suddenly, we're surrounded by a gang of scrawny kids, about nine or ten years old. They cluster around the car, banging their palms on the hood. Fearless. Or maybe just desperate.

Moe blasts the horn and leans out the window. "Scram, you little pissants!"

I spot a row of run-down shops on my side of the street. I tap Moe on the arm.

"Pull over."

Moe shakes his head. "If we stop, the little pricks will slash our tires!"

"I'm pretty sure these tires are slash-proof. Park right here."

Moe rolls to a stop at the curb. As I open the door, I take a deep breath—and turn invisible. I can't resist looking back to see Moe's face. His jaw is hanging down.

He watched me disappear on that first day in the

library, but I'm not sure he really believed it. He does now.

I walk across the sidewalk into a little bodega and head straight for the candy aisle. I pick up an empty cardboard box from the floor and start filling it with chocolate bars, lollipops, bubble gum, licorice sticks. Then I hit the snack aisle. I toss in mini bags of chips, pretzels, cookies, and any other treats I can lay my hands on, until the box is stuffed and overflowing.

The clerk at the front counter backs away when he sees the box floating toward him. I toss a bunch of bills on the counter. I'm probably overpaying by about fifty bucks, but who cares? This guy needs the cash a lot more than I do.

When I walk back outside, the kids are still clustered around the car. But the floating cardboard box gets their attention. Especially when candy starts flying out of it.

The kids run over, grinning and shouting like crazy. There's a lot of bumping and grabbing over the treats, but it's a friendly scramble, and there's plenty for every-body. When the box is almost empty, I drop it on the ground. The kids dive in to grab the rest.

When I open the car door and slide back into the front seat, I decide to stay invisible, just to test my limits. Moe presses back against his window and stares in my direction. I can tell he's still freaked out. When my voice comes out of nowhere, his head just about hits the roof of the car.

"What's wrong, Moe? You act like you've never driven the Shadow before."

CHAPTER 21

MOE DROPS ME off by the front door and pulls the car around back. Margo is waiting for me in the kitchen. She seems impatient, distracted.

"Where have you been?" she asks.

"We went to check out the World's Fair. I wanted to see the spectacle for myself." I pour myself a glass of water and sit down at the kitchen table. "Don't tell Jessica—but I think it shows promise. They have a Ferris wheel design that..."

The look on Margo's face stops me in midsentence.

"What's wrong?" I ask.

"I hate to throw cold water on your fantasy," says Margo, "but the World's Fair happens to be a murder scene."

Margo has a way of getting straight to the point. She sits down across from me at the table. I look around to make sure we're alone, then lower my voice, just in case. "Murder? Murder *how*? Was it the drones? Did they hit somebody on the way in?"

"Not the drones," says Margo. "The killer is a stalker.

Strikes at night. The victims are high school and college kids. Maddy's age."

"Victims? *Plural?* How many?"

"Four so far."

"The fair's not even open yet. What were they doing there?"

"Who knows? Whatever kids do at that age," says Margo. "Drinking. Partying. Having sex. Or maybe just trying to get a sneak peek at the attractions—like you."

"So why isn't this big news?" I ask. Broadcast and social media haven't come back yet, but the underground city grapevine is alive and well. When something important happens—good or bad—word gets around. But nothing about this?

"The city fathers know," says Margo. "But they're keeping a tight lid on it. They don't want to spook people before the fair opens. They're afraid of spoiling the city's image—the big comeback and all."

Of course. The world changes. Politicians don't.

"How did you learn all this?" I ask.

Margo raises her eyebrows. "Do you need reminding? I was a pretty fair detective before I met you."

She's right. In fact, she was my biggest competition before we decided to join forces. At first, all I knew about her was that she was smart and gorgeous. But I was selling her short. I had no idea how resourceful she was and good she was at cultivating contacts and informants. Maybe this is her way of telling me that she hasn't lost it—that she's still in the game just as much as I am.

"Are the police on it?" I ask.

"Sure," says Margo. "But they'll never crack it." She leans toward me across the table. "Not without help."

At this point, I realize that my brilliant wife is playing me like a fiddle. She knows we've got bigger problems to solve, and bigger battles to fight. The Command. The Destroyer of Worlds. Threats to our *own* lives, for God's sake.

But she understands me better than anybody. A murderer is stalking the World's Fair. Margo knows that this is a case the Shadow can't possibly resist.

CHAPTER 22

MADDY LOVES THURSDAYS. Because on Thursdays she only has one class, Dilner's Economics of Crime. Even better, it's a *lecture* class. No active participation required. And it's over by 11:30 a.m. Which leaves the whole afternoon free. As soon as the lecture wraps up, Maddy grabs Deva and they head for the main campus gate.

"So what did you think?" asks Maddy.

"About what?"

"About what Dilner was saying—about street crime being a rational choice. A financial calculation. A business decision."

"Sorry," says Deva. "I nodded off after two minutes. You take notes?"

"Don't I always?"

"Good. I'll need them."

It's a clear, bright day. A few blocks from campus, they reach the green expanse of St. Nicholas Park, filled with New Yorkers savoring the sun. Colorful blankets and beach towels dot the slopes on both sides of the pathway. Deva puts on a pair of sunglasses and tips her face toward the sky. Suddenly, she grabs Maddy's arm and points up.

"What the hell is that? A freaking *vulture*?"

Maddy shields her eyes with her hand and squints. The huge bird is circling a few stories above them, gliding in a slow, circular descent. And rocking its wings. Maddy gets a sour, sinking feeling inside. She has a pretty good idea of what's about to happen. *Oh, shit. Why now?*

"It's a bald eagle," she says.

"I thought they were extinct," says Deva.

"Yeah. Not this one," says Maddy. "Unfortunately."

As they watch, the eagle pulls in its wings and makes a final dive toward the ground. Deva covers her head and screams. The huge bird swoops around them, so close they can feel the rush of air as it passes. It lands on a stone wall and settles like a statue, its long talons hooked over the edge.

Deva tugs on Maddy's sleeve. "Let's go! I'm not waiting to get my eyes pecked out!"

Maddy pulls back. "You know what?" she says. "I left my notebook in class. You go ahead. See you tomorrow, okay?"

Deva gives the raptor one last nervous look as she heads off. In a few seconds, she's around the corner and out of sight.

Maddy walks over to the wall where the massive eagle was perched—where Dache is now sitting. He's wearing baggy slacks with a tucked-in polo shirt.

"You look ridiculous," says Maddy.

"Are you trying to avoid me?" asks Dache.

"If I were trying to avoid you, I'd probably just disappear."

"Wouldn't help. I could still see you."

Dache hops off the wall and gestures down the path into the park. "Shall we walk?"

"It's my afternoon off," says Maddy. "And you're not invited."

"Wrong. It's an opportunity for expanding your knowledge."

Maddy's frustration starts to boil. She stops and leans over her teacher. "Look. You've obviously studied me. My abilities. You know what I can do. I can turn invisible. I can throw lightning from my hands. I can control minds. What more do I need?"

"Your skills are rudimentary," says Dache. "Partially developed. Inconsistent. And there are powers in the universe that extend far beyond what you know."

"Such as ...?"

Dache turns and starts walking down the path. "Such as ... being able to envision the past, or the future."

"Great," says Maddy. "I'd like to envision a future when you're pestering somebody else."

Dache turns and smiles. "I treasure your wit, Madeline."

"Again," says Maddy. "*Not* my name." She's pretty sure he's doing it on purpose now. Maybe it's part of his process. Denying her individuality. Breaking down her sense of self. Or maybe he just likes to annoy her. She follows him down the path.

Dache walks slowly with his hands clasped behind his back. "Would you like to know what I can foresee for *you*?"

Maddy says nothing. Tries to pretend she's not curious. But who wouldn't be? Besides, Dache probably knows what she's thinking anyway. "Okay. *What*?"

"What I see," says Dache, "is a time when your powers will surpass those of Lamont Cranston. You will be a greater force in the world than the Shadow ever was."

Maddy shakes her head. "No. Lamont's the original. I'm just a pale copy. I've known that from the start."

"Right now," says Dache, "your biggest weakness is not trusting your own strength."

"Another proverb from your pile," says Maddy. "You're just bullshitting me."

"Think so?" says Dache. "Let's find out."

CHAPTER 23

THE ANNOYINGLY CHEERFUL monk sets a brisk pace as they walk deeper into the park. Maddy is quiet the whole way. She walks a few paces behind Dache, trying to pretend she doesn't know him. But by the time he stops to wait for her near a renovated playground, the silence just gets uncomfortable.

Maddy realizes there's no way to ditch her tormentor, so she decides to pump him for some family background. Make the time worthwhile. Maybe score some intelligence she can actually use.

"So how are you and Lamont connected?" she asks.

Dache stops. He taps his head—"Here"—and then his chest—"and here," he says. Then he starts walking again.

"Right. I get it," says Maddy, catching up to him. "Not that way. I mean where did you meet? How far back do you go? What's your *story*?"

"I know what you mean," says Dache.

Maddy realizes that's all she's going to get.

She follows her teacher off the path and into a secluded cluster of oak trees, soaring up more than fifty feet. Dache stops in the center of the grove. "Time for today's lesson."

Maddy glances around. "Here?" So lush and peaceful. "Couldn't we just have a picnic?" When she looks back, Dache is gone. Maddy starts speaking into the open air.

"Quit it, Dache. You're obviously here." She turns a full 360. "Unless you took the hint and returned permanently to Mongolia, which would be too good to be true."

Maddy feels a sharp sting on the crown of her head, like she was hit by a pebble.

She spins around and sees a couple with a baby stroller passing nearby. Not the pebble-throwing type. Then it happens again. Another hit. This time she looks up.

On a branch ten feet above, a fat gray squirrel is dropping acorns on her. As soon as Maddy spots him, the animal skitters along the narrow branch, jumps onto the tree trunk, and hops to the ground.

A second later, the squirrel is gone and Dache is back, leaning against the tree. He tents his fingers and points them at Maddy. "Your turn."

Maddy laughs out loud. "Me? A squirrel?"

"Highly useful form," says Dache. "Very sure-footed."

Maddy rubs her head, buying time. She's actually excited by the idea of shape-shifting, but she's not sold on the example. Aren't squirrels just rats with fluffy tails? And deep down, she has more serious doubts. What if she can't do it? What if she can't change back? What if she's permanently deformed? She starts thinking of a hundred things that could go wrong.

"Lamont does cats," she says, still stalling. "I like cats."

"Don't get ahead of yourself," says Dache. "Cats are complex. A hard form to control. Start simple. *Rodentia: Sciuridae* before *Carnivora: Felidae*."

Maddy shifts her feet awkwardly and looks up into

the trees. This is so weird. "Okay. How does it happen? Do I just imagine myself as a squirrel, and then ... *poof*?"

"Not that easy," says Dache. "But you absolutely have it within you to trigger the transformation. You were born with it. Trust me. I'll guide you to it."

Something in his tone makes Maddy stop resisting.

"Look at me," says Dache.

She does. She really *looks* at him. Past the tacky dad wardrobe and the brown, wrinkled skin. She notices that his eyes seem younger than his years—sparkling and alive. And now it's like he's seeing straight through her. Maddy feels her mind going numb. Then, somewhere deep in her brain, something clicks. Her body starts to tighten and twist. It feels like some kind of seizure.

The next instant, Maddy's heart is speeding at three hundred beats per minute. Her muscles feel as tight as compressed coils. And she's almost weightless.

Now she's flat on the ground, sensing the cool grass under her belly. Then, suddenly, she's vertical on a tree trunk, feeling the satisfying grip of claws on bark.

A surge of energy propels her upward, higher and higher. It's a mental and physical rush like nothing she's ever experienced. It's *amazing*!

Her senses are flooded with input. She sees the pattern of the leaves against the sky. She smells the lichens an inch from her nose and the meat in the acorns overhead. Her peripheral vision is phenomenal, like having eyes on the front and sides of her head.

She jumps from the trunk to a low branch, then runs along its length with perfect balance. She leaps to another branch. Then another. Her legs feel like springs. The part of her brain still reserved for human thought is incredulous. But the rest of her is primal instinct and acute perception. She feels totally alert and completely fearless.

Near the top of the tree, the branches narrow and bend under her weight. She senses the tremors from her nose to her tail. While the support is still strong enough, she propels herself toward a thicker limb five feet away. She makes the leap in a full stretch, feeling the air through her fur. But her calculation is off! And now the branch is an inch too far. In less than a blink, she goes from stretching to falling. The ground spins below in a greenish-brown blur and then...*impact*!

The jolt is hard, but surprisingly painless, cushioned by fat and muscle. A shiver shoots through Maddy's body. She gasps. Her heart drops to two hundred beats, then slows to a hundred, then eighty. It feels like dying. Her body is heavy now, and it aches. Human again.

Maddy turns slowly, painfully, onto her back. She shades her eyes and sees Dache leaning over her. "Welcome back, Madeline."

Maddy groans. "You said I'd be sure-footed!"

Dache smiles. "I didn't say immediately."

CHAPTER 24

IT'S ONLY A short walk from our place to the 19th Precinct station house, a compact four-story building with a square tower on top. Under Khan's regime, it was occupied by his secret police, a small army of masked thugs who ruled the city by terror. But today, it's back in the hands of the NYPD and open to concerned citizens, 24/7.

We stop at the sergeant's desk. "Who's the officer in charge?" I ask.

"Who wants to know?" the sergeant shoots back without looking up. Bad start. Reminds me why I went independent in the first place. Back in the 1930s, I wouldn't have even gone to the cops on a case like this. But it's a new day. A new century. And I'm trying to be a team player.

Margo steps forward, calm and polite. "We're private investigators, and we're here to help with the World's Fair murders."

Immediately, I sense a solid presence at my elbow, and a strong whiff of cheap aftershave.

"*What* murders?"

It's a thickset man with a badge dangling from his neck. "I'm Detective Roskow," he says with an upward jerk of his chin. "Can I help you?" Condescending and dismissive. The exact *opposite* of helpful.

"I'm Lamont Cranston. This is my wife, Margo Lane. We're private investigators."

"Private investigators. Yeah. That much I heard." Roskow narrows his eyes and looks me over. I see a spark of recognition. "Cranston," he says, repeating the name slowly, stretching it out. "You live in the big place on Fifth. The old presidential residence."

"*My* old residence, actually," I tell him. "I was there first."

"You fought off Khan. In Times Square," says Roskow. "Impressive."

"Thanks," I say. "But that was a year ago, and…"

Roskow interrupts. "And now, you're what? An amateur sleuth?"

I can feel the heat rising in my neck. "Trust me. We're anything but amateurs."

Margo cuts in. "Are you in charge of the case, Detective? Is there a room where we can talk? About the killings?"

Roskow scratches his pale, thinning scalp. "In terms of any killings," he says, "let the professionals handle it. This is not a hobby."

Margo steps right up to him. "Take us to the highest-ranking officer in the building," she says with a smile. "Then get lost."

Roskow nods and heads for the stairs. I lean over to whisper in Margo's ear.

"Do you know how beautiful you are when you control minds?"

"Somebody has to do it," she replies.

Roskow leads us up two flights to a squad room crowded with metal desks and file cabinets left over from another era. Shirt-sleeved detectives slouch in battered chairs, nursing cups of office-pot coffee. Roskow shows us to a large office in the corner. It has a glass wall with blinds pulled all the way shut. Roskow opens the door without knocking. Margo and I slip into the office as Roskow walks off. The tall woman behind the desk stands up, clearly irritated. Captain Myra Bates, according to the brass plaque near her in-basket. "Roskow!" she shouts, looking right past us. No reply.

I step up close to the front of the desk. "We just need a minute, Captain."

She looks from me to Margo, then back again. "Who the hell are *you*?"

"I'm Lamont Cranston, and this is my wife, Margo Lane." I feel like I'm replaying the same recording. "We're private investigators, and we..."

Bates cuts me off. "How did you get up here? If you have a tip, the front desk will handle it." She sits back down and starts sorting papers. As far as she's concerned, the conversation is over.

"Captain," says Margo, "we know there's a killer loose on the fairgrounds. And we're here to offer our help."

"We understand why you want to keep things quiet," I add. "But killers like this don't stop. You know that. Pretty soon, things will be out of control."

Bates looks up. She's pure ice. "I don't know what you're talking about."

"Yes, you do," says Margo. "Two boys, two girls, over the past five days. Ages sixteen to nineteen. Local kids. From Red Hook and Staten Island. Bodies found on the fairgrounds by security before five a.m. Still in the city morgue listed as John and Jane Does, even though you know perfectly well who they are. No notification to the families. All the parents know is that their kids are missing. Maybe runaways. Which is how you want to keep it until after the fair opens."

Captain Bates stares back from behind the desk. "We don't need any help," she says. "If there's anything going on, we'll manage it."

"We could choose to publicize the crimes ourselves," says Margo. "In the interest of warning the public."

"And I could have you arrested for criminal obstruction."

"So you admit that murders have been committed?"

"Don't put words in my mouth."

We're talking to someone who's stupid or stubborn or both. Or maybe just bending to pressure from above.

"You're making a mistake, Captain," I say.

Bates brushes us toward the door with a curt wave. "Close it on your way out, please."

Clearly, we're going to have to get our information the old-fashioned way. I don't need to say a thing to Margo. She knows the drill. Out in the precinct room, I see her pinpoint the target. I duck into the men's room. It's smelly, but empty. Five seconds later, I emerge—invisible. By then, Margo is leaning close to a young male detective. She has his full attention, making it easy for me to scoop the file off the corner of his desk and tuck it close to my body, where it disappears, too.

I rematerialize with the file next to Margo in the stairwell as we head toward the lobby. A few seconds later, we're out the door and walking down 67th Street, heading for home.

"How much do you think Bates really knows?" I ask.

"Not much more than we do," says Margo. "I think she's trying to maintain her plausible deniability status."

"Nothing ever changes with cops," I say. "Stuck in

their ruts and covering their asses." We stop at the curb at Park Avenue.

"That's why the world needs the Shadow," says Margo.

I take her hand and squeeze it as the light changes. "Don't forget his loyal friend and companion."

She turns and kicks me in the shin.

CHAPTER 25

BACK HOME IN the front parlor, I open the folder and lay the crime scene photos out on a low table. Hard to look at. There's a series for each of the four victims. Margo leans in. "My God, Lamont!" We've both seen plenty of corpses, but these images are sickening and startling.

Victim A is a teenage boy. He's lying on a patch of dirt with tracks from heavy equipment running beneath him. There's a painted wooden survey stake showing in the upper corner. A construction site. His body is splayed at an odd angle, arms and legs bent. His skull has been cratered by a massive blow. His eyes are open and staring.

And his face has been painted with garish green paint. Like some kind of monster.

Margo spreads out the rest of the pictures. The other boy. The two girls. Similar locations. Identical head wounds. Same green faces. Like some sick ritual.

"Is it a copycat?" asks Margo. "Somebody imitating an old Shadow enemy?"

I've got a pretty good memory for crimes, and I'd

never forget something like this. I shake my head. "No. This is somebody new."

We both look up as the front door opens. Maddy walks in with her backpack over her shoulder. She looks exhausted, and her hair is wilder than usual. Margo quickly slides the pictures back into the folder, but Maddy picks up on it. She stops at the bottom of the staircase.

"What's that?" she asks.

"Nothing," says Margo. "Just a local case we're looking into."

"*Another* case?" Maddy shakes her head. "Do you two *ever* stop?"

"How are things going with Dache?" Margo asks.

"Pain in my ass," Maddy replies. "But interesting."

Interesting? I'll take that as progress.

Maddy grabs the banister and propels herself upstairs. Margo slides the folder into a drawer. I follow Maddy and catch up with her in the hallway.

"Maddy. Hold on. I need to tell you something."

"Can it wait?" she says, sniffing her shirt. "I *really* need a shower."

"No, it can't. This is important." I take a step closer. "Listen. I want you to stay away from the World's Fair, okay? Promise me."

Maddy looks at me like I'm out of my mind. "Why the hell would I ever go to the World's Fair?" she says. She turns and heads off down the hall, calling back over her shoulder, "Grandma's right. The whole thing feels like a creep show."

CHAPTER 26

LATE THAT NIGHT, Moe weaves the limo through Manhattan traffic. His grip on the wheel is tighter than usual.

"Don't be nervous, Moe," Maddy calls out from the backseat. "I'll never tell."

"Maybe you haven't heard," Moe replies, glancing in the rearview mirror. "The Shadow knows! He *always* knows."

Maddy is sitting next to Deva on the plush gray leather. And she understands why Moe is so anxious. It's because she's talked him into sneaking the limo out of the garage and being their chauffeur for a girls' night out.

"Where *is* this place?" asks Deva. Moe turns onto the West Side Highway and heads north.

"It's a secret," says Maddy, trying not to show how excited she is. It's rare that she finds a place that Deva hasn't heard of.

"Are you going to get into trouble at home?" Deva asks.

"Nothing I can't handle," says Maddy.

She's borrowed another one of Deva's dancing dresses, this one even more sparkly. But tonight she's wearing shoes of her own—a pair that actually fits.

After a few minutes' drive, Moe pulls off the highway onto a circular road running around the tip of Fort Tryon Park and heads up a steep hill. At the top is a dramatically lit building that looks like a medieval monastery.

Moe pulls the limo to a slow stop in front of the entrance. Maddy leans forward. "Thanks, Moe. You can scoot now. Sneak back into the garage. We'll find a way home."

"Like hell you will," says Moe. "I'm waiting right here."

Deva and Maddy slip out of the backseat and join the stylish crowd on the front steps. Maddy flashes her invite at the door and pulls Deva through the arched entrance, where the experience hits them full force.

"Holy shit!" Deva shouts.

The interior is a dazzling maze of exotic galleries and richly decorated chapels. Gothic. Romanesque. Spanish. The lighting style changes from space to space—from a soft amber glow to pulsing laser beams in neon colors.

Maddy and Deva follow the throbbing music to the central dance floor, set in a room surrounded by marble arches. The walls are marked with huge, pale patches.

"Where the hell are we?" Deva shouts.

"Used to be a museum," Maddy shouts back. "But the last regime stole all the art!"

The swell of the crowd pushes them forward. The energy is insane. The sound bounces off the stone and vibrates through the floor. Maddy is thinking this is what it must be like to be inside a jet engine. Or an active volcano.

Some dancers move in pairs, but most are just soloing,

gyrating and grinding with anybody and everybody in proximity, forming a living mosaic of faces and bodies. Maddy closes her eyes and spins next to Deva, arms over her head. She jumps and bounces and tosses her hips. When she looks again, Deva is several yards away, spinning in an adjacent vortex.

Now a new group swings into Maddy's orbit. A tiny girl with maroon-tinted hair pulls a guy by his belt. She moves with the grace of a ballerina. He's thick and muscle-bound, and taller than his partner by half a foot. His sweaty face is just inches from Maddy's. She can feel the heat radiating from his torso. She tries to avoid his pumping arms, but he takes up a lot of space. Then Maddy realizes that he's looking at her. *Staring* at her.

The guy grabs the maroon-haired girl by the waist. He pulls her close, yelling into her ear. Now the girl is looking at Maddy, too. Maddy spies Deva across the floor and tries to slip through the crowd toward her.

"It's you!" the guy shouts. He's pointing at Maddy, jabbing his finger toward her, almost touching her head. "I knew it!"

Now he's tugging at other dancers. They start looking, too. The guy won't let up.

"It's her! Right?" Slowly, the crowd starts to circle around Maddy. She's feeling trapped.

"Times Square!" a girl shouts.

"Lightning!" shouts another.

Maddy spins left and right, feeling the pressure all around her. Now she gets it. The battle with Khan. The spectators. Hiding in buildings, cowering behind cars. Some of them saw her face. It was the most spectacular event of their lives, and she was at the center of it.

The music is still pulsing, but the dancing has just about stopped. Now people are reaching for Maddy, grabbing at her. "We love you!" She feels like she's about to be torn apart for souvenirs. Deva is just a few feet away now. Maddy grabs her hand. Deva looks excited, then terrified.

"Shoot a bolt for us!" a man yells.

Maddy ducks her head, hooks Deva's arm, and spears her way through the crowd. Behind her, the shouts grow. "Light-ning! Light-ning!"

Maddy shoves her way to the door and pushes it open. The cool night air hits her like a blast. Deva stumbles along behind her.

Maddy looks left, then right.

Moe! Where's Moe? Did he wimp out and head home after all?

The crowd surges out of the club behind them. Maddy pulls Deva down the driveway, just a few yards ahead of the crazed fans. Suddenly, they're hit by the glare of headlights heading right toward them.

The limo pulls up and stops with a jolt. Maddy yanks the rear door open and shoves Deva onto the backseat, then jumps in after her. She slams the door as the crowd surges around the vehicle. She kicks the back of the front seat.

"I hear you're a great driver, Moe! *Prove* it!"

CHAPTER 27

PLAY. PAUSE. REWIND. Replay.

I'm in my study on the second floor, looking at the Destroyer video again, searching for clues. As if I'm going to see something I missed the first hundred times. It's no use. Same blood. Same bodies. Same horror. I click the player off and rub my eyes. I look up at the clock. Two a.m.? Is that possible?

I turn out the lights and walk upstairs to Maddy's room for a bed check. I open the door gently and peek in. The bed is empty. I'm irritated. No. *Angry.* This is the second curfew she's blown through in a week. *Where is she* this *time,* I wonder. I close the door and step back into the hallway.

Wait. Now that I think about it, where is everybody?

I left them all down in the parlor a few hours ago, but I never heard anyone coming upstairs. Margo never goes to bed without telling me. *Never.*

As I start down the main staircase, something makes my neck hairs start prickling. I can't explain it, but something's off. That's not a secret power. Just simple human instinct. I jump down the rest of the steps and head into the kitchen. Empty. When I turn the corner into the front parlor—my heart stops.

I spot Margo first. She's lying on the floor, not moving. There's a shattered martini glass by her hand. I swing right. I see Jessica. She's lying on the carpet by the fireplace next to Bando, both of them as still as death. Burbank is slumped in a chair in the corner, with a shiny stream of saliva running down his chin.

I kick the broken glass away from Margo and drop to my knees. I pull her onto my lap and turn her face toward me. *"Margo! What happened?"* I run my hands over her neck, her back, her legs. No marks. No wounds. I put my arm under her shoulders and raise her partway up. Her chest is moving, but barely.

Suddenly, there's a deep voice from the entryway. "Sorry, boss."

I swivel around, shielding Margo with my body.

It's Jericho. He's pulling a respirator off his face. "I was mixing some knockout gas downstairs. I guess some of the vapors came up through the parlor vents." He waves his hand in front of his face. "Should be gone now. Short half-life."

Across the room, Bando shudders and staggers to his feet. Jessica coughs and raises herself onto her elbows. Burbank blinks and wipes the drool off his chin.

I can feel Margo stirring in my arms. She shudders, then slowly lifts her head.

"Wow," she mumbles. "That was some cocktail."

CHAPTER 28

"I'M FINE," SAYS Deva. "You should get home. Really."

"I know you're fine," says Maddy. "I need the air."

It's no more than a dozen yards from the street to Deva's front door, but Maddy insists on walking her anyway. As soon as they pulled up, she understood why Deva asked to be picked up near school instead of at home.

This is the first time Maddy's seen where Deva lives. And it's depressing. Deva's house is a battered brownstone across from a massive abandoned public housing project—a haven for squatters and worse. It's one of the many pockets of the city that the restoration has skipped over or ignored.

Most apartments in this sector of the city have only one or two working lights. Everything else is dark. No traffic lights. No streetlights. The small patches of greenery are overgrown with weeds, and bins of refuse fill the yards. In this part of town, garbage doesn't get collected; it gets burned. The acrid smell hangs in the air. Maddy can hear the echoes of guard dogs barking down the street.

Deva is clearly embarrassed. "I'm sorry that this is me."

Maddy brushes it off. "Are you kidding? You should see some of the places *I've* lived." She squeezes Deva's arm. "They'll get to this block eventually. You'll see. Just be patient."

Deva reaches for the doorknob.

"Deva, wait." Maddy doesn't want to ask, but she has to. Deva turns around.

"Did you know?" Maddy says.

"Know? Know what?"

Maddy folds her arms over her chest. "About my powers. About what I did. About who I am."

Deva glances down for a moment, then looks up to meet Maddy's eyes. "Of course I knew," she says. "I was there. In Times Square. That day. I saw you. I saw the whole thing. Lightning bolts and all."

Maddy gets a twinge in her belly. She runs her fingers along a rusted railing. "Why didn't you ever say anything?"

Deva takes a step toward her. "Because I didn't want you to think that's why I wanted to be friends."

"Are you sure it's not?"

"Yes," says Deva firmly. "I'm sure. It was never about that." She leans in and cracks a smile. "It's because you let me cheat off your Criminal Procedures quiz."

Maddy laughs. True or not, she'll take it. "Okay," she says. "That's definitely a solid basis for a friendship."

"So, we're good?" asks Deva.

"Absolutely," says Maddy. "I'm sorry. It's stupid. I just had to ask."

"No problem," says Deva. "I wouldn't want you to feel I liked you for the wrong reason." She moves a step closer.

Before Maddy realizes what's happening, Deva moves in tight and kisses her on the mouth. Gentle, but passionate.

Maddy freezes for a second, then starts to pull away. Then her arms wrap around Deva's shoulders and she starts to kiss back. Her heart is racing. She's surprised. Excited. Confused. Has she been missing signals this whole time? Or maybe ignoring them?

Deva gently breaks off the kiss and cups Maddy's face in her hands. "Great night," she says. She quietly opens the door and slips inside. Maddy just watches. Her heart is pounding. Her head is swimming.

She turns toward the street. In the glow of the limo's dome light, she sees Moe's head whip around to face front. She walks down the sidewalk and reaches for the front passenger door. She pulls it open and slides into the front seat, then just sits there for a few seconds, breathing out and breathing in.

"Home?" asks Moe.

Maddy nods.

Moe eases the car slowly away from the curb. Maddy can still feel the blood flushing her cheeks. "Not one word," she says.

"About what?"

"About what you just saw."

Moe shrugs. "My eyes aren't what they used to be."

CHAPTER 29

DAWN IS BARELY breaking when I walk out of my bedroom in my robe the next morning. I heard Maddy come in at four. She'll get a few choice words from me when she wakes up. Margo is still sound asleep. As I make the turn toward the stairs, I see Burbank pacing in the hall. He looks nervous or happy, or both. Burbank is a hard man to read, even for me—and I consider myself an expert. He looks up when he spots me.

"I need to show you something," he says.

"Pre-coffee?" This better be important.

He nods. Clearly, it is. At least for him.

I follow him down the hall and up the back staircase to the third floor, where my live-in help used to reside. Cook. Housekeeper. Valet. Those were the days.

"So how do you feel?" I ask. "After the accidental sedation?"

"Fine. No cobwebs."

I can't remember the last time I was on the third floor. Probably a hundred and fifty years ago. Burbank shows me toward a cramped space under the attic stairs—an architectural dead end. Always bothered me.

I stop in the doorway and look in. I was not expecting this.

Burbank has made the place his own.

There's a metal table with a desk chair against one wall. On the other side, the wall is lined with heavy-duty shelves, packed edge-to-edge with electronic devices. Controllers. Monitors. Meters. Scanners. The room is glowing from dozens of blinking LEDs. Wires and cables poke through ports in the walls and loop in fat coils on the floor.

"What do you think?" asks Burbank.

I take a step inside. "Where did all this come from?"

"The basement. It was a gold mine."

"What about the power?" Residential voltage is still being rationed, even on the better streets like ours.

"I'm siphoning off the main municipal feed," says Burbank. "I doubt we'll trip any alerts. This stuff is pretty light on amps."

"What the hell is *this*?" It's Jericho, peeking in from the hallway. His room is directly underneath us. He must have heard our footsteps.

A few seconds later, Moe pops in right behind him. "Jesus! I *wondered* what Burbank was hiding up here," he says. "I thought it might be a blow-up doll."

I can see that Burbank isn't happy about Jericho and Moe intruding. He seems to get anxious in close quarters—and this room is barely big enough for two people.

On the other hand, he clearly wants to show off. I think he wants to prove that he's every bit as sharp at communications as the *original* Burbank.

I wave my hand toward the wall of gear. "Okay. I'm officially impressed. What have we got?"

Burbank adjusts his glasses and checks off the devices, shelf by shelf. "Alarm system. Comms panel. Video decks. Police channel. International tap. Network interface..."

"You've got *internet* up here?" asks Jericho, incredulous.

"Rudimentary," says Burbank. "I can probably hack into the few networks that are still functioning, depending on signal strength and bandwidth." He rattles on with a bunch of terms that are just gibberish to me. *Transmission protocols. Packet-switching. Asynchronous transfer mode.* But Moe and Jericho know exactly what he's talking about, and I can see they're amazed.

"And check this out," says Burbank.

He taps a few buttons and a panel of video monitors lights up with rotating views of my whole property—from the front entrance to the back garden. On a monitor covering the rear lawn, we can see two figures clearly. One is Jessica, leaning on a stone railing. The other is Bando, forcefully relieving himself.

"You better not have a tap in my *bath*room," says Jericho.

From what I can see, this has to be one of the most sophisticated comms setups in the city. Definitely the best I've ever seen.

"Nice work, Burbank." I pat him on the shoulder. He flinches slightly.

Suddenly another monitor sounds a chirping alert. Our heads swivel to a screen on the top shelf. It's showing a bird's-eye view of the front driveway. As we watch, three armored vehicles pull in around the paved circle, leaving a wide space in front of the door.

A squad of men in dark uniforms jump out of the vehicles, guns in their hands. But they don't move toward the house. They just scan the area and wait. Two seconds later, we see what they're waiting for.

A fourth vehicle—an even heavier one—swoops up the driveway and slides into the empty space. A couple of the gunmen fall back to guard the new arrival's rear door.

Jericho turns for the hallway. "I'll get the shotgun!"

"Wait! Hold on." My eyes are fixed on the screen. "Nobody move. I'm going down alone." I nod to Burbank as I back out of the room. "No matter what happens, record *everything*."

If I'm about to get shot or dismembered, at least they'll have something to remember me by.

CHAPTER 30

AS SOON AS I open the door, I'm confronted by a wall of armed men. Then the wall parts, and I'm staring at a face I never expected to see in person. I do my best not to appear stunned. But I am.

The man standing in front of me is Lucian Diaz, president of the Americas, now the most powerful politician in the Western Hemisphere. What the hell does he want with me?

Before I can ask, two of the bodyguards pull my arms out to my sides and pat me down, shoulders to ankles, under and over my robe. Diaz stands politely at the threshold, smoothing his bespoke suit. When the guards finish, they step to the side.

"I apologize for the indignity, Mr. Cranston," says Diaz. "May I come in?"

For most citizens, a visit from Lucian Diaz would be the next best thing to having Abraham Lincoln himself show up on your doorstep. But I have an instinctive distrust of politicians, even one who's as popular and beloved as this one.

I give the president a nod and wave him in. "No sense wasting a good body search."

Diaz moves into the center of the foyer. The guards take up a protective formation around him.

"I'm aware this is a surprise, Mr. Cranston."

"Yes, Mr. President, it is. Which is why you caught me in my bathrobe."

Diaz has a light brown complexion and an accent so suave and worldly it almost sounds fake. Born in Ecuador, raised in Texas, educated in Boston. I guess he has a right to sound eclectic.

"I'm here because of your reputation, Mr. Cranston. I know that you were instrumental in eliminating the prior regime. In a way, I owe my office to you."

Diaz is one of the many global politicians who stayed low during the Khan years, hoping for an opening while they tried to avoid being assassinated. With the dictator gone, strongmen of various stripes emerged to consolidate their power. The West was hungry for Diaz's mix of purpose and principle. And his movie-star charisma didn't hurt. After uniting a mix of constituencies, he now governs almost half of the planet, from Alaska to the tip of Cape Horn. As rulers go, Diaz is pretty highminded. And very popular.

"You won the election in a landslide, Mr. President. The people are behind you. What do you need from me?" I doubt that he's here to offer me a cabinet post.

Diaz clasps his hands in front of his chest. "I'll come to the point, Mr. Cranston. You've heard of the Command?"

I'm not sure how much I should reveal, or how much he already knows. So I hold my cards close. "I've seen their work."

"Well, then, Mr. Cranston, my ask is simple: I want your help to erase them from the planet."

My eyes keep flicking to the armed men behind Diaz. "Sorry if I seem antsy. The last president who stood where you're standing tried to kill me."

Diaz laughs, showing the same dazzling smile that beamed from a million campaign posters. "*Kill* you? Mr. Cranston, from everything I've heard, that would be a criminal waste of talent."

His laugh makes me relax a little. "Well, then you probably know that I'm primarily an investigator. I gather evidence. I follow leads..."

"Spare me the modesty," says Diaz, his smile evaporating. "You are far more than an investigator. You have powers none of my scientists seem to be able to decipher. Supernatural abilities. The power to summon fire and lightning." He leans in with a low whisper. "The power to shape-shift at will."

I don't like where this is headed. For decades, I kept my special abilities secret. Only my closest associates ever knew what I was capable of. Putting my powers on display for the whole city to see a year ago was not my choice. Khan had to be defeated, and he picked a very public place for the battle. But the fact that a politician's staff knows my entire skill set is not reassuring. In fact, it's unnerving.

"So show me," Diaz says.

"Show you what?"

"Shape-shift for me. Turn into something else. I want to see it for myself."

This gets my back up even more.

"With all due respect, Mr. President—I'm not a trained monkey."

Diaz stiffens slightly and his expression clouds over. He's clearly not accustomed to being turned down.

"Understood," he says. "Then let me show *you* something. I insist."

CHAPTER 31

BURBANK, MOE, AND Jericho are standing stiffly in the hallway when I walk upstairs with the leader of half of the world. They've obviously been watching and listening on the monitors, but from the expressions on their faces, they still can't believe this is happening. It's safe to say that Lucian Diaz is the first president any of them has ever met. I make the introductions short and sweet.

"Mr. President, my associates. Druke, Shrevnitz, and Burbank."

"Do they need to be here?" asks Diaz.

"Yes, they do. They know what I know."

Diaz waits impatiently as the guards give all three the same vigorous pat-down that I got. Then he pulls a video stick from his jacket pocket and holds it up.

"Somebody play this."

Burbank nervously plucks it from the president's fingers. "Follow me, sir." He leads the way to his homemade comm center. Diaz steps in behind him. The rest of us crowd in as Burbank slides the video stick into a slot in the video console. A large monitor blinks and brightens.

The scenes are even more disturbing than the footage

my source sent me, and the video has been sharpened and enlarged to make the horror even more visceral. And unlike the videos I received, this one has sound. The tiny room fills with the roar of military machines. Then gunfire, explosions, and screams of pain.

Diaz lets the horror play out for a half minute or so, then reaches past Burbank to slide the volume down. The images keep playing in the background.

"Bad as this is," says Diaz, "we believe it's just a sideshow. Destroying resources and setting populations against each other is just a way of masking the real threat."

He nods to Burbank. "Freeze it here."

Burbank taps a key.

"Now roll it back. Slowly."

Burbank reverses the footage, frame by frame.

"Stop," says Diaz.

Burbank freezes on the image of a figure in black ducking into a cement bunker. The location appears to be somewhere in the Asian highlands. Maybe Pakistan. Maybe Tibet. The subject is only visible in a few frames, and even with enhanced video, it's hard to see much. He's draped in flowing tribal robes from head to toe, and the view is from the back. We can't see a face. There's not enough to catch much body movement.

If I had to testify in court, I'd say that the person of interest was tall and thin. Beyond that, I'd be guessing.

"Who the hell is that?" asks Jericho. Never afraid to speak up.

"We never saw this guy before," adds Moe, drafting off Jericho's nerve.

Diaz ignores them both.

"You think that's the Destroyer of Worlds?" I ask.

"That's my opinion," says Diaz. "It's the only image we have."

I lean in toward the screen. "So this one person runs the Command? He's orchestrating all this insanity?"

Diaz nods. "The Destroyer is stirring the pot to prepare for something bigger. We believe that he's close to perfecting a superweapon, capable of wiping out entire populations in seconds." He leans toward me. "And we have to find it before Toor Bayani does."

I'm trying not to show it, but this is worse than I thought. Toor Bayani rules Chinasia—the forced union of China, Japan, and the entire Asian subcontinent under one totalitarian regime. Bayani is a brutal despot, and a bitter rival to his counterparts in Europe and the West. Diaz is content to run one hemisphere. Bayani wants to run the whole world. With a mega-weapon in his hands, he'd be a big step closer.

"What's the technology?" I ask. "Who's working on it? Where's the factory?"

"If I knew any of that," says Diaz, "I wouldn't need you." He looks at me as if we're the only two people in this uncomfortably stuffy room. "So. Are you with me, Mr. Cranston? Will you help?"

It would be hard to say no. But before I answer, I feel the need to do one thing.

Suddenly, the guards are jumping toward the president, guns out. Can't blame them. Because I'm now sitting on his shoulder, having shape-shifted into a chattering rhesus monkey.

"Well," Moe chuckles, "you wanted a demo, right?"

As the guards grab for me, I jump to Jericho, clinging to his thick arm like it's a tree branch. Jericho elbows the guards aside until he's face-to-face with Diaz.

"We're in," he says. "All of us. Whatever it takes."

Exactly what I would have said. If monkeys could talk.

CHAPTER 32

Singpa, Bangladesh / Midnight

THE MOON IS obscured behind heavy clouds. The embers of cooking fires are the only bright spots in the darkness. The tiny jungle settlement is swollen with refugees, huddled in makeshift shelters.

The young mother, just seventeen, is exhausted after a twelve-hour trek with her baby boy, just two months old. Lines on maps are meaningless to her. All she knows is that her village on the other side of the river is gone, the men and boys taken. She feels lucky to find shelter here in the middle of the rain forest.

While the mother suckles her baby, the old woman whose tiny tent they're sharing sits smoking in the corner. They'll be safe here, the old woman says. No roads.

Boats are the only way in. No army will find them. Not even Toor Bayani's.

The air outside is alive with the clicks and chirps of insects. As the mother shifts her baby to the other breast, she hears the buzzing intensify, as if some huge hive had suddenly been stirred.

The old woman steps forward and parts the tent flap. There's a loud zipping sound and the back of the tent is splattered with blood. The woman drops with a heavy thud, her head split open like a melon. The teen-age mother crawls to the opening, clutching her baby to her chest. The buzzing is louder now. She sees red lights coming through the darkness, weaving through the trees.

Suddenly, the village is raked by a stream of bullets. Tents and huts are demolished as if sliced by a scythe. Screams. Panic. The mother pulls her baby tight and starts to run. But now the whole village is surrounded by flames. And the flying machines with the red eyes are everywhere. No escape. There is only one small mercy for the young mother. She doesn't see her son die.

She dies first.

CHAPTER 33

I CAN FEEL my eyes glazing over as I watch the fire crackling in the parlor fireplace. The hundred-year-old Scotch is having its effect. Numbing. Pleasant. Then I hear Dache shout from the other side of the room. "Park Place! Pay up!" I turn to see Jericho handing over a thick stack of pastel-colored play money.

I hate board games. Always have. Too much luck, not enough logic.

So while the rest of the household is immersed in a fierce Monopoly contest, I'm content to just sip my drink and observe. I guess it's a good sign that Maddy didn't protest when Dache decided to hang around after their lesson. Maybe she's getting used to him. The monk is sitting on the floor with the others—Maddy, Margo, Jessica, Jericho, Moe, and Burbank—like it's a normal family night. And from the stack of pretend cash in front of him, he appears to be winning big.

Bando leans his head against my seat cushion. I reach down to scratch him between the ears, his favorite spot. My mind is warm and fuzzy. I should be thinking about the president's challenge, about a way to tackle the

Command, about a plan for tracking down the World's Fair killer. Instead, I'm just thinking how lucky I am to have the people who mean the most to me in one room.

One evening off can't hurt, right?

Suddenly, I hear a blast from outside. The weakened windows shatter. Lines of black holes appear on the parlor wall, blasting off thick chunks of plaster. Armor-piercing ammo. Blasting through Khan's reinforced glass. I hit the floor and crawl toward the others. Everybody flattens themselves on the carpet. Everybody except Dache. He sits perfectly still as furniture splinters around him.

"The damn drones!" yells Jericho. "They're back!"

Dache shakes his head. "Chinasian commandos," he shouts over the metallic bursts. "Highly skilled. And relentless."

I guess the president's visit was no secret. And being on his team put a bounty on our heads. "Nobody move!" I shout.

The gunfire gets more intense. Multiple shooters. Multiple angles. Light fixtures explode. Glassware shatters. Books are blasted into confetti. I'm waiting for a pause, deciding when to make a move. I see Dache reaching for Maddy's hand.

"Come, Madeline," he says. "Let's show them who you are."

Maddy pushes herself up from the floor and stands in the middle of the room, as bullets whiz around her. I grab for her leg to pull her back down. *"No!"*

Margo screams, "Stop! Don't do it!"

Dache puts his arm around Maddy and walks her across the floor toward the front entrance. He yanks her to the side as another stream of bullets blasts through the shattered windows. He looks back at us, his voice calm, but firm. "If you don't trust me, how can she?"

He nods to Maddy. She opens the door.

CHAPTER 34

MADDY WALKS OUT onto the dark lawn with Dache at her side. For a moment, the shooting stops. She feels the adrenaline rush that always accompanies fear. But there is no fear. Instead, it's a feeling she couldn't describe if she wanted to. Her mind now separates from the danger—from the obvious fact that there are killers in the darkness. And that they want to see her die.

As her eyes adjust, she sees black-masked commandos filtering out from behind foliage and walls. A dozen, maybe more. Long metal magazines hang from their flat-black guns. The man in the lead raises his weapon and points it at her face. He pulls the trigger. Maddy's in another zone now—a zone where she can actually see the bullets as they leave the barrel of the gun. She stares, unblinking, as the slugs stop an inch from her face, then watches them drip onto the grass like beads of mercury.

She hears Dache call out an order in Mandarin, which she somehow understands. His voice is calm and assured. The commandos stop in mid-step and lower their weapons, letting them dangle from straps around their shoulders. One by one, they walk to a storm grate near the entrance and slide their weapons into the opening. Maddy hears the rattles and splashes from the sewer chamber beneath the street.

Dache whispers into her ear. She calls out a phrase in perfect Mandarin, which she can now speak. The commandos move back onto the lawn, peeling off their tactical outfits until they're down to their black underwear. All at once, they drop to their knees and bow in prayer, as if in a temple.

"Good job," says Dache, waving his arm over the group. "New converts."

"You have a weird sense of humor," says Maddy.

Dache gives her a respectful bow. "Coming from you, Madeline, that is a true compliment."

CHAPTER 35

AT MIDNIGHT. I'M the last one still up. I'm staring at the shattered parlor windows, wondering how long our luck can hold out. A man's home is his castle, but this place is starting to feel like a shooting gallery. For tonight at least, we're all still breathing. Thanks to Dache and Maddy.

A few hours ago, Dache lined up the Chinasian commandos on the front lawn and sent them on their way, single file, to a monastery upstate. A fifty-mile overnight hike. I wanted to question them first, but Dache said it would be a waste of time. The commandos had been trained by Toor Bayani, and they were as mindless as Dr. Mocquino's bloodsuckers. They had nothing in their heads but the mission. And now, not even that. Dache says none of them will ever touch a weapon again.

I take one last look out one of the broken windows and then head upstairs. As I walk down the hallway, I hear voices and laughter from Maddy's room, like she's having some kind of slumber party. I knock on the door, announce myself, and peek in. The laughter is coming from Dache, high-pitched and silly. He's sitting cross-legged on the floor with Maddy's antique tape player in his lap, volume up full. Maddy is sitting across from him, clearly enjoying his reaction.

They're listening to one of the old Shadow radio shows from Maddy's collection, and Dache is clearly eating it up. Maddy obviously knows the script by heart. She's mouthing every word from every character. She must have heard this tape a hundred times.

She must not have heard me. Neither did Dache, who's listening to the program intently, moving his body in sync with the action—*feeling* every twist in the drama. As the episode ends, the radio announcer intones, *"As ye sow evil, so shall ye reap evil. Crime does not pay. The Shadow knows!"*

Dache throws his head back in delight, clapping and whistling.

Maddy reaches over and clicks the player off.

"I thought you'd like it," she says.

"Like it? Madeline, I *loved* it." He hands her the tape player and rests his palm gently on her knee. "Perfect end to a perfect night. You did well." And then he disappears.

I close the door softly. Earlier, I asked her what happened to her out on the lawn. I saw what she did, but I wanted to know how she did it, what it felt like. She told me that was between her and Dache.

I admit that stung a bit, but I guess I should be happy that they've formed such a close bond, even if it makes me feel like a third wheel. If there's anyone in the world I can trust with Maddy, it's Dache. That's why I asked him to come in the first place.

I still think of him as my father and my brother. That hasn't changed. Not even after ten thousand years.

CHAPTER 36

THE NEXT NIGHT is the grand opening of the World's Fair, and Margo and I are headed for the scene of the crimes. Moe insists on driving us in Khan's limo. He knows that Margo enjoys her creature comforts, even if they're left over from a madman.

She runs her hands along the cushioning in the back-seat. "I hate that we're sitting where that maniac sat, but this leatherwork is exquisite."

We can see fireworks shooting into the sky as we approach the fair site. It's the first time I've been back since my visit with Moe, and the difference is amazing. The crews have obviously worked overtime to get the place ready, and the venue looks spectacular.

The huge main pavilion seems to glow from within, and the news crawl around the peak spells out WELCOME! in a dozen rotating languages. The engineers must have rerouted a large portion of the city's electrical supply, because every pavilion and pathway gleams.

"Omigosh!" says Margo. "You weren't kidding!" Through the car window, she's getting her first glimpse at the invisible Ferris wheel. It's hard not to be impressed.

The ride looks even more spectacular at night, with spotlight beams shooting up from below as riders circle in midair, a thousand feet up. I slide out of the backseat and help Margo out. "I *told* you it was amazing."

Moe gives us a wave and drives off to wait in the parking lot. Margo and I walk through the arched entrance. No admission charge. New York and the rest of the world are paying for everything.

The fair is set up as an oversized village, with winding pathways leading through all kinds of pavilions—science, art, technology, music. The air is filled with the aromas from a hundred different outdoor bistros and food booths. The fireworks pop overhead and reflect on the surface of the East River below.

"Think he's here?" asks Margo. "The killer?"

"How could he resist?"

Over the past week, the sites of the murders have no doubt been paved over. All evidence erased. But predators tend to stick with territory they know. He could be part of the crowd or one of the thousands of workers, hiding in plain sight. It will take us hours to do a walkthrough of the whole fair.

But first things first.

I grab Margo's hand and pull her toward the massive Ferris wheel. The closer we get, the higher it looks. The riders at the top of the arc are just dots in the sky. Margo is generally fearless, but I know she's not crazy about heights. She looks up at the floating benches and pulls back on my arm.

I pat her gently. "C'mon! It'll be like flying!"

"Right," she says. "Which is one step away from falling."

The crowd gets thicker as we move toward the attraction. A lot of people are walking with their eyes tilted up. We sidestep a couple of collisions. Just ahead, I spot a young man gliding purposefully through the crowd, head swiveling, arms loose. I recognize that kind of body language in an instant.

I nudge Margo. "Straight ahead, blue denim jacket."

"I see him. You think he's working?"

"Just watch."

We pick up our pace until we're just a few yards behind him. I keep my eyes on the young man's right hand. He eases himself between two couples and presses close to a woman holding an ice cream cone. Her purse is hanging loosely from her left shoulder. Without looking down, the man dips two fingers into the purse and lifts out a wallet.

"Slick," Margo whispers.

The man pockets the wallet and heads for a trash bin. That's where he intends to ditch the wallet and palm the cash. I take a few long strides to catch up to him. When he reaches to pull the wallet out, it's gone. Already in my hand. He whips around, but I'm now ahead of him. Margo brushes by me. I slip the wallet to her. She sidles up close to the woman and drops the wallet back into her purse.

Margo smiles as I catch up to her. I could do this all night. No special powers required. Kind of fun. But we're not here to frustrate pickpockets, and we both know it. We're here to find a killer.

That is, after we take the ride of our lives.

CHAPTER 37

AT THIS MOMENT, Jon DeLeon is feeling like the luckiest high school sophomore in New York. The World's Fair opening was the hook that finally got Britta Lofton to go out with him, and it was definitely worth the wait.

As they walk along the main path through the fair, Jon sees other guys turning their heads to catch a look at his date. Red dress. Long legs. Wavy black hair. Best of all is her laugh—full-throated, with a hilarious little squeak at the end. He can't believe he's actually here with her.

When Britta threads her fingers through his for the first time, Jon feels like his head might explode. From that moment, the displays and pavilions are just a haze. All he wants is to be alone with her. Too bad they're surrounded by a few thousand people and more bright lights than he's ever seen in his life.

They walk along the winding pathways, past food stands and exhibitions, until they reach the Amazon rain forest—actually, a small sample of it. According to the sign over the entrance, the enclosed two acres of transplanted jungle represent the amount of rain forest being burned and cleared by loggers every single second.

But the two eager teenagers pay no attention to the sobering ecological message. And they're not thinking about the massive engineering and irrigation effort it took to bring the exhibit to life. All they know is that the trees are tall and the foliage is thick and it looks like a good place to make out in privacy.

Ten yards in, they're surrounded by ferns and kapok trees and the chatter of jungle birds. The ground is spongy with moss. The artificial canopy far above mimics the night sky, blocking the light from the rest of the fair. They head deeper into the exhibit, until they reach an isolated niche overhung with vines and thick fronds. A small stream winds through the tree roots nearby, creating a subtle rush of white noise. They don't even need to close their eyes to imagine they're alone in the Amazon basin. The illusion is that perfect.

By now, their clothes and hair are damp from the humidity. Britta grabs the hem of her dress and playfully pretends to wring it out. She laughs her fantastic laugh. Then abruptly, she stops. She points over Jon's shoulder then presses against him, her eyes twitching with fear. Jon turns and spots a quick movement in the thick foliage.

Then, in a blur, he sees a raised arm and a contorted green face.

CHAPTER 38

MARGO AND I are being held in our bench by an invisible magnetic belt. The seat is transparent and our legs are dangling in midair. We're nearing the top of the arc, gravity be damned. Margo is clinging to my arm so tightly that I can feel her fingernails through my shirt. A few minutes into the ride, she still has her doubts.

"Lamont, are you sure this thing can be trusted?"

I look down at the massive battery housing at the center of the apparatus, and the emergency generator below. "As long as the magnets hold out."

We're nearly seventy stories up, the height of a skyscraper. The whole fair is spread out below us like a field of light. The ascent felt thrilling and perilous. Here at the top, it's amazingly peaceful, like being part of the sky. On the floating benches above and below us, the riders are mostly silent, just taking in the view. I feel Margo relax a bit. She leans her head against my shoulder and snuggles in.

"Remember Chicago?" she asks, looking out over the river.

I run my hand across her soft hair. "I do. Seems like another lifetime."

When Margo and I traveled together to the 1933 World's Fair, we barely knew each other. In fact, it was our first trip together. Terrible times for the country and the whole world. In the midst of the Great Depression, the fair was the one bright spot in the gloom. A CENTURY OF PROGRESS, the posters said.

That was the weekend when I first understood that Margo was going to be the best partner I ever had, in every possible way. On the train to Chicago, we had separate sleeping compartments. On the way back to New York, we only needed one. We've been together ever since.

I wrap my arms around Margo's shoulders and lean over to kiss her cheek.

"Don't get frisky," she says. "You'll give me vertigo."

By now, we're way above the murmur of the crowd and the sounds of traffic on the highway below. But there's one sound that carries in open air like nothing else.

A female scream.

CHAPTER 39

BY THE TIME I get there, security has a small corner of the rain forest blocked off. Two nervous guys in white uniforms are setting up portable screens near a small artificial stream. Another guy is intercepting visitors on a nearby path and escorting them back toward the main entrance. There's already a sign outside saying CLOSED FOR ROUTINE MAINTENANCE. Fair patrons are just walking by without a second look.

I have a perfect view of the whole scene, and nobody's bothering me. Nobody even *notices* me. Why would they? I'm just one more parrot in the jungle.

From the branch where I landed, I can see two teenagers lying next to each other alongside the stream. They're young. Maybe their first date. Definitely their last one. Their skulls are caved in. Exactly like the kids in the police photos. I hop to another branch for a better angle.

The water leading away from their shattered heads is tinted red. Except for bloodstains and mud, their clothes are intact. It doesn't look like a sex crime. What it looks like is a horror movie. Both kids are lying with their mouths hanging open and their hands clawed into the ground. From their necks to their hairlines, their faces are covered in bright green paint.

I'm feeling jumpy and guilty. If I hadn't been so determined to take a joy ride with Margo, maybe we could have been around to stop it. Or maybe the killer spotted us and waited until he knew we were out of the way.

I hear thrashing in the underbrush, then three more men burst into the clearing. I recognize Detective Roskow right away. A couple of young uniforms follow right behind him with body bags. Roskow practically shoves one of the security guys out of the way to get to the victims. He stops just a few inches from the deceased.

"Goddamnit!" he mutters.

The detective squats for a few seconds between the two corpses, then looks up at one of the security people. "What's the closest way out?"

The security guy looks nervous. "Should we wait for the medical examiner?"

Roskow brushes a wad of wet leaves off his shoe. "You want somebody to pronounce them dead?" He waves his hands over the bodies like a cheap magician. "Okay. Presto. They're dead." He stands up and clicks off a couple of photos of the bodies with a digital camera, then turns to the two cops. "Bag 'em."

He steps up to one of the security guys. "As soon as we're gone, lose the screens and rake this area. Back to nature. One hundred percent."

And that's it. No crime scene markers. No search for weapons. No pathologist to take body temperatures or check for hidden wounds. No crime scene investigators. The cops place the two black vinyl bags flat on the damp ground and lift the kids by their underarms and ankles. First the boy, then the girl. Their legs and arms are folded inside the plastic, then the zippers are pulled up over the faces. One lock of the girl's black hair is still sticking out when one of the cops throws her over his shoulder in a fireman's carry. The other cop takes the boy the same way.

I make the short flight through the trees from the murder scene to the back exit.

When the cops get there, I'm perched on top of the barrier that hides a paved service road. There's no ambulance waiting. No hearse. Just a black unmarked van. The two cops load the bodies into the back and climb in with them.

Roskow pounds the side of the truck twice with his fist and the truck takes off down the narrow road. He leans back against the barrier and pulls out his walkie.

"Yeah. Tell Bates we got two more. All clean. No witnesses."

I make a short hop to a pole directly above where Roskow is standing. Suddenly, I have an irresistible urge to shit on his head.

CHAPTER 40

Kalu Ganga River, Sri Lanka

THE CEREMONY BEGINS at dawn in the shadow of a huge stone dam, seven centuries old. A temple built from the same stone sits at the base of the dam, surrounded by thatched cottages.

As the first flicker of light kisses the river, clerics and families wade into the gently flowing water. They're all dressed in colorful gowns with flowered headdresses. The head priest stands thigh-deep in the green current and raises a long ceremonial stick over his head. He starts chanting in a low singsong cadence. The others echo him, slowly building in confidence and volume. The only sounds in the deep valley are the rising voices of the worshippers and the gentle rush of water.

Suddenly, the air is split by a series of loud booms. Flames and smoke belch from the center of the looming dam. The stone towers collapse and the belly of the structure bows out. Then the river blasts through.

Two seconds later, the foamy torrent hits the worshippers with the force of a hurricane, propelling two-ton stones like pebbles. Everybody turns toward shore, but nobody reaches it. Many are crushed to pulp before being swept away in the powerful current.

In seconds, the temple is gone. The cottages are gone. Everything is gone.

The high priest swirls downstream in a pinwheel pattern, impaled on his sacred stick.

CHAPTER 41

"ARE YOU SURE?" says Dache. "This is a step beyond."

I nod. I'm *more* than sure. I'm itchy and impatient. The skill I'm about to learn is called *chuanghu*. In my boyhood training, it was known as a forbidden skill, considered out of our reach. Dache has made it clear that it's powerful and dangerous. But I don't care. Let's get *moving*!

The two of us are in the middle of the garden behind my mansion, sitting on opposing stone benches. We're surrounded by flower beds and decorative trees. My senses are on full alert. I can smell the lilacs and crab apples. I can hear the twitters from ten different species of birds. Just being in the presence of Dache has always made me more aware and attuned. When I'm with him, I'm eager to absorb all I can.

If I'm being totally honest with myself, I realize that I'm a little jealous of all the new skills Dache has been teaching Maddy. Stupid, I know, to be competing with a nineteen-year-old. Maybe I miss the feeling of being the star pupil. But what I mostly want is to find the World's Fair killer. And Dache says this technique might help— as long I'm willing to risk losing my mind.

I settle on the bench, bare feet flat on the soft grass. Grounded and steady. But my heart is pounding hard. "What will it feel like?" I ask. "What will I see?"

"If I knew that, I would tell you," says Dache. "Chuanghu opens a channel based on something you've already experienced, or a place you've already visited. It allows you to see what happened there through the eyes of somebody else who has been in the same place, like tapping into another person's memory. A parallel past."

"*Whose* past?"

Dache shakes his head. "I can help you open the window. I cannot control what you see. Or who you become."

"And the risk?" He told me before, but I need to hear it again.

"The risk is that you don't come back. The risk is that your mind becomes somebody else's mind. And that your mind ceases to exist."

Dache is right. That's a truly terrifying concept—to be alive, but not myself. I worked hard for my life. Spent a century and a half in a coma waiting to live again. Maybe there's another way. Something that's not quite so radical. But, like I said, I'm impatient. And I didn't live this long by *not* taking chances. I don't have time for any more second thoughts.

I nod to Dache. "Do it."

He stands up and walks behind me. "Eyes closed," he says.

I feel his hands on both sides of my head, cradling my temples. I can remember the same feeling from when I was a boy, when Dache was trying to get me to focus on something important. "Do you have the place?" he asks.

"I do." I'm picturing the Amazon rain forest—the snippet of it that ended up at the World's Fair.

"Don't say it," Dache whispers. "Just think it."

At first, I feel nothing. As I start to form another

question, there's a bright flash and a small pop in my brain, like a bulb exploding.

Suddenly the scents and sounds of the garden are gone. I'm inhaling the thick atmosphere of the jungle. The air is heavy. The ground is spongy and damp. I feel myself walking, but in someone else's body. I'm human, but heavier and taller, and my breaths are coming from a bigger, deeper chest.

I'm following two shapes into the underbrush. My vision sharpens. Not perfect, but enough to see the shapes resolve into a tall boy and a girl in a red dress. I've never seen them before tonight, but I've chosen them. That much I understand. I can smell his sweat and her perfume. I can hear their supple young hearts beating. They're perfect.

I'm following them through the humid foliage, deeper and deeper toward darkness. A buzz of excitement rises in my belly, like an urgent tickle. When the girl turns around, I freeze. I feel heat rising in me. The girl grabs the boy. Now he turns to face me. There's no waiting. I need to move. *Now!*

In an instant. I see their expressions shift—from surprise to terror. They know they're about to die.

I know it, too.

I'm the one who's about to kill them.

CHAPTER 42

"WHAT THE HELL did you do to him?"

It's a woman's voice. Familiar, but foggy. My eyes are still clamped shut. I'm lying on the ground with hard pebbles pressing into my back. I'm not sure where I am, but I'm in my own body again. At least I think so.

"He pushed too far too fast." A man's voice.

"You're the teacher, dammit! *Control* him!" Another woman. Younger. As soon as she speaks, the haze in my brain starts to clear. I open my eyes and look up. I'm in my garden, with Margo and Maddy kneeling over me. Dache is sitting on the stone bench, hands folded in his lap. Margo turns on him.

"Dammit, Dache! He *always* tries to do too much. You know that. It's the way he's always been. That's why he's always just one step away from disaster. He *trusted* you!"

"I cautioned him," says Dache. "We discussed the risks."

"You should have *stopped* him!" Margo fires back.

I blink and run my hands over my face. I jerk my hands away, expecting to see blood. But I don't. Now I remember what just happened to me. Most of it, anyway.

I sit up and look at Margo. "I was there!"

"Where?"

"At the murder! The two kids at the fair. Last night. I just saw it."

I see Maddy's eyes narrow. "*What* murder?"

"We'll explain," says Margo.

But Maddy is way ahead of her. "Is this why you didn't want me at the fair? You knew somebody was going to be killed?"

My head hurts. I'm in no mood for an argument. "We knew it might happen, yes. And we didn't want it to be *you*!"

"Who did it?" asks Margo. "Who's the killer?"

I put my head in my hands, still a little shaky and confused. "I was. It was me."

Margo glares at Dache. "What's he talking about?"

Dache slides off the bench and helps me to my feet. "Lamont didn't kill anyone. He just saw it through the killer's eyes."

I pull away from Dache. "I'll go back! If I can see it from one of the victims' point of view, I can ID the killer."

"Over *my* dead body," says Margo. "The only place your brain is going is inside to rest."

Maddy is standing with arms folded over her chest. I know a sulking pose when I see one. She's angry at being kept in the dark about a case this important. And I guess she has a right to be. Was I just keeping her away to protect her—or to show her who's boss?

Dache steps up to distract her.

"Madeline," he says. "It's time for your training. You need to…"

Margo puts a hand up to stop him. "Forget it," she says. "You've done enough damage for one day." She puts her arm around my shoulder and leads me toward the house. Maddy turns toward Dache with fire in her eyes. I can tell she's about to give him a piece of her mind, too.

But before she can say a word, Dache is gone.

All that's left is a gently fluttering butterfly.

CHAPTER 43

BY THE NEXT morning, I feel pretty much back to normal. Maybe *better* than normal—the way you feel when you've lived through something that could have wrecked you. For a while after, all the regular activities of life seem more significant and meaningful.

Like picking out the right suit and tie.

"Lamont, for God's sake, slow down!" Margo is sitting up in bed, watching me get dressed. I can tell she half expects me to topple over.

"We need to go," I tell her. "The speech is at ten, remember?"

I'm switching gears again. I have no choice. Because along with trying to find the World's Fair killer, we also need to deal with the Command. And to do that, we need to keep the president of the Americas alive. He's scheduled to speak before the general assembly at United Nations Headquarters this morning, and Burbank picked up some chatter that somebody might try to kill him there. Big stage. Big opportunity. The chatter might be bogus, but I can't take that chance.

"Lamont, the man has his own security. So does the UN, I'm pretty sure."

"Not enough. We can't trust anybody else."

"Then talk Diaz out of speaking. He sought you out. Maybe he'll listen to you."

"Not on this he won't."

Most world leaders—good and bad—have an unquench-able need to show their faces in person. It feeds their ego and demonstrates their power. It lets people know who's in charge. It makes a statement. And makes them juicy targets. If somebody wants to kill one of the few decent leaders left on the planet, the United Nations would make a pretty historic setting.

"Margo, he asked for our help."

"Yes. By figuring out how to disarm the Command. Not by becoming his personal bodyguards."

I slip into my jacket and press an extra dimple into my pocket square. "I promise, he'll never even know we're there." I picked the dark gray pinstripe suit with the European cut. Like any cookie-cutter diplomat. "How do I look?"

Margo gives me a once-over. "Like you're ready to settle a border dispute."

I tap my watch.

Grumbling, Margo throws back the bedcovers, then straightens her nightgown over her long legs and shuffles to her dressing table mirror. To me, Margo is never anything less than beautiful—even now, when her face is a little puffy and her hair is matted on one side of her head. She leans toward the mirror and rubs her eyes.

"Give me ten minutes," she says. "I can't save the world looking like this."

CHAPTER 44

EXACTLY TEN MINUTES later, we're sitting in the back of the limo, headed toward UN Headquarters on the East River. Margo is sitting next to me, with only her beautiful blue eyes showing through a silk chiffon niqab—her idea for blending in.

As Moe drives, Jericho's head pops around the passenger seat headrest. "Feeling better, boss?"

"Will everybody please stop asking me how I feel? I'm fine. Focus on today."

In the back of my mind, I'm thinking of ways to lure the World's Fair killer into the open without risking my brain again, and without getting anybody else killed. But the *front* of my mind is focused on even bigger problems. World-shaking problems. Maybe world-*ending* problems.

Jericho faces front and does a quick comms check with home base. As we ride, Burbank is sitting in his tiny communications center under the top floor staircase, keeping track of everything, including us.

When we reach the corner of East 44th and UN Plaza, I see the iconic building looming ahead. But it's not what it used to be. The glass exterior is laced with vines, and some of the reflective panels have been replaced by plywood. Others are cracked and bowed. I guess we're lucky it's still standing at all.

During his regime, Khan had no use for diplomatic relations or peacekeeping missions. In a symbolic gesture, he had the UN's most revered statues thrown into the East River. The same civic committee that supervised the World's Fair burnished the building just enough to make it presentable again—or at least not a total embarrassment.

Moe pulls around the circular fountain in front of the building. As we slow down in front of the entrance, a guard pounds on the hood and waves us forward. "No stopping!" he shouts. He's jumpy, pistol at the ready.

When I turn around and look through the rear window, I see why. An imposing motorcade is sweeping into the circle right behind us. The president of the Americas has arrived.

The motorcade stops. We all watch as the security team jumps out and secures a pathway to the entrance. Lucian Diaz emerges from the rear seat of the middle vehicle, buttoning the jacket of his suit. He gives onlookers a flash of his broad smile before reverting to his purposeful demeanor. A small crowd of civilians behind a police barrier shouts and waves frantically, as if they were watching Jesus stroll on the Sea of Galilee.

"He looks pretty confident," says Margo.

"Right," says Jericho. "Let's see how long *that* lasts." He climbs out of the passenger side and opens the back door. Margo slides out first in her flowing floor-length garment. It's simple, but elegant. Pure Margo.

Before sliding out of the backseat, I lean forward toward Moe. "Okay. We're going in. You know the drill."

He turns with a grin and repeats the mantra of the

getaway driver. "Stay close. Stay awake. Keep the motor running."

I reach out and pat him on the shoulder. He's great behind the wheel, just like his ancestor. And more important, he's a good man—as good as they come.

I watch him pull away toward a VIP parking area and then I head into the entryway with Margo and Jericho. The instant we cross the threshold, we're no longer in the United States. We're in international territory. Normal rules no longer apply. Especially these days. I'm not sure what to expect.

As we pass through the metal detectors, the guards only give our forged passports a cursory look. A lot of wasted effort on Burbank's part, and a bad sign for security overall. Seems loose and uncoordinated.

As we walk up the sweeping ramp to the second level, I can see how impressive this place must have been. I've heard about the great things that were achieved here. Now it feels like a relic. The walls are cracked and I can see ugly water stains crawling across the ceilings. The recent efforts were a touch-up, nothing more. Sad.

The official delegates are already moving into the huge Assembly Hall. The reception space is packed with minor diplomats and aides, speaking a dozen languages. Whispers of new attacks and mass graves are racing around the room. I can only catch snippets of conversations, but it's clear things are getting worse, not better, all over the world.

Margo is better at languages than I ever was. I glance at her to see if she's picking up anything meaningful. She shakes her head. No surprise. Trying to follow a conversation in this hubbub is like trying to pick one buzz out of a hive.

I spot Diaz's security detail standing in front of a door just off the lobby. A few seconds later, the man himself emerges from the room and walks toward the entrance to the Assembly Hall. He pauses for a moment, straightens his shoulders, and nods. When the doors open for him, the diplomats inside rise to their feet. Nothing but respect as Diaz strides down the green-carpeted aisle toward the podium.

Time to split up. It's our best chance of spotting any danger. There's no way three people can cover the entire complex, but with Burbank's help, we'll do our best. The threat to Diaz could be totally fake, or totally real. And if it's real, it could come from any direction.

I nod to Jericho and Margo. Then I disappear. Right there in the middle of the UN lobby. The four men chatting next to me don't even notice. As soon as I'm gone, Margo heads down the main aisle to take a seat in the audience. Jericho starts making his way toward the elevator bank. I know we're spread too thin. I really wish I had Hawkeye and Tapper along with us. If they're anything like the men they were named after, they'd add solid skills and sound judgment.

But right now, I'm not sure they even exist.

CHAPTER 45

BACK AT THE mansion, Burbank is totally focused—and totally content. He prefers working alone. That's when he feels most secure and centered. Huddled in his tiny chamber under the staircase, he's unencumbered and in control. No distractions. He feels like himself. His *best* self.

He doesn't mind the company of animals, though. When Bando wanders in and starts sniffing around the console, Burbank gives him a scratch between the ears and lets him settle down under his chair.

"Okay, buddy, let's see what we can see..."

Burbank taps a keypad. The console lights up.

Hacking into the security system at United Nations Headquarters was a lot easier than it should have been. Some of the technology was almost a century old, and even the modern software hadn't been updated in decades. The hodgepodge of wired and wireless circuits had lot of weak links, easy to exploit, even with Burbank's Frankensteined equipment.

He managed to tap into a fair number of security cameras, especially the black-and-white antiques.

He's also got a setup for biometric scanning, to detect NanoDevices in temperature. A lot of the UN audio scramblers, however, are airtight. They block incoming communication in large chunks of the building. In those spaces Burbank can see the team, but he can't communicate with them. The one clear channel he has is to the limo. He toggles the mic button. "You hear me, Moe?"

"Loud and clear."

"What's the mood?"

"If Diaz talks as good as he looks," says Moe, "hugs all around."

"Stay put," says Burbank. "I'll let you know when to move."

"Don't worry," says Moe. "I've got my seat reclined and the AC on full. I'm not going anywhere."

Burbank scans the array of small monitors in front of him, each one connected to a series of visual and thermal taps. Some of the connections are clearer than others, but he's got a fair overview of the building—in bits and pieces.

On one screen, he sees Margo taking her seat in the General Assembly Hall gallery. Her resplendent garment is a clear marker, even without the tracker sewn into the hem. On another screen, Burbank spots Jericho headed toward a rear staircase.

Burbank's eyes flick to the view backstage, where human security is tightest. Men with automatic weapons stand in the wings like a small army, braced for trouble.

Burbank adjusts his glasses and squints at the screen. He toggles a key to zoom in over one of the agent's shoulders. He smiles. Sure enough. There's Lamont, right where he said he'd be, just a few yards behind the podium, taking up almost no space at all.

An actual fly on the wall.

CHAPTER 46

IT'S TIME.

The crowd in the large auditorium settles into their seats behind rising rows of curved desks. As Burbank watches, Diaz mounts the short step to the rostrum and takes his place behind a podium with the UN emblem emblazoned in gold on the front.

At least half of the delegates place headsets over one ear to hear the simultaneous translation. Every seat is filled, except for a row of chairs directly in front of the podium. All of those spaces—about fifty of them—are vacant. Diaz lets the murmurs settle until the room is as silent as a cathedral. Then he begins to speak.

"Madam Secretary General. Delegates. Fellow citizens of the world. I'm grateful for your invitation to address you today in this temple of peace." The audio feed is good, and Diaz has one of those booming voices that would carry even without a microphone.

Amplified, it rattles the speakers in Burbank's tiny enclosure.

"All of us in this grand hall hold positions of power and

influence, but we are not the most important people here today. Far from it."

Diaz gestures toward the back of the assembly hall. Every head turns. The massive doors open. Burbank switches to a wide view of the chamber as a solemn procession heads down the center aisle.

A procession of children.

Some are teenagers. Some are as young as four or five, nervously holding hands with older companions. The group includes children of every race and hue. And every single one is broken in some way. Some are limping or walking with canes. Some are marked by brutal scars. Others are missing hands or arms. Several propel themselves in wheelchairs. The delegates turn, wide-eyed and silent, as the procession passes by them.

"These are the important ones," says Diaz. "The children of conflict and hatred. The orphans. The maimed. The ones who will never see again, or walk again. They are not here to elicit your pity. Pity is cheap. They are here to bear witness to our decisions—to the path we choose from here. They are here to ask if we will unite against evil, or be consumed by it."

One by one, then in whole groups, the delegates and spectators rise and begin to applaud. Burbank sees Margo stand along with the others. As the procession reaches the front of the hall, the children file left and right to fill the spaces in front. They settle with their faces turned up toward the podium.

"In this room, we speak in many tongues," says Diaz. "But these children have a common language. The language of grief, loss, and pain. This language knows no borders. And it needs no translation. We all understand it. The question is, are we bold enough to do something about it?"

"Damn, he's good," Burbank mutters.

Suddenly a beep sounds from one of the thermal monitors.

Then another.

Burbank leans forward, sweat popping on his forehead. The scans are too primitive to reveal much detail. All he can see is that there are two new human heat signatures in the building—in places no human should be.

CHAPTER 47

TWO THREATS. TWO different levels of the building. Burbank quickly reviews his options. Lamont, in his present form, is unreachable. For now, Burbank will have to rely on Jericho and Margo. He leans forward and speaks into the console mic. "Two intrusions. Levels three and four."

On his screen, he sees Jericho and Margo stiffen slightly as they get the alert in their earpieces.

"I'll take four," says Jericho, moving quickly along a fourth-floor corridor. "Location?" His reply is scratchy, barely audible.

"I'll guide you," says Burbank.

On another screen, Burbank sees Margo stand and slip out of the back of the gallery. "I'll take three," she whispers. On the main monitor, Diaz is still speaking. Burbank turns the volume down. The president's smooth baritone is now just a low background in the tiny comms room. The threats are what matter now. Finding them. Eliminating them. Keeping the president alive.

The first heat signature is in the ductwork directly over the rostrum—seventy-five feet above Diaz. The thermal image appears as a reddish-orange blob. Organic and alive, for sure. But no clear definition. The second thermal image is on the third level, moving quickly along a restricted corridor. From the size and density, definitely human.

"Target one is in the ceiling vents," says Burbank.

"How high up?" asks Jericho.

"As high as you can go."

Margo is now in the foyer just outside the General Assembly, where scattered aides and visitors are watching the president's speech on huge wall-mounted monitors.

"Where am I headed?" she asks, chin dipped toward the mic in her collar.

"Secure corridor. One level up," says Burbank. "You'll need access."

Burbank watches as Margo walks purposefully toward the staircase at the far end of the foyer. She brushes past a security guard. For a second, his stout body is obscured by Margo's flowing garment. When he emerges into the clear again, his key card is missing from his belt.

"Got it," says Margo.

Burbank swivels back to Jericho's screen. But Jericho's gone. Out of sight. Out of range. Burbank slaps the console, hoping to jostle the connection back to life. But it's no use. Contact lost. *Dammit!*

Jericho is on his own.

CHAPTER 48

THE FOURTH-LEVEL CORRIDOR is nearly empty. Jericho waits for a few workers to disappear around a corner. Then he scrambles up a metal ladder mounted to an inside wall. He pushes open a ceiling hatch and muscles his way into a transverse aluminum ventilation duct. He clicks on a small flashlight and grips it between his teeth.

"Which way?" he mumbles to Burbank.

No reply.

Jericho can hear the voice of the president of the Americas booming through the sides of the metalwork. There must be a speaker column mounted near the ceiling.

He starts crawling through the narrow duct. He doesn't even know what he's looking for. He squeezes his broad shoulders toward his ears and inches forward, knees against the cold metal, fighting his growing claustrophobia. He feels like a mouse passing through the gullet of a snake.

Suddenly, a rivet pops underneath him. A narrow seam opens between two sections of the duct. As Jericho squirms past the break, he gets a glimpse of the audience four stories below him. Then he hears another sound.

This one is coming from around a bend in the duct ahead. A shuffling, scurrying sound.

Something or someone in a hurry.

Margo presses the key card against the entry plate. The lock releases with a loud click. She pushes the door open. The corridor is empty. The walls are stainless steel and the floor is grooved rubber. The door closes behind her. No sound from the Assembly Hall below. All she can hear is the low hum of heavy machinery. Margo hugs the wall and moves down the corridor.

"Which way?" she asks Burbank. No answer.

Jericho contorts his body to squeeze around the bend. The duct narrows again.

No way he can get through. Not with his bulk. He starts to move in reverse. His chest pounds as he imagines being stuck in here forever. Then he stops and looks ahead once more. He squints. His narrow flashlight beam illuminates an obstruction in the middle of the next section. Like a stack of clay bricks.

C4 explosive!

"Bomb!" shouts Jericho. His voice reverberates in the duct. But nobody else can hear. He forces his body forward again and feels the sides of the duct compressing his shoulders and chest. Sweat drips from his forehead and runs down his nose. He grits his teeth and frees one arm. He stretches it forward, straining his muscles until he feels like they might rip.

Margo catches a flash of clothing a few yards ahead. A black burka. She looks around the hallway for a weapon she can use. Something heavy or sharp. But the walls are seamless.

She runs to the end of the hallway. Sees a door ajar. Jerks it open and steps into a dimly lit utility space—a corridor behind the corridor, lined with cables and junction boxes. The figure in the burka is moving around a corner at the far end. Margo follows, inching sideways, her back pressed against the wall. She projects her thoughts, trying to control the intruder's mind and get him to stop. But in return she gets only a dim, primal current. More animal than human. Totally nonresponsive.

Jericho's fingers scratch at the base of the explosives, attached to a small electronic packet. His flashlight wobbles in his mouth, slippery with saliva. He looks for a timer, but sees only a receiver. The bomb is wired for remote detonation. He spreads his legs as much as possible to distribute his weight. His thumb and forefinger are an inch from the mechanism. He makes one final painful lurch and plucks two wires from the receiver. He holds his breath, praying that he didn't trip a backup circuit. Nothing happens. He wipes his brow and rests his head on his arm. The silence is golden.

Margo rounds the corner and sees the veiled figure on a ladder, head and shoulders hunched over a seam between the wall and ceiling. The stock of a rifle is nestled against her armpit. Margo leaps up and grabs for the waist. They both fall backward. The shooter's head cracks hard against the cement floor, and her body goes limp. Margo yanks the head covering off the unconscious figure, expecting to see a Middle Eastern woman.

Not a scrawny white man.

"Margo! Jericho!"
Burbank shouts into his mic, even though he knows they can't hear him. The trackers are blocked. He's getting no audio signal at all. All he can do is watch. And what he sees is confusing.

There are now two thermal images in the inner corridor on the third level. Only one is moving. In the duct high above the gallery, one thermal image is dead center over the podium. Another is moving quickly down the space between the inside and interior wall. But who's who? Are the threats neutralized or active? Are Jericho and Margo alive or dead? No way to tell.

Frantic, Burbank switches to the camera view from behind the podium. The president is still speaking. In the front row, a slender teenage girl in a wheelchair puts a water bottle to her lips, her eyes locked on Diaz. When she lowers the bottle, the mouthpiece stays between her lips. Burbank zooms in. The girl stands up. She points the mouthpiece at Diaz!

Burbank jumps up from his chair and puts his hand on the screen, as if that would help. *Where's Lamont?* The girl leans forward, puffing her cheeks. Suddenly, a steel plate appears in front of the president. Bodyguards swarm Diaz, shoving him down behind the podium. Two agents leap from the rostrum and tackle the girl, flattening her on the carpet as the other kids cower and scream.

As Burbank watches, the steel barrier dissolves. A needle-thin dart floats lightly in midair—as if it's being held in an invisible hand.

The Shadow's hand.

CHAPTER 49

I'M HUDDLED WITH the president of the Americas in a safe room in the subbasement of the UN building. The walls are designed to withstand a nuclear strike, and we could live for weeks down here on the supplies in the storeroom. But the president is ready to leave. Right now.

"Let's move!" he says. "I feel like a goddamn gopher in a hole!"

The head of UN security is standing near the door, sweat seeping through his light gray suit. "Please. Give us a few minutes, sir. We're still securing the building."

Jericho glares at him. "A little late for that, isn't it?"

The security boss has no comeback.

Margo is sitting in a chair next to the president with the top of her niqab peeled back over her head. I can see the fire in her eyes. She wanted to question the two assassins, try to work her way into their minds. But they're already on their way to a maximum-security detention center. If they're anything like the Chinasian commandos, I doubt there's much left of their minds anyway.

"What about the bomber?" asks Diaz.

"So far, no trace," says the security chief. "We've established a perimeter."

"I'll tell you one thing," says Jericho, rubbing his chafed shoulders. "You're looking for somebody really thin."

Across the room, the head of the president's security detail puts down a phone and steps over to report. "It looks like the man and the girl are mercenaries, trained in Hangzhou. First-timers. Doubtful they know anybody beyond their handlers. If they even know that."

"And the other kids?" asks Margo.

"All clean, as far as we can tell. The girl infiltrated the line after they left the holding room. The dart was a synthetic polymer. Hard to detect."

"And the poison?" asks Jericho.

"Batrachotoxin. About a thousand times more potent than cyanide. Natural and untraceable."

That would have been one painful stick. And a very quick death.

Suddenly, I hear Burbank in my earpiece.

He shouts one word. One syllable. I turn white.

"Open the door!" I shout at the guard. He stiffens and plants his feet. I turn to the president. He looks at my face and nods. The guard presses a release mechanism and swings the massive door open. I step into the underground corridor and wave my security pass at the sentry posted outside.

"Which way out?"

The guard points down the hall. "That way. Thirty yards."

The corridor flies by in a blur. For a second, I think about shape-shifting into a cheetah or a greyhound. But that would take some concentration. And right now I can't concentrate at all. All I can do is run—as fast as my human legs can carry me.

I head for an exit. ALARM WILL SOUND, it says. I push through it. A piercing siren blasts. I'm outside on the north side of the building, river at my back. In the parking area, smoke is billowing from behind an emergency vehicle, lights flashing. UN firefighters are jumping off the truck with hoses and extinguisher canisters.

My lungs are heaving as I sprint across the grounds. Two security guys try to intercept me. I shove through them like they're not even there. On the other side of the truck, I stop cold.

Moe's limo is wrapped in flames. The whole frame of the car is bent, and the hood is up and partly detached. The roof is practically blown off.

One of the firefighters has a heavy tool wedged between the driver's-side door and the frame. He throws his full weight into it. The door flies open, releasing another plume of black smoke. The firefighter reaches in and slices the shoulder strap and belt with a sharp blade.

I get to the car just as Moe topples out, his face bloody and blackened. His suit and shirt are in shreds and I can see deep, oozing wounds in his chest and belly.

The firefighter grabs his ankles. I grab his wrists. We drag him a few yards away and lay him on the pavement. Smoke is billowing around us and we're soaked with water and foam.

"Moe!"

I lean down over his shattered skull, and see his pinkish brain leaking out. I scream his name again and again, louder and louder.

As if I had the power to wake the dead.

CHAPTER 50

LAMONT'S MANSION IS lit by hundreds of flickering candles. Tall torches illuminate the garden. Giddy guests in formal wear circulate through the first-floor rooms and pause to chat on the rear balconies. Waiters move from room to room carrying trays of elegant canapes. A man in a pork-pie hat sits at the piano, pounding out a bouncy accompaniment to the festivities.

The conversations are all about one thing. Prohibition. Or, actually, the end of it. What better cause for a celebration? Copies of that morning's New York Times *are stacked in the foyer. December 5, 1933. "City Toasts New Era," the front page says.*

The party has two full bars, one in the parlor and one in the library, staffed with red-vested bartenders. Legal booze is in short supply, but Lamont apparently still has plenty of bootleggers on call. And tonight, they definitely delivered.

As the guests swirl and mingle, Lamont stands quietly near the fireplace, sipping his Scotch. In a sea of formal black and white, his midnight-blue tux stands out like a beacon. Even with all the Broadway actors at the party, he's by far the best-looking man in the room.

His girlfriend Margo is gorgeous, too. She moves from group to group in a high-waisted satin gown, her bright red lipstick setting off her brilliant white smile. At one point, she kicks off her high heels and shows off a few sinuous samba moves in her bare feet. A cluster of guests applauds. In mid-step, Margo looks up and spots Lamont leaning against the mantel.

She picks up a flute of champagne from a tray and walks toward him. They lock eyes through the crowd, and some kind of visual warp opens between them, turning the rest of the room into a buzzing blur. She slides her arm through his and brings her lips to his ear. Lamont grins, then turns and kisses her gently on the neck. Then he does it again. As if they were the only two people in the room.

"That's enough," says Dache.

Maddy blinks. Back to present reality. She's blushing.

"Wow," she says. "It *worked*! I was really there!"

"You did well," says Dache. "Now rest."

"Lamont and Margo," says Maddy. "I *saw* them! In this house!"

"Of course," says Dache. "You were a guest at their party."

Maddy leans back on the bench, her heart still pounding. Dache had told her the risks of inhabiting the past, but she had insisted. And it was totally worth it. Now she's back with her mind intact. "It's *embarrassing* how in love they were," she says.

"Are," corrects Dache. "Not everything fades with time, Madeline. Some things get even better. Even if you can't always see it."

Maddy grabs Dache by the arm. "I want to go back! I want to see more."

"Not today," says Dache gently. "Pace yourself. I warned you—chuanghu can be dangerous, even for the best students. The past has a way of…" He stops in mid-sentence.

Maddy looks up. Lamont, Margo, and Jericho are standing at the top of the garden path. Margo is in the middle, clinging tight to the men. Her lips are ashen. Lamont's pants and shirt are streaked with blood.

Maddy stares at Lamont. She gets a sudden stab in her gut.

In that split second, she knows.

CHAPTER 51

IT'S NOT MUCH of a wake. I don't even have a photo of Moe to display. But Jessica filled the whole parlor with candles, which makes it feel kind of like a chapel. Moe wasn't religious. In fact, he probably would have called the whole thing silly. But we had to do something.

Margo is sitting across from me in a high-backed chair. Her eyes are red. "It's amazing how alike they were," she says.

"Who?" asks Jericho.

"Moe and his ancestor."

"Those Shrevnitz genes were strong," says Burbank from his seat in the corner.

He's right. I think back to the original Moe Shrevnitz—the New York cabbie who became my confidant, my spy, and my escape driver back in the 1930s. I can't even count how many times he got me out of a jam or helped me crack a case. Moe could be crusty at times, but he had street smarts like nobody else. And I always knew he'd take a bullet for me, if it came to that.

The Moe we just lost was exactly the same. I know how proud he was to be on the team. And I know how much he adored Maddy. In just one week, they'd built a special connection. Everybody saw it. Across the room, Maddy is curled on the sofa, her head buried in Jessica's lap.

I have no doubt that the bomber who blew up Moe's car was the same one who tried to blow up the building during Diaz's speech. It was a message. If they can get to one of us, they can get to any of us.

I uncork a bottle of brandy and fill seven snifters. I pass the glasses around the room and set the last one on the mantel.

I raise my glass. "To Moe."

"To life," says Margo.

"To the team," says Jericho.

Maddy stands up from the sofa and pushes her hair back from her face. She downs her drink in one gulp.

"To revenge," she says.

CHAPTER 52

AT 1:00 A.M., Margo and I are the only ones still up. The fifth of brandy is almost drained, and the two of us are the main culprits.

"So what happens now?" Margo asks, leaning back in her chair. She knows the answer. She just needs to hear it from me, out loud.

I swirl what's left of my brandy in the bottom of the glass. "What happens now is, we go on. We find out who's behind all this damage, and we eliminate them. Same for the killer at the World's Fair. We do it all for Moe."

Margo nods quietly, then reaches for my hand. She fights a yawn, but the yawn wins. "Lamont, I'm sleepy."

I put down my snifter and push myself up out of my seat. "Me, too. Half a bottle of Rémy Martin will do it every time." I help Margo up from her chair and we head upstairs with our arms wrapped around each other. Margo's leg wobbles on the second step. Neither of us is too steady at the moment. She gives me a little smile and grabs me tighter.

"If I go down, you're coming with me," she says.

"Joined at the hip," I tell her. "Forever."

We make it to the top of the staircase and head down the hallway. Everybody else has been tucked away for hours. As we pass Maddy's room, Margo tugs on my shoulder. When we stop, I hear it.

Sobbing.

Maybe we should just leave her alone, I think. Let her feel what she's feeling, give her some space to grieve. But Margo already has her hand on the doorknob. No way she's not going in. She pushes the door open slowly. I follow her.

In the slice of light from the hallway, I can see Maddy hunched under the covers. Margo reaches out and rests one hand gently on her shoulder. Maddy flinches and rolls toward us, barely awake, her cheeks glistening with tears.

Margo sits on the bed and slips off her shoes. Maddy sits up slowly and wraps her arms around Margo's neck.

"I could have saved him," Maddy sobs. "If I'd been there, nobody would have gotten near that car. *Nobody!*"

Margo cradles Maddy's head against her chest.

"They would have found another way," she says, "another time."

"I can't lose anybody else," Maddy sobs. "I *won't!*"

I get the distinct feeling that I'm really not needed here. Or maybe it's my discomfort at seeing Maddy in pain. It cuts me to the core. I can feel myself inching back toward the door. Margo looks up and nods, giving me permission to go. Or maybe asking me to.

As I ease the door closed, I see Maddy lie back down again. Margo slides onto the bed and folds herself around her, like a mother around her baby.

I walk across to the other side of the hallway. My throat is burning from the brandy—and the anger. I agree with Maddy. I want payback. I'm standing in front of the hall window that overlooks the front of the house. The only light outside is from the lamps near the front door, and from the sliver of moon overhead. The air is still. No movement in the trees.

That's when I spot them.

Two figures rustling a row of juniper bushes.

In a split second, my drowsiness evaporates. My bloodstream spikes with adrenaline and my vision sharpens. I look again. No mistake. There's somebody out there.

I take the stairs three at a time. I head down the back hallway and down into the basement. When I reach the exit to the front lawn, I open the door slowly and slip outside. Invisible.

The figures haven't moved. Two of them. Maybe looking for a clear shot through one of the windows, or getting ready to detonate a bomb. Whichever it is, they picked the wrong night.

I move quickly along the hedgerow until I'm close enough to feel them breathing. Then I reach through with both arms. My hands close around their collars and I pull both intruders through the branches to my side, landing them on their backs.

"What the *fuck*?" one of them shouts.

The other one whips his head side to side. But there's nothing to see.

They're military types, dressed in camo from head to toe. Their faces are painted in broad strokes of gray and green. They're looking at each other with wide eyes, not understanding what's happening. There's no one to fight.

They both scramble to their feet, but I take them down again with kicks behind the knees. The guy on the right gets up again and takes an aimless swing. I pound my fist into his solar plexus and he goes down again. His partner pulls a knife from his belt and slices the empty air in front of him. I kick the knife out of his hand and then deliver a roundhouse to his temple. He drops next to his buddy. They're both alive, but barely conscious.

I grab their chins and turn their faces toward the light. Then my heart freezes. I take a step back, breathing hard.

The two men lying on my lawn are Tapper and Hawkeye.

CHAPTER 53

BY THE TIME their senses start to come back, I've got them both tied to chairs in the parlor. I roused Jericho and Burbank and they're standing alongside me, staring.

"Gentlemen, meet Hawkeye—and Tapper."

"Holy shit," says Jericho.

"The missing links," says Burbank.

I start pacing the room, furious and fuming. "I invited them to join our team, but they apparently decided to come after us instead." I lean into the prisoners' faces. "I caught them outside the house. My *house*!" I'm so raw from losing Moe, I could snap their necks with my bare hands.

"Hold on," says Tapper, straining against the ropes. "We got your goddamn invite."

Hawkeye twists in his chair. "We weren't in a position to reply."

I lean in. "So what were you doing in my bushes with high-powered rifles?"

"Waiting for daylight," says Tapper. "We figured you had the place trip-wired."

"We should have," says Jericho.

"So where have you been?" I ask. "I tracked you both to Zurich."

"Right. We were there," says Hawkeye. "Spying on the Command."

"From the inside," adds Tapper. "Switzerland. Then Tibet. Saudi Arabia. Senegal. Working our way up. Gaining their trust. Getting the assignment to kill you. The Command sent us. They think we're mercenaries, out for a buck."

I reach over and grab him by the hair. "How do I know you're *not*?" I jerk his head around toward the mantel, where the single brandy snifter is still sitting. "See that? It's a memorial. One of us got blown to bits yesterday. And I'm ready to kill both of you right now. I won't like it. But I'll do it."

"Moe Shrevnitz," says Tapper. "We know. Look. We've lost people, too. Buddies, relatives. We understand what the Command is doing. We've seen it. Smelled it. That's why we're in this fight. We're *with* you. Not against you."

I catch Hawkeye looking over my shoulder. I turn. Margo is standing in the entryway. She walks across the room slowly in her bare feet, stopping right in front of the prisoners.

"Holy shit, it's her," mutters Tapper.

"Hello, Margo," says Hawkeye.

Margo reaches out and places two fingers under Hawkeye's chin. She tilts his face up to the light. Then she does the same with Tapper. "Amazing," she says. "You're carbon copies of your ancestors."

I pull her back by the arm. "One big difference. I knew I could trust the originals."

Margo stares at the prisoners for a few seconds. I can see her taking command of their minds. "My husband sometimes jumps to conclusions," she says. "If you're telling the truth, prove it."

Tapper nods. "My vest. Inside pocket."

Margo reaches in with two fingers and pulls out a video stick.

I nod to Jericho and Burbank. The three of us herd Hawkeye and Tapper upstairs to the comms center after untying them. I slide the stick into the console. Burbank takes over the controls. The first few scenes are of men in ratty uniforms stacking piles of ammunition.

Another scene shows a row of dust-covered military vehicles under camo netting. The next shot is sunny bright, like a vacation photo.

"Freeze it," says Hawkeye.

This is no war scene. It looks like paradise. We're looking at a gorgeous villa with marble columns and a massive fountain in front. Seventeenth-century vintage or earlier. Stately. Magnificent. It looks twice as big as my house. Maybe three times.

"What's this?" I ask.

"Headquarters," says Hawkeye. "For the Command."

Tapper nods at the screen. "That's where the Destroyer of Worlds is hiding out. It's as close as we could get."

Burbank extracts the coordinates from the image and converts them to a map.

In a second, we're looking at a satellite view of France.

"It's in the countryside near Chartres," says Hawkeye. "Security is unbreachable."

I glance at Margo. I can tell she already knows what I'm thinking. So do Hawkeye and Tapper.

"Look," says Hawkeye. "We can get you a plane."

"And I can fly it," says Tapper.

Based on what I know about their skills, it could all be true. Or it could be a trap.

It's possible the Command has managed to warp their minds—to make fiction seem like fact.

I look over. Margo nods. Decision made. We're going.

I grab Tapper by the throat. "If I find out you're double-crossing us..."

Tapper twists away. "You're the goddamn Shadow," he says. "If we're not on the level, you've got plenty of ways to kill us."

I relax my hand and let it drop to my side.

"You're right. I do."

CHAPTER 54

VERY EARLY THE next morning, Maddy is walking north on Morningside Avenue, closing in on the City College campus. Sunlight is just starting to peek between the buildings, painting bright stripes on the sidewalk.

Maddy is alone. She managed to get out of the house before anybody else woke up, and before Lamont could insist on escorting her. The last thing she wants today is to be shadowed by the Shadow.

She's already missed the last two days of school, and at the moment classes don't feel that important. Going in today is just a means to an end. She just wants to see Deva, and school is where they always meet. She needs to tell her about Moe, and about the World's Fair killer. But mostly, she needs to talk about the other night.

A lot has happened since that kiss on the porch, but Maddy's mind is still in a swirl about it. She's not clear about what it meant, or what she wants it to mean. She knows that she truly loves Deva. Her best friend. Probably her *only* friend. But that's a scary thought. Right now, it feels dangerous to be close to anybody.

A few minutes later, Maddy walks into the amphitheater-style classroom for the Principles of Forensics lecture. She's the first one there by a mile. No problem. She sits by herself, eyes closed, enjoying the silence.

Maddy thinks back to the first day of class. She was sitting in the aisle seat when a pretty girl with long black hair walked up and introduced herself. *"Hi. I'm Deva Keane. Do you mind switching places?"* Maddy shifted one seat over. *"Tiny bladder,"* Deva whispered. *"Sometimes I need a quick exit."* They've occupied those same seats ever since.

Gradually, other students start filtering in to the classroom, filling the long, banked rows that rise from the front. At exactly one minute before the hour, the instructor walks to the lectern and sets down his binder. He clicks on the mic with a gentle pop.

But no Deva. Strange. She's never missed a class—not once. As Maddy pulls out her notebook, her temples start to throb. She fumbles with her pen. Almost drops it.

"Quiet, please!" calls the instructor, a reedy man with a nasal voice. He leans forward with both hands on the lectern, his nose an inch from the slender mic. The murmur in the class fades. Maddy keeps one eye on the door, expecting Deva to burst through at any minute, hair flying.

"Who can tell us the Golden Rule of crime scene preservation?" asks the instructor. He rakes his gaze across the long rows of groggy students. No answer. He slaps his hand down hard on the lectern right under the mic, making a sound like a gunshot.

Maddy jumps in her seat. Everybody's awake now.

"Don't touch anything," a man calls out from the back.

"Thank you," says the instructor. "That is correct. Leave everything as it is until it can be catalogued, marked, and photographed."

"What about bodies?" asks a woman near the front of the room.

"*Especially* bodies," says the instructor.

"What if you're not sure they're dead?"

"Fair question," says the instructor. "Put on your gloves and check for a pulse. If you see signs of life, look for injuries or wounds. Call for medical and render any necessary treatment in the meantime. If the subject is deceased, leave them in peace and wait for the ME. Make a note of how and where you touched the body."

The instructor taps a button on the lectern. The large screen in front of the room lights up. "Okay. What's wrong with this picture?" The photo on the screen is grim. It shows a man's body lying at the bottom of a staircase. His neck is bent at an unnatural angle and blood from a gash in his head forms a dark, irregular puddle on the floor. Three male investigators are leaning over the splayed figure.

"The tall guy isn't wearing gloves!" comes a shout from the back.

"True," says the instructor. "What else? Look closer."

"The shoe!" somebody shouts.

Maddy leans forward. Sure enough. The tip of one of the investigator's wingtips is resting on the outer margin of the pooling blood, a few inches from the victim's cracked skull. The instructor zooms in on the infraction.

Suddenly, Maddy feels a sheen of perspiration on her forehead. Her chest tightens and her belly heaves. She lurches out of her seat and runs down the aisle to the door, saliva pooling in her mouth. She shoves the door open and lunges at a trash can on the other side of the hall. It feels like it's a mile away.

She gets there just in time to vomit her guts out.

CHAPTER 55

MADDY STRAIGHTENS UP slowly, wiping her lips as she gasps for air. She feels dizzy and weak. Her mind is spinning. She staggers outside and sits down on the curb at the edge of the parking lot.

Her heart is racing. What's going on? God knows she's seen dead bodies. She passed them on the street every day when she was growing up. Why should the image of a corpse on a classroom screen set her off? Why today?

She grinds her fists against her temples, irritated and anxious. She needs to talk to Deva. Right now! Where the hell is she? Why did she pick this morning to ditch school? Was she out late last night? Did something happen at home?

Maddy's out of patience. She wants an answer. And she knows just how to get it.

Chuanghu. She sits up straight, closes her eyes, and gets ready to look into the past, just like Dache taught her. She doesn't care how dangerous it is. She just needs to go back about twelve hours. To wherever Deva was last night.

Maddy folds her hands in her lap and shuts down all nonessential parts of her awareness. She blocks out the warmth of the sun on her cheek, the sounds of cars moving through the parking lot, the smell of the lawn behind her. She breathes deep into her belly. Suddenly, the vision fires up, like her own private movie.

She's walking through a ribbon of lights. The image is blurry. She feels heavy, not herself. She's surrounded by people. Men, women, children. But she doesn't recognize any of them. Then a figure blows past her, black hair waving.

Maddy follows, but not too close. She's weaving through crowds and past flashing lights, like a nightclub. But outdoors. Maddy feels her pulse thumping.

The vision is like a dream, foggy and imperfect, like her visit to Lamont and Margo's party. Maddy knows she's not in her body. She's trapped in somebody else's memory. That person now doesn't know Deva, but follows her anyway. Drawn to her. Excited by her.

Deva walks through an entryway. Maddy is a few yards behind, seeing through the follower's eyes. The space inside is dark. Maddy blinks. Deva's body is gone. Only her skeleton remains. But the skeleton is upright. Still walking! Another pulse of light. Then total darkness again.

Maddy hears footsteps. Her own. Running. Chasing. There's a flash in her brain. Then the sound of a scream.

Light returns in a series of flashes. Deva is directly beneath her now—on the ground and still. The flesh is back on her bones, but there's no breath inside her body. Her skull is crushed. Her features are contorted and coated in fresh green paint. Like the face of a grisly, broken doll.

Maddy gasps and falls forward. Her knees hit the hard pavement of the parking lot. She gags but nothing comes up. A tingle shoots through her. She's fully back in the present—and someone is watching her.

She looks up and sees Dache standing on the other side of the parking lot, his hands folded in front of him. His face is impassive, his body relaxed.

Maddy struggles to her feet and jabs her finger at him, shouting furiously across the space between them. "*You!* You see everything! You know everything! You could have stopped it!"

"Not my place," says Dache calmly. "I observe. I don't control."

"The hell you don't! You control *me*!"

"No. I teach you to control yourself. At least I try."

Maddy is frantic with fear and anger. The vision felt like a nightmare, but she knows it was real. Deva is dead. Murdered. Mutilated. And she wasn't the first.

"Get out!" shouts Maddy. "Go!"

"Go where, Madeline?" asks Dache calmly.

"The past! The future! Or to *hell*! I don't care! Just... *leave me alone*!"

Maddy thrusts her hand forward. A fireball blasts from her palm. It shoots across the parking lot and explodes into a pillar of flame, engulfing Dache. The blast knocks Maddy back onto the grass. When she looks up, Dache is gone.

Maddy pounds her fists against her forehead, not sure what's real anymore.

Was he ever really there?

CHAPTER 56

"FAIR WARNING. THE coffee is pretty strong."

Margo carries a huge carafe over to the table as the team settles in for breakfast—Jericho, Burbank, and our two latest arrivals. Margo made scrambled eggs. I fried the bacon. Enough for a small army. Which is what we are, I guess. I'm just hoping that what we lack in numbers, we make up for in determination.

Tapper and Hawkeye grab for the platters and start piling food onto their plates. Jericho and Burbank sit back politely and wait their turn. I can tell they're not entirely sold on the new members of the team. I can't blame them for being a little wary. I am, too. But the proof will come soon enough.

I hear panting and scratching from outside. When the back door opens, Jessica breezes in with Bando. She stops short when she sees the two muscular strangers.

"More company, Lamont? I didn't realize we were running a barracks."

I lift partway out of my chair to make the introductions. "Jessica, this is Tapper, and this is Hawkeye, two more associates of mine."

"The two we've been waiting for," adds Margo.

Jessica pulls up a chair. "Strange," she says, "I didn't hear you gentlemen arrive."

"We came in late," says Tapper, his mouth full of bacon and eggs.

"We didn't want to ring the doorbell," adds Hawkeye. The side of his face is still purple from my punch.

"So what's the plan?" asks Jessica, boring in on them. "How do you intend to catch the criminals who killed Mr. Shrevnitz? I assume that's why you're here?"

I lift the carafe and fill Jessica's cup. "Tapper and Hawkeye brought us some valuable intelligence on the Command. A specific target."

"As a matter of fact," says Margo. "Lamont and I are on our way to France tomorrow."

"France?" says Jessica. "How?"

"By air," says Margo. "Tapper says he's a flyer."

Jessica leans across the table toward Tapper and narrows her eyes. "How many hours?"

"To France?" replies Tapper, spooning another helping onto his plate. "It depends on the type of plane my friend Hawkeye steals for us."

"No," says Jessica. "I mean how many flying hours do you have?"

Tapper puts his spoon down and wipes his mouth. He stares at Jessica. She stares back. "Two-thousand-plus," says Tapper evenly. "Last time I checked."

"Instrument rated?" asks Jessica.

"Since high school."

"Good. I won't have my family going off with some bush pilot."

"Glad we cleared that up," says Tapper. He digs back into his food.

I hear the front door open, then slam shut. When I look up, Maddy is standing in the kitchen archway. Her face is pale and her eyes are bloodshot.

I jump up from the table and walk her into the parlor, my arm around her shoulders. "Maddy, what happened?"

She jerks away and glares at me with her jaw set. *"How many?"* Her voice is tight and her tone is cold.

"How many what?"

"How many people have been murdered at the World's Fair?"

I'm not sure what's going on here, but I know I need to come clean. I let out a slow breath and clear my throat. "Six, that we know of."

"Wrong," says Maddy. *"Seven.* My best friend died last night."

I take a step toward her. "Maddy, I'm…"

"It wasn't even reported, was it?" she says. She slams her hand hard against my chest. "It's not *going* to be reported, *is it?*"

I grab her wrists and hold them tight. Her eyes are brimming with tears. "Maddy, it's political. The authorities are keeping this thing a secret. It's sick, I know, but it's not our choice. They're trying to keep up appearances. Prevent panic. Make sure the fair succeeds. That's why we told you to stay away."

"You're serious? People are dying, and you're trying to protect the attendance numbers?"

Now Margo is at my elbow. "Who was it?" she asks Maddy. "The girl you go dancing with?" Maddy twists away from my grip.

"Deva. Her name was Deva. She died because of all these secrets. This city has way too many secrets. So does this family!"

"Maddy, I'm so sorry," says Margo. "We were just trying to protect you. We'll solve this case. I promise. We'll catch whoever did this."

Maddy looks back into the kitchen and a flicker of

recognition comes over her face. "Oh, my God. That's Tapper and Hawkeye in there, isn't it? More descendants? What's going on?"

I nod. "They arrived last night. They're here to help us fight the Command."

Maddy turns abruptly and walks toward the staircase. "Perfect. You guys solve the world's problems—the Shadow and his elite team of experts. I'll find Deva's killer." She heads up the staircase. "I'm going to the fair tonight. *Alone!*"

Margo grabs my arm and whispers softly. "Like hell she is."

CHAPTER 57

IT'S JUST AFTER dark. The three of us are walking through the fair entrance together. A united force. It took some talking, but once Maddy realized that there was no way we were letting her go off by herself, she came around.

She understands our combined powers are a lot stronger than hers alone. Not that our powers have done much good on this case. So far, our most impressive feat has been to watch people die—after they're already dead.

Maddy does a slow turnaround, taking in the expanse and spectacle of the fair for the first time.

"Pretty, isn't it?" says Margo.

"Yeah, sure," says Maddy. "For a slaughterhouse."

I know how she feels. The first time I visited the site with Moe, all I saw was promise and potential—a city trying its best to get back to normal. I was blinded by the lights. Now all I see are the seams of darkness in between. This place feels anything but normal. Anything but hopeful. It feels menacing and evil.

As we walk together down the midway, I spot a few

men and women moving purposefully through the crowd—some solo, some in pairs. Undercover cops. I guess Captain Bates has decided that an ounce of prevention is better than a ton of cover-up. But the killer is way too cagey for this kind of surveillance. I should know. I've been inside his head.

I'm looking at faces, checking body language, sorting for clues. But it feels impossible. The killer could be anybody here. Or nobody.

Maddy speeds up and walks ahead of us. She stops at the entrance of a massive pavilion. The roofline soars high above the walkway. On either side of the entrance, I see gigantic tiered platforms filled with mounds of fresh fruit—apples, pears, oranges, kiwi, grapefruit—all lush and colorful. Margo and I catch up as Maddy walks inside. A few steps later, we're in a different world.

The air is thick with floral scents and the sound of falling water. From the ground level to the ceiling hundreds of feet above, the space is filled with spectacular hydroponics displays. Curtains of flowers and vines drape down over rocky cliffs. Waterfalls plummet from ten stories up. On every side, canopied groves bloom with tangerines, mangos, and bananas. It looks like a scientifically enhanced version of Eden.

"Jesus," says Margo. "This is one fancy fruit farm."

We wander through rows of hybrid flowers and specimen trees, and past long white troughs of cultured seaweed. Workers in white uniforms pile harvested produce onto huge stainless-steel carts. It looks like this place could single-handedly end world hunger.

Suddenly, out of nowhere, I get antsy. The exhibit is stunning. But three pairs of eyes in one place seems like a waste of resources. I pull Margo and Maddy aside next to a miniature orchard. "You two take your time in here. I'm heading across the way."

"Don't get lost," says Margo.

I look Maddy in the eye. "Stay together. Never out of each other's sight. Clear?"

"Okay, okay," she says. She sounds like she means it.

I turn and head for the exit—like something's pulling me.

CHAPTER 58

AS SOON AS I step out of the garden pavilion, I know exactly where to go. About a hundred yards up the path is an exhibit that caught my eye the other night. Something about the "magnificent isolation of outer space."

Sounds dark and mysterious. And maybe a good place for a killer to lurk.

A minute later, I'm passing through an electronic entry curtain with a group of fellow enthusiasts—a few couples and one large family. For about half a minute, we all wait in a large, dark chamber. The kids can hardly contain themselves. Then one whole side opens and we step out onto a rocky surface with the whole universe surrounding us. Disorienting, but thrilling. Like nothing I've ever felt.

According to the readout floating in midair in front of me, I'm standing on an asteroid, hurtling through the Black Eye galaxy, twenty-four million light-years from home. The illusion is amazing, and totally complete. All I'm missing is a spacesuit.

Some kind of audio effect has canceled out the sound in the room. I can see the kids nearby squealing with excitement, but in total silence. Eerie. I turn slowly on the jagged rock surface. The asteroid is a mere fragment, maybe a few hundred yards across. We're surrounded by glittering stars—and billions of miles of endless black. Filaments and particles shoot past us, creating a sense of movement, like we're surfing through space. Incredible! Time seems to stand still. Minutes seem like hours. Or maybe eons.

Suddenly, a comet shower passes overhead like fireworks. Then, in the distance, a giant sun explodes, blasting outward in concentric circles of yellow and orange, brighter and brighter. For a moment, the whole universe is whited out.

In that split second, my mind flashes back to the murder scene in the rain forest—those two terrified kids an instant before they died. But now I see something else. I see what *they* saw. The killer's face! Blurred and dark. Feral. Monstrous. With grotesque green features.

I drop to my knees on the hard rock and squeeze my eyes shut, trying to get more detail. Then, suddenly, I'm seeing myself from above. My heart freezes.

I'm being watched.

I open my eyes and spin around. But when I look up, all I see are stars. The imaginary asteroid is moving through a multicolored aura, like passing through the middle of a kaleidoscope.

The exhibit goes dark.

And then it's over.

A wall lifts at the far end. Soft blue lights guide us through a passageway to the exit. My ears pop as I pass through a final electronic curtain and back into the noise and chaos of the midway. Back to Earth. My head is pounding.

I see Maddy and Margo walking toward me. I run over to grab them.

"I just saw him! The killer!"

Margo looks over my shoulder at the exhibit I just came out of. "In there? In fake outer space?"

"It was in my mind. But I *saw* him. And he saw me."

Maddy grabs my arm. "Who was it? What did he look like?"

I rack my brain for a description, but only four words come out. "Dark. Powerful. Not human."

I can read the frustration on Margo's face. "You and Maddy should have come by yourselves," she says. "You should have turned invisible. Or shape-shifted into... whatever. You could have covered more ground. Gotten into more places."

I rub sweat from my forehead and lean forward to catch my breath. I feel totally drained, as if someone had just sucked the life out of me. "Wouldn't matter. Whatever the killer is, he's onto us. He sees everything we do. Whatever form we're in."

When I look up again, Maddy is walking away from us—heading toward the huge Ferris wheel in the distance. I can see from her body language that she's frustrated and angry.

"Maddy!" shouts Margo. "Where are you going?"

Maddy turns and jerks her thumb toward the main attraction. "We're getting nowhere down here," she calls out. "If the killer wants to see us, let's give him a real good look!"

I straighten up. Margo takes my hand. We follow Maddy toward the giant gleaming circle across the fairgrounds. No question, there's something irresistible about it. I felt it the first time I saw it.

Maybe Maddy just wants to go for a ride.

Or really wants to be bait.

CHAPTER 59

A FEW MINUTES later, we're all on a single invisible bench suspended eighty feet in the air, Maddy's in the middle, leaning against me so tight I can feel her heart pounding. I know how brave and strong she is, but right now she feels small and vulnerable, almost like a little girl. I think deep down, she knows how much she needs our help and protection—even if she won't admit it.

"Lamont, look!" says Margo, pointing down to the right.

Far below and a few miles away, a huge section of Brooklyn just lit up, finally back on the grid. Street by street, block by block, the electricity is being switched back on. It's about time.

From where we're sitting, the whole city shimmers like a field of bright candles. But I know there's a murderous monster somewhere under our feet. Maybe looking at us right now. Or waiting to follow another victim into the dark.

When I look out over Long Island toward the ocean, another chill runs through me. Because in a stately villa a few thousand miles across the Atlantic, there's an even bigger threat—and we have to face it tomorrow. I wrap my arm tighter around Maddy, and around my wife.

"It's a beautiful world from up here," says Margo softly.

I agree. It is. So why would anybody want to destroy it?

CHAPTER 60

MADDY WALKS SLOWLY up the uneven stone pathway to Deva's front door. Even in broad daylight, the neighborhood feels menacing. A few houses down, a pair of fierce-looking dogs growl and strain against their chains. Across the street, three shirtless teenage boys lounge against a loose metal fence. Maddy can feel their eyes on her the whole way.

She hates that she needs to be here. She hates that she's the one who has to do this. But there's nobody else.

Maddy knocks. After a few seconds, she hears shuffling from inside. The door opens partway. A woman's face appears in the gap. Her black hair is fringed with white. Her jowls sag. Her eyes are rheumy and red. Her breath carries a stale waft of liquor.

"What the hell do you want?" she asks, hands clawed around the edge of the door.

Maddy inhales and lets it out slowly. "Are you Mrs. Keane? Deva's mom?"

"Why?" Suspicious. Noncommittal.

"My name is Maddy. Maddy Gomes. I'm a friend of hers from school."

The woman opens the door wider and leans against the frame, arms folded across her chest. "Great. Then maybe you can tell me where the hell my daughter is. She hasn't been home in two nights." The woman fingers the collar of her housecoat and waves one hand dismissively. "Not the first time. Probably passed out at some damn club. I keep telling her that if…"

"Mrs. Keane," Maddy interrupts. "I'm sorry to stop you. Deva isn't at a club. I hate to have to say this, but— Deva's dead. She was killed. Murdered. At the World's Fair."

The woman freezes for a second, then slumps against the door. Maddy reaches out and grabs her. Maddy wraps her arm around the woman's shoulders and leads her through the gloomy foyer. The small living room is littered with dirty plates and empty bottles. Maddy helps the trembling woman to a worn sofa and eases her down.

"Who would kill Deva?" the woman asks, her voice shaking, her chin lowered toward her chest. *"Why?"*

"I don't know yet," says Maddy. "But I'll find out, I promise you."

The woman lifts her head slowly and jabs a finger toward Maddy's face. "Wait. I know who you are," she says. "You're the magic girl. The one with the superpowers. The girl from Times Square. Fire and lightning. Deva talked about you."

Maddy manages a tight smile. "Deva knew me pretty well. Maybe better than I know myself."

The woman's brittle voice turns bitter. "So you saved the whole city, but you couldn't save my girl?"

This hits Maddy like a punch. "I'm so sorry, Mrs. Keane. I'm sorry I wasn't with her when she…I loved Deva. I really did."

"She called you her personal hero," the woman mutters. Then she shakes her head. "Some goddamn hero."

Maddy pretends to ignore the insult, but it cuts deep. "Is there a neighbor I can get for you? A relative?"

"No. Nobody. It was just me and Deva. Leave me alone."

"Should I stay with you? Can I get you anything?" Maddy looks at the empty bottles. "Do you have enough food?"

The woman appears to gather all her strength and then projects it in a single word. *"Go!"*

Maddy stands up slowly and walks toward the front door. She pauses at the threshold. "I'm sorry, Mrs. Keane," she says again. "Very sorry."

No response. Deva's mom is tipped on her side, her face buried in the arm of the battered sofa. Weeping.

CHAPTER 61

WHEN MADDY STEPS back onto the porch, the three shirtless boys are standing at the edge of the yard, tossing a battered football back and forth, heaving it hard into one another's chests with painful-sounding thuds.

Maddy takes one last glance back at the house and then heads down the path toward the sidewalk. When she turns back, the boys have moved into the yard, blocking her way. One holds the ball under his arm.

"Not as hot as her friend," sneers the kid in front.

"You like to dance, too?" asks the one with the ball.

Maddy just keeps walking, eyes straight, ready to push right past them.

"You wanna dance right now?" the third boy asks. Leering. Ominous. As Maddy walks by, the boy grabs her arm.

Maddy flinches. Then disappears.

Suddenly, the boy is holding on to nothing—and staring into thin air. He spins around. "What the hell ...?!"

The boys look up just before a metal trash can comes crashing down, knocking them to the ground and showering them with rancid, wet garbage. The football wobbles off against the curb.

The boy who had his hand on Maddy now feels rough hands on *him*. Hands he can't see. They yank his baggy jeans down to his ankles, exposing his scrawny belly and threadbare gray briefs.

Then a voice comes out of nowhere, fierce and determined, whispering in his ear.

"If any of you assholes *ever* come near this house again, I will find you, I will slice off your tiny testicles, and I will kill you. In that order."

"It's a goddamn *ghost*!" shouts one of the other boys, wiping a gob of wet garbage off his chest.

"Screw this!" shouts the third.

The boy with his pants down struggles to his feet and yanks on his waistband. Tripping and stumbling, he scrambles across the street with the others. In a second, they're all through the fence and running toward a cluster of abandoned buildings.

Maddy watches until the boys are out of sight, then turns and heads down the sidewalk, walking slowly. She's still stung by what Deva's mom said. She feels useless, powerless. She just scared off three skinny kids. Big deal. She's a few blocks along before she remembers that she's still invisible.

She stops at the gate of a run-down playground. Probably left over from the last century. She walks past the broken swings and climbs to the top of a rusted, skeletal dome.

As she perches on top of the structure, she materializes again. She closes her eyes and pictures Deva. Her face. Her hair. Her laugh. She flashes back to the night in the subway club. Pulsing music floods her brain. She sees Deva through the crowd, looking straight at her, eyes bright and teasing. Full of life.

Maddy takes a deep breath and shakes off the vision. No looking back anymore, only forward. She stares up into the sky and focuses her mind. Her feet press hard on the narrow bars of the play dome—and transform into black talons.

Seconds later, she's soaring across the city toward home. A sharp-eyed hawk.

Her first attempt at this form. As the warm air passes under her wings, the part of her brain that's still human feels both fury and freedom. Who needs Lamont or Margo—or the useless cops?

She'll catch this sick animal on her own. Whatever it takes.

CHAPTER 62

I'M STANDING WITH Margo, Jericho, and Burbank at what's left of JFK International Airport. Rising sea levels have almost submerged it. Most of the airfield is now covered by the waters of Jamaica Bay, but one long runway is still in operation. And sitting at our end of it is an aircraft like I've never seen.

"I promised you a plane," says Hawkeye proudly. "And here she is."

I'm not sure how to react. The last plane Margo and I flew in was a DC-3 twin-prop in 1933. Newark to LA in twenty hours, with four stops along the way. The machine sitting on the tarmac looks more like a missile. It's about thirty feet long and no more than four feet across, with a pointed snout and a single giant engine in back.

"This is incredible," says Burbank, running his hands over the raked wingtips.

"No way this thing gets off the ground with three people," mutters Jericho.

"Almost ready," Tapper calls out. He's under the black fuselage making an adjustment. Hawkeye brings out two nylon jumpsuits, one for me and one for Margo. Bright yellow, with zippers up the front.

Margo shakes out her jumpsuit to its full length and holds it up by the shoulder seams. "Lamont, this is *hideous*!"

"Thin, but insulated," says Hawkeye. "You'll thank me at fifty thousand feet."

With a sour face, Margo slides her feet into the attached booties and slips her arms into the sleeves. I suit up next. Tapper is walking toward us, wearing a bright red version of the same outfit. He's rubbing goop off his hands with a towel. "Well. What do you think?"

I step up to the plane and place my hand on the tailfin. It feels as flimsy as a tin spatula. "Are you sure this thing is airworthy?"

"I won't lie. It's experimental," says Tapper. "But it's supersonic. Should get us to Paris in two hours."

He walks to the side of the fuselage and presses a lever. Two clear canopies flip open—one over the cockpit, and one over the impossibly small passenger compartment. Forget luggage or weapons. There's barely room for us.

"All aboard for *Paris*," Tapper says, one leg inside the aircraft. Burbank, Hawkeye, and Jericho move back onto the runway apron. *Way* back.

"Lamont, are you sure about this?" asks Margo.

"What I'm sure about is that we need to get to France. And this is the quickest way to do it."

"Fine," says Margo. She walks to the fuselage and steps into the compartment, easing herself down into the seat until only her blond hair is peeking above the side of the fuselage.

My turn. Looks like a very tight fit.

"Should have brought a shoehorn, boss!" yells Jericho.

I zip my jumpsuit up tight to my throat and squeeze into the open seat directly in front of Margo. My knees are bent up toward my chest and my feet are pressed against an aluminum bulwark. Through an open hatchway, I can see Tapper in the pilot's seat, turning dials and flipping switches.

I hear the whine of a small motor. The canopies lower over us. There's a small sucking sound as the gaskets seal, then a gentle hiss as the onboard air supply kicks in.

I feel a hard lurch. My seat starts to vibrate. When I look to the side, we're rolling toward a white centerline. Tapper fine-tunes the maneuver until the nose of the plane points straight down the runway.

"Do we have parachutes?" Margo calls out.

"No room!" says Tapper.

"Ejection seats?" I ask.

"Just mine!" Tapper replies. He lowers a dark visor over his face and grabs a large lever at the base of the console.

"Clench your sphincters," he calls out. "She's got a kick."

The main engine behind us rises in pitch, from a loud whine to a guttural roar. Suddenly, I'm slammed against the back of my seat and the runway is shooting past in a gray blur. The nose of the aircraft tips at a sharp angle and we shoot up into the sky. More like a launch than a takeoff. I feel a heavy thud from underneath my seat.

"Wheels up!" shouts Tapper above the engine noise. "Enjoy your flight!"

I hope I didn't make a mistake when I let this guy live.

CHAPTER 63

MADDY IS IN a deep sleep when she feels a warm tongue slurping at her face. She presses a pillow over her head. "Bando! Quit it!" But the terrier won't give up. He tries to root underneath the covers, sniffing and whining, begging for attention. A moment later, Maddy feels a gentle hand resting between her shoulder blades. She lifts the pillow to see her grandmother sitting on the edge of the bed.

Jessica snaps her fingers. "Bando, down." The dog hops off the bed and curls up on the floor. Maddy props herself up on her elbows.

"Are they gone?" she asks. "Margo and Lamont?"

Jessica nods. "On their way to France."

Maddy isn't sorry for not going to the airport for the send-off. She still hasn't forgiven Lamont and Margo for keeping quiet about the World's Fair killings, or for leaving town before Deva's murder is solved. At the thought of her, Maddy's eyes brim with tears again.

Jessica reaches out and grasps her hand. "You miss her. Your dancer friend."

"I do," says Maddy, sniffling through tears. "So much."

Jessica leans in and whispers. "You know who else loved to dance?"

Maddy shakes her head.

"Your mother."

Maddy sits back and wipes her eyes. "Really?" Jessica rarely speaks of Ellen, Maddy's mom. And Maddy hardly has any firsthand memory of her. All she knows is that her parents both died young, and that Jessica raised her on her own. Maddy looks at Jessica and realizes that her grandmother knows exactly what she's thinking.

"It's okay," says Jessica. "Go back."

Maddy sits up. She had told her grandmother that she was learning chuanghu and she had to disclose the risks, so she never expected this. "When to?" she asks.

"Your third birthday," says Jessica.

Maddy clears her mind, then brings her focus to the first day of May, sixteen years ago. Forget the dangers of chuanghu. She'd risk anything for this. And with her grandmother's hand on her arm, she somehow feels safe.

One second later, she's there—in a tiny living room in a small apartment. From somewhere, music is playing. A woman with long hair is leaning down, holding the hands of a small girl with blond hair. The woman moves gracefully, hips swinging to the rhythm. The child does her best to follow her steps.

The smells are familiar and comforting. Cooking oil. Roasting vegetables. Soap. Tobacco. Perfume. There's a small birthday cake on the table and a few colored balloons resting against the ceiling. Maddy watches from a corner as the woman picks the girl up and holds her in her arms, spinning her around the room in time with the music. The girl giggles with delight, her blond hair flying with each turn.

Maddy can't tell whose eyes she's seeing through. Maybe her grandmother's.

Doesn't matter. All she knows is that the little girl loves being held, and that she wants to be held this way forever.

Bando yips. The vision evaporates. Maddy comes back to the present, startled and gasping. Jessica wraps her in her arms. "Did it work?" she asks. "Did you see her?"

Maddy can't speak. She can only nod as she hugs her grandmother tight, clinging to the feeling she just experienced.

The last time she was truly happy.

CHAPTER 64

I HAVE TO say I'm impressed. Our landing is a lot smoother than the takeoff, and Tapper's time estimate was right on the money. Just two hours in the air and now we're taxiing down a runway somewhere in France. At least I *think* it's France.

I crane my head from side to side. No other planes in sight. No people or vehicles, either. Just a rusted metal hangar in the distance. The whole airfield is overgrown with stubby brown grass. Looks like it hasn't been used in years. When the plane comes to a stop at the end of the runway, there's a hiss from the ventilation system and then a rubbery pop. The canopies release and lift open over our heads.

I smell country air mixed with jet fuel.

"Lamont! For God's sake, pry me out this thing!" Margo was quiet for most of the flight, but now she's clearly out of patience. I climb out of my seat and offer my arm for a handle as she pulls herself up.

"Frankly," she says, "I preferred the *Queen Mary*."

I help her step out of the fuselage onto the cracked tarmac. Tapper is already on the ground, running his hand back and forth under the fuselage.

"Looks good," he says. "Nothing fell off."

"You're surprised?" I ask.

"Maybe a little."

"Where in God's name *are* we?" asks Margo. "I thought we were landing in Paris." She gazes around at the bleak landscape, then grabs my forearm. "Lamont. Please tell me this is not Paris!"

Tapper laughs. "Don't worry. Paris is still Paris. But this is as close as I'm comfortable getting."

"So where do we go from here?" asks Margo. "I'm not wearing my hiking boots."

"There's a train station about a half mile that way," says Tapper, pointing past the hangar. "And the villa is about two hours north." He reaches into his pocket and hands me a wad of currency. "Here. Take some euros."

"Wait," says Margo. "You're not coming?"

"I'm a wanted man over here," says Tapper. "If they got to your friend Moe, they've probably figured out that me and Hawkeye were spies on the inside." He pauses. "And we all know what happens to spies."

I glance at Margo. "Tapper's right. We don't need a fugitive slowing us down."

"Also, I can't leave the aircraft here," says Tapper. "Too much of a target. I need to fly it somewhere safe. Burbank will figure out how to contact me when you're ready for pickup."

Margo doesn't look happy. I think she expected to have Tapper's muscle along on the mission. "Fine," she says. "Take your toy and go."

"Good hunting," says Tapper, stepping back into the cockpit. He waves us off to the side. "Watch out for the blast."

I pull Margo back onto the grass alongside the runway. Tapper settles into his seat and lowers the front and rear canopies. The plane makes a slow turn at the near end of the runway until it's pointed back in the direction we came from. Margo and I press our hands against our ears. The main engine starts up—like a cannon firing.

In two seconds, the plane is shooting down the runway. When it's just about at the end, it tilts up and spears into the sky at a forty-five-degree angle. We watch it disappear into the clouds, like it was never even here.

Now it's just the two of us. Like the old days.

Margo takes a slow look around the airfield. "Lamont, look at this wasteland. Do you think it's a trap?"

I shake my head no. "Think about it. If Tapper wanted to set us up, he didn't need to fly us all the way to France to do it."

Then I feel a tremble. A slight vibration in the air.

I squint into the distance, past a line of trees. Just below the clouds, a small speck appears in the sky. My heart starts thumping. Maybe I was wrong. Maybe it *is* a trap. Maybe Tapper meant to leave us here like two sitting ducks.

"Drone!"

CHAPTER 65

I PULL MARGO by the arm. We start running toward the hangar—the only cover in sight. Margo stumbles. I catch her just in time to keep her from falling. I gauge the distance. No good. The drone is moving too fast. Margo looks over her shoulder. Sees it coming.

"Lamont!"

I look around. Nothing but flat ground. No cover. I take Margo by the shoulders and push her down onto the grass. "Don't move. Protect your head!" She curls into the fetal position and squeezes her forearms against her temples.

The drone is heading straight for us. I whip my arm around. A fireball blasts out of my palm. The drone swings to the side. Quick and nimble. The flame shoots right past it and flickers out in midair. The drone dips lower. Point-blank range. *A wall!* We need a wall! I try to shape-shift, but my energy is drained. My body tightens up. I drop to my knees.

"Lamont!" Margo shouts. "Go! Run! Disappear!"

Maybe I could. It's my simplest skill. But there's no way I'm leaving my wife. If our time is up, we're going together.

The drone is only a few yards away now, hovering about six feet off the ground. It feels like it's taunting us. The rotor blades sound like a hornet hive. I feel around for something to throw. A stick. A rock. *Anything!* But there's nothing but dry grass and hard-packed dirt.

The drone starts beeping. Like a bomb counting down.

I wrap myself around Margo and whisper into her ear, "I love you." I feel her body tighten as she squeezes my hand.

"Joined at the hip," she says. "Forever."

The beeping stops.

I look up.

A slot on the underside of the drone slides open.

A small envelope drops out and falls to the ground. It lands just a couple of feet from our faces. Margo turns around and looks up at me. I stretch out to pick up the envelope. I can feel the hard wind from the rotors on the back of my neck.

Margo uncurls herself and gets onto her knees. "What the hell is this?"

I open the envelope and pull out a cream-colored card. Elegant script. All in French. Margo translates.

"It's an invitation," she says.

"From?"

Margo points to the bottom of the card. The signature is also in elegant script, but bolder.

Destructeur de Mondes.

"I'll give you one guess," says Margo.

There's a quick *thip* from the drone. Margo crumples back onto the tarmac. *No!*

Another *thip*. I feel a sharp sting in my neck.

And then . . . nothing.

CHAPTER 66

MADDY WALKS THROUGH the entrance of the World's Fair at the stroke of midnight—alone and determined. The visit with Lamont and Margo two nights back showed her the lay of the land, and Lamont's vision gave her a few hints about the killer. All-seeing. Hideous. Powerful. But she left that night feeling discouraged and useless. Nothing was solved.

Tonight will be different, Maddy tells herself. Very different. She knows that Lamont and Margo would stop her if they could. But they can't. They're on another continent. This time, it's just her.

At this late hour, most of the families with kids are gone. The main thoroughfare is packed with young couples and rowdy friend groups, most of them drunk. Maddy passes a gaggle of twentysomething women, slurring and stumbling, their faces sparkling with glitter from a makeup booth.

As she heads down the main concourse, Maddy is amped up and alert. The killer is here somewhere. She's sure of it. Maybe watching her right now. She feels her neck hairs tingle at the thought of something behind her, or above her. Somehow, she needs to lure the murderer into the open. Whoever it is—*whatever* it is—she's going to find it and kill it. No mercy.

The crowd thickens as patrons pour out of a pavilion exit in front of her. Maddy angles her way through, trying to stay on course, looking through small gaps in the throng.

Something catches her eye. About twenty yards ahead.

A young woman. Slim. With long, dark hair.

She looks again. No. Not possible!

Maddy feels a blast of adrenaline—so strong it stuns her. For a second, her breath stops in her chest. Her heart is racing now. She elbows her way through the crowd, trying to keep her eyes locked on her target.

The young woman is walking fast. Black pants. Bright blue top. Maddy knows that top. It was the one she lent to Deva a week after school started. She never got it back. *Dear God . . .*

"*Deva!*"

Maddy breaks into a run, crazed with relief. Her vision at school must have been wrong. Some kind of misfire. She shoves people aside, almost tripping as she goes. "Sorry! Move!" Signs and lights and kiosks pass by in a blur.

"*Deva! Stop!*"

But she doesn't.

What's wrong? Why won't she turn around?

Maddy breaks through the other side of the crowd and freezes. She's in the middle of the concourse now—surrounded by strings of bright lights. Drums pulse from a pavilion just ahead.

But Deva's gone. Vanished.

Maddy looks left and right. The drumming is getting louder, blocking out all other sounds. She hurries to the pavilion entrance and walks through, as if she's being pulled.

She can't stop.

The entrance leads into a tunnel lined with black canvas. With every step, the drumming gets more and more intense. Maddy can feel it from her temples to her toes.

She's almost at the end of the tunnel now. She sees light through a half-open flap in the canvas just ahead. She steps through and...*bam*! She gets walloped by a blast of sound and human heat.

It takes a second to register. She's in a stadium. The biggest she's ever seen. Packed with thousands of people. The stage at the far end is filled with costumed dancers—spectacular and acrobatic. The performers and the audience are all thrashing to the rhythm pounded out by a battalion of drummers on a platform above the stage. The energy is insane! Wild. Ecstatic. The drum pattern is Asian, then African, then everything at once—the pounding of a global tribe.

Maddy stands at the top of one of the main aisles. The bleachers shake from thousands of feet stomping in unison. She looks across the stadium.

There!

A lone figure is moving down another aisle about twenty yards to her right. For a split second, the figure is illuminated by one of the spotlights sweeping the audience.

Black hair, blue top.

It's her!

Maddy races toward the stage and cuts across the front of the stadium. Her ears are throbbing. The tempo of the drums is building, faster and faster. Maddy speeds up, too. The figure she's chasing is now just a silhouette. The stage lights pulse in sync with the drums. On the final deafening beat, the stage goes black. The roar from the crowd rises like a physical force.

The figure is gone.

Maddy spins, trying to get her bearings in the darkened space. She pushes through another curtain. She's backstage. A flash of blue disappears into an exit tunnel on the other side. Maddy is breathless now, not thinking—just running, dodging, jumping, until she's in another passageway, lined in black, just like the entrance.

She sees Deva just ahead. Shouts her name again. Why won't she answer?

Maddy makes one final lunge for her friend's arm, spins her around—and staggers back in shock.

The face is not Deva's face. It's green and hideous. And the body is no longer human. The creature lunges at Maddy, swiping at her with sharp claws. The jaws are open, showing blackened, blade-like teeth. Maddy ducks and turns, covering her head. A claw rips through her hair, slicing her scalp. She bends over, wincing in pain. She rocks backward, trying to clear her head. She needs to do something! Needs to fight back! The monster moves forward to strike again. Maddy shields her eyes with her arm.

Suddenly she feels a powerful grip around her waist. She's lifted off the ground and propelled through a fabric flap into the outside air. Maddy whips her elbows back, striking hard muscle. But the grip around her midsection only gets tighter.

"Hey, hey, hey! Stop! It's me!" A man's voice in her ear. Maddy stops flailing. "I'm letting go now," the voice says.

Maddy feels the pressure ease around her torso. She twists free and spins around to see . . .

Jericho?!

CHAPTER 67

MADDY BENDS FORWARD, hands on her knees. Her chest is heaving. Her head stings. She blinks the sweat from her eyes and looks up at her rescuer. She pants out the words, "You've been *following* me?"

Jericho nods. "Shadow's orders."

Maddy shakes her head, her breaths coming in quick gasps. "You've got to be kidding," she mutters. After all this time, Lamont still won't stop treating her like a baby.

She hesitates for a second, then gets onto her toes and tries to rush past Jericho, back into the pavilion tunnel. He blocks her with one arm and holds her back.

"Maddy, *quit it*! Whatever the hell was in there, it's gone."

Maddy's furious. She tries to wrestle free. "You don't know that!"

"Yeah, I do. It disappeared the second I grabbed you. Otherwise I would have whipped its ugly goddamn ass."

Maddy stops struggling. But Jericho still has a tight hold on her.

"Let it go, Maddy," says Jericho. "Let it go."

Maddy's head drops. She relaxes her fists. She feels the anger and adrenaline slowly drain out of her. Then she realizes that she's feeling something else. Something foreign and odd. Something she hasn't felt in a long time.

In this moment, she feels safe.

Maddy looks up at the huge man looming over her. Strange. In her brain, she knows this isn't the same Jericho Druke she grew up reading about, but somehow it feels that way. Exactly the same. Just like she always imagined. It feels like she's known him forever. She's starting to understand why Lamont trusts him so much.

"Promise me you'll stay still," says Jericho.

"Fine."

"Look. Maddy. I'm sorry about your friend. I truly am. But chasing some shape-shifter around the fair tonight won't bring her back. Let's head home, okay? Fight another day."

Maddy steps back and stares at him. "You do realize that I could turn invisible right now and leave you here in the dust?"

"You should have thought of that before you left the house," says Jericho. "Would have made you a lot harder to track."

"Okay, bodyguard," says Maddy. "Let's go."

They slip out of the cramped space behind the pavilion and find their way back onto the main concourse. The walkway is filled with concertgoers, still energized from the show. Suddenly, there's a loud crack from overhead. Fireworks. Splashy and bright.

"You're welcome, by the way," says Jericho.

"For what?" says Maddy. "Stopping me when I was about to catch the killer?"

"For stopping you when you were about to get torn to shreds."

"I think you're just hoping for a gold star from Lamont."

"And I think you have some trust issues."

Maddy nods. Pretty perceptive. Just like the Jericho in the books. "You're right," she says. "I do."

CHAPTER 68

MY HEAD IS swimming. I have no idea where I am. It takes me a few seconds to realize that I'm actually still alive. No pain. Just a significantly altered state. I turn my head to the side. I'm in bed with Margo. Her eyes are just starting to flutter. The whole world is moving in slow motion.

"Lamont? What happened?" Her voice is a croaky whisper.

I squeeze my eyes shut. It comes back to me in small pieces.

The airport. The drone. The envelope.

I lean over toward Margo. It feels like I'm talking through molasses. "Sedated. We were...sedated."

I try to push myself up, but there's almost no resistance from the deep mattress.

It's like pressing against a giant cotton ball. I can see that we're at one end of a palatial bedroom. The walls are stone. The floor is polished oak. A huge fireplace is set into one wall.

Margo lifts the bedcovers and peeks underneath. Her voice sounds as numb and groggy as mine. "We're still in our jumpsuits."

"Are you okay?" I ask. "Are you hurt?"

"All in one piece," she says slowly. "You?"

I swing my legs over the side and stand up. The room spins. I grab the bedpost for support. I walk carefully across the room and lean against the window. We're on a high floor. Out front, I can see a circular gravel drive and a massive fountain. I feel a click in my brain. My focus sharpens.

I know that fountain. I've *seen* that fountain.

"Where the hell *are* we?" asks Margo, struggling to sit up against the headboard.

I turn back from the window. "We're in the villa. The Destroyer's villa."

"Christ," says Margo, rubbing her head. "So much for catching him by surprise."

I try lifting one of the window sashes. No use. Welded shut. The glass is thick and ballistic. Unbreakable. I move to the door and wiggle the handle. Locked from the outside. I start pacing around the room, pressing on panels and baseboards, as if I'm about to find some secret exit. But I know it's a waste of time. Nice room. Nice prison.

There's a knock on the door. The lock clicks.

I tighten up, ready to take on whoever comes through, but my arms feel like noodles. I doubt I could even land a solid punch. I wait a few seconds. Nothing happens. I touch the door handle. It turns freely now.

I open the door a crack. Nobody there. But resting on the carpet outside is a silver tray with two French presses and a basket of croissants. I pull the tray inside and set it on a bedside table.

There's a small card leaning against the basket. BIEN-VENUE A LA DOMAINE DE SOL, it says at the top. Elegant type, like fancy hotel stationery. Below is a handwritten note. Margo plucks the card off the tray and reads it.

"Looks like we're about to meet our host," she says.

She holds the note up to let me read it. *La Chambre Jardin, 9 a.m.*

I take a stab at a translation. "The Garden Room?"

Margo rips up the card and lets the pieces flutter onto the carpet. "Maybe the Destroyer of Worlds has a green thumb."

CHAPTER 69

THE STAIRCASE IS a massive granite spiral with a wrought iron balustrade. When we reach the ground floor, I hear birds chirping. We walk through a massive reception hall, the size of a medieval throne room. Margo points straight ahead. "There." At the far end, a set of French doors opens onto what looks like an atrium. La Chambre Jardin.

On the way, I look around for guards, housekeepers, butlers. But the place looks totally empty. I have a sick feeling about this. We flew here to find the Destroyer. Instead, he found us. And now we're meeting on his terms. Not good.

The sunlight hits my face as we walk into the atrium. The walls and ceiling are all glass—thick panes connected by seams of brass. The room is filled with bright flowers and leafy plants in terra cotta planters. In the center of the room is a sitting area with a large wicker sofa and two high-backed wicker chairs. The air feels thick and cool. It smells like jasmine.

I wipe the condensation off one of the glass panels with my sleeve and look outside. The setting is gorgeous—manicured lawns and long stone walls. At the top of a small knoll, I can see an ornamental railing surrounding a bunch of very old headstones.

Margo steps up beside me and looks out. "Maybe he's got a couple of plots picked out for us."

"Bonjour!" A woman's voice. Then the click of heels on the tile floor. "I trust your medication has worn off."

Margo and I both turn as she approaches—a slender Eurasian woman in an elegant silk suit and stylish high heels. Very attractive. Stunning, actually.

Why is she here? To prep us for our meeting? She seems way too refined to be a mere assistant. Maybe head of security or chief of staff. Maybe a pretty assassin.

"Good sleep, I trust?" she asks. Cantonese accent, mixed with Maghrebi and a touch of French.

"How did we get here?" I shoot right back.

The woman smiles. "In total comfort, I assure you. Much better than sweltering on that miserable train for two hours."

She takes a step closer. I'm waiting for her to introduce herself, but she doesn't. She just stands there, staring at me. Suddenly, I feel my chest tighten, like there's a fist closing around my heart. My mind flashes to the video we watched with Diaz. That fleeting image of the figure in the desert. The dark robe. The tall, slim profile...

I inch closer to Margo, ready to push her behind me. I gather my strength for whatever happens next.

I realize in that moment that the Destroyer isn't coming.

She's already here.

CHAPTER 70

"BLACK IS NOT my favorite color," she says. "But it works in the desert."

I realize she knows what I'm thinking—the exact scene I'm picturing, the image I used to ID her. She bends to pluck an orchid from one of the pots. Sniffs it. Crushes it between her fingers.

"*Destroyer of Worlds*. Yes. I know that's what they call me." Her smooth brow wrinkles. "It sounds so harsh in English."

I glance over at Margo. I can tell that she's trying not to react. Or overreact. "If it's you," she says, "you've more than earned the title."

The Destroyer folds her long body into one of the wicker chairs and crosses her legs. She gestures toward the sofa. I sit down next to Margo, our hips touching, ready for anything. The Destroyer gets right to the point.

"I know how you found me," she says. "I know the names of the informants."

A shiver passes through me. I taste bile in my throat. What am I waiting for? I should blast this bitch through the wall before she can kill anybody else, including us. The world would instantly be a better place. I feel my fists clenching, my blood rising. I plant my feet solidly on the floor and center myself, ready to move. She's just sitting there, brushing a wrinkle out of her suit.

"Don't embarrass yourself, Mr. Cranston. Your powers are considerably diminished at the moment. Aftereffects of the sedative."

She's right. I can sense it. I'm trying, but I can't muster the energy.

"If you know what I'm thinking," I ask, "why bother with a conversation?"

"Conversations come in many forms, Mr. Cranston. For example, I can read your mind, but you can't read mine." She flicks her eyes toward Margo. "And you can't control me, Ms. Lane. You can stop trying."

I lean forward. "So why are we here? Just so you can watch us die in person? Instead of sending your drones?"

"Don't be crude, Mr. Cranston. I'm a businesswoman."

"You're a mass murderer," says Margo, her jaw tight. "A genocidal maniac. A war criminal."

The Destroyer doesn't flinch. "The world is the world, Ms. Lane. It's collapsing without my help. Things have been building to this conflagration for centuries. All these petty jealousies over land and religion and resources. *Ridiculous*. I'm not the prime mover. I'm just a witness to the carnage. Like both of you."

"Then why do you need a world-ending weapon?" I ask.

Silence. Then . . .

"*Touché,* Mr. Cranston." She gives me a disarming smile. "Everybody needs a little extra insurance."

She stands up and walks toward me. I get up to face her. She looks right into my eyes, as if she and I were the only two people in the room. I feel my chest clenching again. Is she trying to intimidate me? Hypnotize me? Break me?

"Am I right, Mr. Cranston? Or is it *Le* Shadow?" She frowns. "So silly, these cartoon names. They diminish us." She steps closer, invading my space. "Tell me something, Lamont. Be honest. Do you think you're a match for me?"

Her energy is overwhelming. Her fragrance goes right to my brain, like another kind of drug. It's all I can do to hold my ground. Suddenly, Margo elbows her way between us, eyes flashing.

"Lamont's already met his match," she says. "You're looking at her."

Instantly, the Destroyer's tone shifts. She reaches out and strokes Margo's cheek. Just for a second. "Indeed," she says. "True love. *Lasting* love." Her smile widens and her tone turns gracious. "I have an idea. You've come all this way. I want you to enjoy a special dinner tonight, at the finest restaurant in France. Just the two of you. *C'est moi qui offre.*" *My treat.* Then she looks straight at me again as if Margo's not even in the room. "We'll do business later," she says, *"toi et moi."*

She turns and walks toward the door. I feel sick and dizzy. Like I've been punched in the head. At the threshold, she turns and looks us up and down. First me. Then Margo.

"Forty-two regular, and size two," she says. "We'll find you some actual clothes."

And then she's gone. I'm foggy, but furious. I turn to Margo. "Business? *What* business? Does she think I'm here to make some kind of *deal*?"

"Really?" asks Margo. "You don't get it?"

"Get *what*?"

She shakes her head. "God! Men can be so *thick*."

"How? What am I missing?"

"Lamont. The Destroyer of Worlds wants to go to bed with you."

My stomach flips. My head throbs. "What? That's... *sick*!"

Margo slides her arm through mine and squeezes. "Don't worry. She'll have to go through me first."

CHAPTER 71

MADDY PACES BACK and forth in Burbank's tiny comms room. "Are they okay? What the hell is happening over there?"

Hawkeye leans over Burbank's shoulder as they try to get a bead on Lamont and Margo's location. Maddy can feel Jericho hovering behind her, like a 250-pound babysitter.

"Give me some space," she says. "I promised I wouldn't disappear on you."

Maddy hasn't given up on finding Deva's killer—or Moe's—but right now, she's more concerned about Lamont and Margo. They've been out of contact for nearly twelve hours. According to Burbank, the plane touched down, but that's about all he knows.

Maddy watches as he taps his keyboard and tweaks his dials. But nothing seems to be working. Burbank looks harried and frustrated. "Look," he says, "this system wasn't designed for transatlantic transmission. I can barely get a reading from their sensors."

Maddy leans in close. "What kind of sensors?"

"Biometric tags," says Burbank. "Very primitive.

Attached to their scalps, under their hair." He points to two meters with wavering, red-tipped indicators. "All I can say for sure is that they both have pulses."

"What about Tapper?" asks Hawkeye. "Where's my goddamn jet?"

Burbank checks another device, taps his keypad. A set of coordinates appears on a screen. Burbank does a quick conversion. He glances at Hawkeye. "Do you know anybody in Lycksele, Sweden?"

Hawkeye looks relieved. "Lycksele? Yeah. I do. Old army buddy of ours. Runs an airfield there. That's where Tapper must be hiding out. Can you reach him?"

Burbank shakes his head. "Nothing but static."

"I'm not worried about Tapper," says Hawkeye. "If I know him, he's huddled somewhere in a bunker, taking a nap."

"What's this?" Jericho reaches around Maddy to pick up a video stick from the console.

"Another video. Delivered last night," says Hawkeye. "More of the same."

Maddy watches as Jericho plugs the stick into the console. The screen lights up. Hawkeye's right. These scenes are starting to look way too familiar. Blackened buildings. Shallow graves. Bloated corpses. She reaches to turn off the monitor. "Enough of this crap. I'm sick of watching things we can't do anything about."

Hawkeye grabs her hand before she can touch the switch. "Hey. Lamont and Margo are working on it. They're doing something right now."

"Right," says Burbank. "We just don't know what it is."

"Hold on!" says Jericho. "What's this?"

He's pointing at the screen. Right in the middle of the scenes of misery and mayhem, there's a brief shot of a New York City street. No more than twenty frames.

Easy to miss. Surveillance video of a heavy-duty vehicle, surrounded by bodyguards.

Hawkeye rewinds and freezes the image. He pokes Burbank in the arm. "Did you see this?"

Burbank looks up. Shakes his head. "Looks like an editing glitch."

"It's not a glitch," says Hawkeye.

"Who's this?" asks Jericho, tapping the image of a man emerging from the car.

Burbank unfreezes the video and lets it inch forward, one frame at a time. Everybody in the cramped space leans in.

"Holy shit," says Hawkeye.

Jericho squints. "What?"

"That's Toor Bayani."

Burbank rocks back in his chair, scratching his scalp. "What the hell is the ruler of Chinasia doing here?"

"You mean the repressive, asshole *dictator* of Chinasia," Maddy retorts. She knows her world affairs—and her world despots. It was never on the school curriculum.

Banned material. So Jessica taught her at home—the whole truth about power and corruption. No matter how ugly.

For decades, Bayani's regime controlled the lives of more than three billion people, from the Indus River to Oceania. Like every other world despot, he was subject to the whims of Shiwan Khan. After Khan's defeat a year ago, Bayani reasserted his grip.

"That's nuts," says Jericho. "Bayani never leaves his compound. *Never.*"

"You're right," says Hawkeye. "Why would he risk coming out of his cocoon?"

"To enjoy the World's Fair?" says Burbank. Silence. "Sorry. Bad joke."

Hawkeye stops the video on a frame of Bayani in

the middle of the sidewalk. "There's only one reason a guy like this shows up this far out of his comfort zone. He's been summoned—by somebody he's afraid to turn down."

"Only one person in that category," says Jericho.

"The Destroyer of Worlds," says Maddy.

"Hey!" Burbank interrupts. "I'm getting something."

Maddy looks down at the console. Needles are bouncing and new coordinates pop up on a blurry printout.

"It's them," says Burbank. "Lamont and Margo."

Maddy grabs the arm of his chair and shakes it. "What's going on? Did something change?"

Burbank leans forward and checks his readings. "I can tell you three things," he says softly. "They're alive. They're excited. And they're in Paris."

CHAPTER 72

IT TAKES A lot to impress Margo. But I can tell that she's dazzled tonight. There's no way she can hide it.

"Wow!" she says, "I've never seen Paris like this!"

Neither have I.

Spring of 1937. That was the last time Margo and I were here. Back then, the Eiffel Tower was the tallest structure for miles. Not anymore. The restaurant we're sitting in is perched at the top of a 110-story skyscraper. At this very moment, we're actually looking *down* at the famous Eiffel spire. From here, the whole tower looks like a shiny toy.

The dining room is a large circle, with clear glass panels up to waist level all around. Above the panels, the sides are totally open to the air. Overhead, there's a clear glass canopy with a beautiful view of the night sky. It feels like we're floating.

Paris is more beautiful than ever. But it can't hold a candle to my date, especially in what she's wearing tonight.

When we got back to our room after our meeting in the garden room, our evening wear was already hanging in the wardrobe. For me, a perfectly fitted tux. For

Margo, a strapless white gown with lace trim. Stunning. Like something she might have picked out herself in the Triangle d'Or. Same for the high heels and beaded clutch. And the elegant diamond necklace. The ride from the villa was luxurious, too—in a vintage 1990s stretch limo. Another truly guilty pleasure.

I lean across the table and put my hand over Margo's. "I'll deny I ever said this. But the Destroyer of Worlds has excellent taste."

Margo adjusts her lacy bodice. "Sure beats a jumpsuit."

Out of nowhere, a waiter appears at our table. *"Madame et monsieur, bonsoir."*

He's slim and elegant, with his dark hair combed straight back from his Gallic face. "Welcome to Ciel. Tonight the chef is preparing for you a special tasting menu. Nine courses, with wine pairings." His English is as smooth as his French.

"Nine courses?" says Margo. "I'll burst a seam."

The waiter smiles. *"Pas du tout, Madame."* *Small plates.* He gives us a slight bow and backs off as a stately sommelier approaches, cradling a bottle in his hands. He presents it like a small treasure. Which it is. "Chateau Lafite Bordeaux. 1937. A spectacular vintage. Compliments of the house."

1937. Nice touch.

He pours a small amount into my glass. I hold the base against the tablecloth and swirl for a good twenty seconds. No rush. A wine this mature deserves a little extra time to wake up.

I raise the glass to my lips and take a small sip, letting it roll around my tongue before I swallow. My eyes go wide. I look at Margo. "He's right. It's fantastic."

The sommelier pours for both of us and leaves the bottle on the table. Margo picks up her glass and sniffs. "You don't think she'd try to poison us, do you?"

"We're perfectly safe."

"How do you know?"

"I never told you? It's an aftereffect of cryogenic suspension. The chemicals that kept us alive for all those years included some serious antitoxins." I lift my glass for a little pronouncement. "We are fully and permanently inoculated against ingested poison."

"Well, then," Margo clinks her glass against mine, "here's to one less way to die." She takes a sip then closes her eyes in bliss. "Oh, Lamont. That's *incredible*."

The wine warms and relaxes me. I almost forget that we're here as the guests of the most despicable human being on the planet. Obviously, she has her reasons for keeping us alive for at least a little while longer. Which buys me some time to figure out our next move. But for right now, I'm trying to just sit back and savor the company of my beautiful wife. As long as we're together, everything feels right. Always has.

Every table in the room is full. Our fellow diners are spaced around the perimeter—far enough apart that I can't hear conversations, just accents. From where I'm sitting, I'm picking up French, Spanish, Russian, maybe Greek.

Two tables away, a man with a lined face and upswept silver hair shares a table with a woman in a spectacular blue dress. She looks young enough to be his daughter. If it weren't for Margo, she'd be the most beautiful woman in the room. Margo snaps her fingers in front of my face. Caught me looking.

"Lamont! Eyes front. What's the plan? Are we actually going back to the villa tonight? I'm telling you right now, there's no way I'm letting you meet with that killer on your own. She's a man-eater. Among other things."

Waiters are circulating through the room, serving succulent-looking morsels on elegant plates and small platters. My stomach is growling. "I seriously doubt that she's still there. I think she wanted us out of the house so that she could sneak off."

"So we're just letting her go?"

"She confirmed that she has the weapon. With any luck, she'll lead us right to it."

Margo takes another sip of her wine. "Always the optimist, Lamont."

Out of the corner of my eye, I see the girl in blue excuse herself and slide out of her chair. Her companion leans back from the table, a white napkin resting on his lap. His eyes flick our way. His right hand slides across his thigh.

I jump up and grab Margo's arm.

"Gun!"

CHAPTER 73

MARGO HITS THE floor hard. I flip our table onto its side and pull her behind it. Bullet holes explode through the wood. Across the room, a bottle shatters in the sommelier's hands. He flies backward, a hole in his belly. Two waiters topple behind Margo, blood spraying from their necks. From under another table, two women start shrieking.

The shooter is on his feet now, firing from the hip. Machine pistol. Long clip. How many more rounds. Thirty? Forty? He steps forward. I lunge for him. The next shots strike the ceiling. Glass rains down in thick pebbles. I hit him in the midsection and feel the air go out of him. He staggers back, trying to grab me for balance. The gun comes loose. I knock it away. He goes for my neck. I shove my hands up under his armpits and push. He's two hundred pounds, easy, but I'm so amped he might as well be a sack of groceries.

I force him back to the edge of the room. He tries to get traction, but his soles are smooth and I've got momentum on my side. With one final push, I heave him over the glass panel and into the air. He lets out one quick scream—all he has time for. A second later, he hits the top of the Eiffel spire and impales himself on an antenna, twitching like a bug on a pin.

"Lamont!" Margo crawls from behind the table. Her white dress is splattered with blood. Her hair and face, too. I run over and yank her up onto her feet. I scan the room for other threats as we run toward the elevator.

"Go! Don't look! Just go!"

On the other side of the lobby, the door to the ladies' room swings open. The girl in the blue dress steps out and stops short. Her hand whips out from behind her back.

She points a gun at Margo's face.

I reach for the girl's arm.

Too late!

Margo's already knocked her out cold.

CHAPTER 74

WE'RE HALFWAY ACROSS the Pont d'Iena before we see that nobody's chasing us. At least not on foot. I look left and right over the Seine, searching for drones in the sky. Nothing but stars.

Behind us, we can hear police sirens heading for the crime scene. My chest is heaving from the run. I stop and sit Margo down on a low wall. She's panting, too. And barefoot. She kicked off her heels the second we got out of the elevator. Under the light of a street lamp, I can see the streaks of red on her cheeks and forehead. Her white dress is splotched with dark stains. I run my hands over her back and sides.

"Are you sure you're not hit? No grazes? That's a ton of blood."

She shakes her head. "Everybody's but mine."

We stand up and start walking. I hold Margo close, hiding the gore as we head for the Trocadéro district on the other side of the river. As we move along the walkway, we pass tourists and locals out for late-night strolls. Just ahead, a college-age kid sets his backpack against the wall and points a small camera toward the river. As we pass, I dip down and lift a plastic water bottle from his backpack sleeve.

On the other side of the bridge, we find an empty bench tucked under a tree in front of a huge park. Margo cups her hands as I pour water into her palms. Using her fingers, she scrubs the blood from her face, leaving light pink smudges on her pale skin. I've got a few scrapes of my own, but nothing major. I wet my hands and wipe the blood from her hair. I probe deep into her scalp until my fingers feel something hard.

I give a quick tug. Margo squirms and grabs my hand.

"What the hell, Lamont! Are you operating on my skull?"

I hold up a tiny electronic device encased in an adhesive patch, with a few blond hairs attached. "I need your biosensor."

"For what?"

"For this." I drop the sensor onto the ground and crush it with my heel. "Bang. You're dead."

"I don't get it."

"That's the sign."

"What sign?"

"If one of our hearts stops, Burbank gets a message to Tapper, and Tapper comes to extract the survivor. That's how we set it up. It's crude, but it's clear."

Margo rubs her head. "Good God, Lamont. Any cruder and we'd be using smoke signals."

I hear a bell jangle. I whip around to see a young boy on a bike heading straight for me. He's scrawny, no more than ten. He skids to a stop two inches from my knee. I slam my hands down on his handlebar. "Hey! Watch where you're going!"

He just looks at me. Doesn't say a thing. He reaches into his pocket and hands me a folded note. Then he jerks the bike out of my grip, turns around, and rides away, standing on the pedals to build up speed. Margo calls after him. *"Attendre! Arrêt!"* But he doesn't even look back.

I open the note. It's in English. I recognize the penmanship.

> *My dear Lamont—*
>
> *No need to investigate what happened this evening. It was me. I sent the assassins. Your wife was the target, not you. She's in the way, Lamont. You must know that.*

I hand the note to Margo. She reads it, then tears it up.

"Do me a favor," she says. "Try to be a little less irresistible."

CHAPTER 75

"THAT'S IT. GOOD boy!"

Maddy averts her eyes while Bando does his business at the edge of a flower bed—his favorite spot. The routine has been set since the family moved into the mansion a year ago. Jessica handles the morning walk. Maddy takes the after-dinner shift. The sun is already setting over the front of the building, casting long shadows over the garden.

Bando does a cursory cover-up of his mess with his back paws, then takes off to chase a squirrel around the base of a tree. Maddy smiles. Thanks to Dache, she could *be* that squirrel.

She hasn't seen her teacher in three days—not since she threw the fireball at him. If that was really him. Now that she could really use his help in finding a killer, he's nowhere to be found. Is he trying to teach her a lesson? Maybe he's done with her for good. Considering her past attitude, Maddy realizes that she really couldn't blame him.

She sits on the garden wall while Bando takes a few more laps around the garden, then claps her hands to call him back. "Let's go, Bando!" As they head for the rear entrance, she gives him a vigorous scratch behind the ears. Then she looks up to see Jessica standing in the doorway.

Something in her grandmother's expression makes Maddy tremble. When she reaches the back entrance, Jessica wraps her arms around her.

"Grandma. What is it?" She feels Jessica's grip tighten around her shoulders.

"Go upstairs," she says. "It's Margo."

CHAPTER 76

FRANTIC, MADDY RUNS up the back staircase to the third floor. She bursts into the tiny comms room. "What happened! What went wrong?"

The whole team is there. Hawkeye and Jericho step back to give her room. Burbank shrinks in his chair as Maddy steps up and pounds her fist on the console. She scans the screens and readouts. The biosensors! Lamont's needle is bouncing in the green zone. Margo's indicator is all the way to the left, in the black. Not moving.

Maddy feels Jericho beside her. "They were in Paris," he says. "About eleven p.m. their time. Both pulses shot into the red for a few minutes. Then hers just stopped."

"It's a malfunction!" says Maddy, kicking the base of the console. "Goddamn this second-hand patchwork piece of *shit*!"

"The sensor leads are pretty simple," says Burbank softly. "On or off."

Maddy turns on Hawkeye. "Find another plane! *Do it!* I need to get there!" Hawkeye doesn't move. Maddy pounds her fists against his chest. "Now! I mean it!"

Hawkeye absorbs the blows without blinking, then grabs her wrists.

"Maddy, *stop*! Even if I could find another plane, there's nobody to fly it. Tapper's the only jet pilot we've got. We're trying to reach him right now."

Maddy's mind is reeling. *Planes. Wings. Flight.*

Wait! *She* can fly!

Who needs a jet? She can shape-shift into a bird right now and launch herself across the Atlantic. She spins the idea out in her head for a few seconds, then comes back to reality. Three thousand miles over open water? She wouldn't make it. She's not that strong. Not yet. Maybe not ever.

Suddenly, the shortwave speaker crackles. A burst of static. Then, a male voice, garbled and faint. Maddy whips around. "Who the hell is that?" The voice starts to cut through—stronger, but incomprehensible.

Maddy leans in. "What is that? Norwegian?"

Hawkeye reaches across Burbank and grabs the microphone. "No," he says. "Swedish." Burbank slides over and adjusts a dial on the radio panel. A second later, the static clears. The Swedish voice is gone.

"Hello. New York base. Anybody there?" It's Tapper.

"Tapper! Hawkeye here. Extraction Point Echo. Repeat. Extraction Point Echo. Code Four. Do you copy?"

"Extraction point Echo. Copy." Then a long pause. "Code Four? Confirm."

Hawkeye repeats it, his head drooping. "Code four. Confirmed."

"Dammit!" says Tapper. "How did ... ?" His voice dissolves in another flood of static. Burbank twists the radio dial again but it doesn't help. A second later, the line cuts off. Hawkeye puts the microphone down.

"He got the message," he says. "He'll get it done."

Maddy grabs his arm. "Extraction point? *What* extraction point? What the hell is Code Four? Why are you talking like goddamn spies?"

Hawkeye sets his jaw and looks straight at her. "Because that's what we are," he says. "We can't use the same airfield they came in on. It's not safe. The pickup is at a spot Lamont knows—just across the French border, in Belgium. Remote and secure. At least it should be. Nobody's used it for a long time."

Maddy is burning with anger. First Moe. Then Deva. And now *Margo*? Not possible. Not after all that's happened, after all they've been through together. "Don't worry," says Hawkeye, "Tapper will bring her home. Dead or alive, nobody gets left behind. That's the code."

On the word *dead,* Maddy falls back against the wall and sinks to the floor, head in her hands. She starts sobbing. The room goes quiet for what feels like forever. When Maddy lifts her head, all three men are gone. But her grandmother is here.

Maddy feels Jessica's arm around her shoulder. Warm. Strong. Steady.

Like when it was just the two of them.

CHAPTER 77

The Western Front, Belgium / 1918

DEATH IS EVERYWHERE. By now, he's numb to it.

The lieutenant shifts his boots under six inches of muddy water and human waste. The private crouching next to him in the filthy trench is a green replacement—assigned to the platoon just that morning. Now it's midnight, and in this winding seventy-foot stretch of the Allied forward line, they're the only two left alive.

The lieutenant breathes through his mouth. It doesn't help. The smell of dead bodies rises like an invisible fog. Most of the platoon is in bloody pieces, hardly recognizable as human. He's got a five-inch shrapnel gash in his leg from the last explosion. He barely feels it.

For the past hour, the German artillery has been mercifully silent. But the lieutenant knows that it's only a temporary reprieve. A parachute flare lights the sky over the trench for a few seconds before fizzling out. The kid fumbles with his Springfield rifle.

The lieutenant snaps at him. "Don't drop that."

The kid tightens his grip. "No, sir."

The officer pulls out a cigarette, lights it. Passes it over. The greenhorn is even younger than he is. The only thing to do now is to keep him talking, keep him thinking, keep him sane until the relief column shows up. Or until the next shell ends them both. Whichever comes first.

"You from New York, Private?" Easy guess, based on the accent.

The private nods. "Yessir." He takes a deep, grateful drag on the cigarette.

The lieutenant eases his back against the wall of the trench. "Me, too."

"Manhattan?" the private asks.

"Upper East Side."

The private grins nervously, exposing crooked teeth. "You a rich kid, sir?"

"Black sheep," says the lieutenant. He plucks the cigarette back.

"So that's why you're here, sir? Instead of at some debutante ball?"

"Never cared for debutantes," says the lieutenant. "No sense of adventure."

For a few moments, the trench is quiet, except for the echo of gunfire crackling in the distance.

The private clears his throat and pipes up again. "Hey, Lieutenant. If you get back, you should look up my big brother. Moe Shrevnitz. From Brooklyn. He drives a cab."

The lieutenant sucks down one last drag and flicks the butt away. "It's a big city, Private," he says. "And I don't take many cabs." He cocks his ear toward the top of the trench, then yanks the kid back tight against the dirt wall.

The sounds are coming from the field above. Jangling metal and heavy boots. Men muttering in German. Getting closer. The lieutenant unshoulders his rifle and turns to tighten his bayonet.

When he looks back, the private is halfway up a wooden ladder, climbing toward the lip of the trench.

"Get down!" the lieutenant mutters, his jaw clenched.

"I'll see how many there are, sir," the private whispers back, moving up another rung. The lieutenant grabs for the private's belt just as he pokes his chin over the edge. A sharp crack. The private falls back off the ladder, arms wide, helmet flying. He lands hard in the bottom of the trench. The right half of his head is gone.

The lieutenant turns. He hears the slosh of boots from the north side of the trench. Reinforcements? No. Enemy. He raises his rifle and shoots the first attacker in line. He hears movement from behind him. He whips around. More gray uniforms. He fires again. The trigger just clicks. The Germans move in slowly from both sides, rifles pointed at his chest.

It's over. There's nothing more he can do here.

The lieutenant drops his gun, takes off his helmet—and disappears.

CHAPTER 78

"LAMONT. WHAT ARE we doing here?"

The cemetery is smaller than I expected—just a few hundred white crosses on a neat lawn surrounded by green hedges. I realize that a graveyard is a strange place to visit when you're running for your life, but it's on our way, and I probably won't get this chance again.

We haven't slept for twenty-four hours. Margo and I hid out in the park overnight and picked up some secondhand clothes this morning. We hopped the train from Paris to Ypres, then another from Ypres to Kortrijk, then rented bikes for the final leg to the pickup point. I insisted on this one extra stop. It's important to me.

Margo doesn't get it. Not yet. "What is this place? Where's the airstrip?"

I can hear the frustration in her voice. She thinks I've gone nuts.

"Hold on," I tell her. "I'm looking for something."

I move down the line of crosses, checking each one as I go. My vision is blurry from lack of sleep. It's hard to focus. And I know we're short on time.

There! Last man in the row. The lettering is etched

deep into the marble: *Leo Shrevnitz / Pvt / 106 Inf / 27 Div / Sept 25, 1918*

Margo comes up alongside me. "Who's this? Did you know him?"

"I did. A long time ago. For about twelve hours."

I run my hand over the name. Margo leans forward and squints for a better look. "Wait. *Shrevnitz?*" She steps back. "Is that a coincidence?"

"Coincidence?" I hold on to the top of the cross for a few moments. "No. I'd call it fate."

There's a low whistle and a rumble from overhead. We both look up. It's Tapper's jet, swooping in low on its approach. We hop on our bikes and start pedaling like crazy toward a place I remember from over a hundred years ago.

It only takes a few minutes to find it, off a dirt lane past an old windmill. There's no tower. Not even a proper runway. Just a bare grassy strip in the middle of the Belgian countryside.

When we ride up, I see Tapper crouched under the fuselage. He peeks out, then stands up slowly. He walks toward us, looking stunned. "Margo? Jesus Christ! You're *alive?*"

Margo lays her bike down and pulls off her cap. "I am. Minus a few hairs."

Tapper looks over at me. "What the hell *happened* here?"

I drop my bike next to Margo's. "You and Hawkeye were right about the villa. The Destroyer was there. And the intelligence from Diaz was solid, too. There's some kind of super-weapon in the works. She pretty much bragged about it."

Tapper nods, then cocks his head. "Hold on," he says. "She? She *who?*"

"I'll explain in the air."

Tapper pulls a jumpsuit from the cockpit. Just one. He's embarrassed. "Sorry," he says. "I thought..."

I grab the yellow outfit and toss it to Margo. "You take it. I'll use the body bag."

Margo steps into the leg holes and zips the suit up. Tapper helps her into the plane, then climbs into the cockpit. I settle into my seat in front of Margo and strap in. I spread the thick black vinyl bag across my torso and tuck it in around my waist. Not the most comfortable blanket, but better to be under it than in it.

Tapper looks back at me as we start to taxi. "Hey, boss. How did you even know this strip was here?"

I gaze out the window as the rutted field rolls by. "I spent some time in Flanders."

It's a short runway. It was built for biplanes, not jets. But Tapper doesn't need a lot of running room. The takeoff is as explosive as the first time. In a few seconds, we're thousands of feet up. I look down at the green fields and tidy towns as we climb. When I close my eyes, I see the same landscape. But now it's blackened with craters and strung with barbed wire.

Like most people in the world, I thought the Armistice would bring an end to the insanity once and for all. After the Great War, humans would never be that careless or cruel again.

Clearly, I was wrong.

We all were.

CHAPTER 79

WE TOUCH DOWN on the runway in New York just as the sun comes up. On the way, Tapper managed to transmit the good news about Margo. I can already see the happy welcoming committee at the end of the runway. Maddy and Jessica are standing arm in arm on the apron. Jericho and Hawkeye are waiting by a huge military-style Humvee.

As soon as the canopies pop open, I see Maddy running toward us. Margo barely has her feet on the ground when Maddy grabs her in a tight hug. They hold each other for a long time. "I thought you were gone," says Maddy, her face pressed against Margo's shoulder. "I really did."

"Don't worry," says Margo. "I'm only a fashion casualty." She steps back and uses Maddy's shoulder for support as she unzips her jumpsuit. "Hold still while I climb out of this damn thing." She extracts her arms and legs and drops the outfit in a heap. "Good riddance."

While Tapper sets the chocks on the jet wheels, I walk over to Hawkeye and Jericho. They're not the hugging type, but I can tell that they're both relieved to see us all home and still breathing.

"You gave us a little scare there, boss," says Hawkeye.

Jericho shakes his head slowly. "We thought Margo was…"

I nod. "I know. She almost was."

Hawkeye leans forward. "Is it true, what Tapper radioed? The Destroyer is a *female*?"

Before I can answer, Margo steps up beside me. "That's right. She is. And she's one green-eyed bitch."

Jericho looks confused. "Green? Like a cat?"

"Green, like envy," says Margo. "She has some perverse fascination with Lamont, and she wants me out of the way."

Jericho pats the massive vehicle. "In that case, I'd say the best place for you is inside an armored-plated chariot."

He opens the door to the electric Humvee and climbs behind the wheel. Hawkeye takes the front passenger seat. Margo and I scoot into the middle row. Maddy and Jessica slide into the back. We're just waiting for Tapper to finish securing the jet.

Jericho's right. The vehicle is a beast. The doors and sides are reinforced with thick steel, and the windows are bulletproof. "Found this baby in Khan's garage," he says, pressing the ignition. "All it needed was a charge."

Hawkeye turns from the front seat. "More news, boss."

Just what I need. "About what?"

"Toor Bayani is in New York."

"That murdering *thug*?" It's Jessica from the backseat. Strong opinion, as usual.

"What's he doing here?" I ask. "He's a homebody."

"Not sure," says Hawkeye. "All we got was a glimpse. We think maybe…"

I cut him off. "We should be tracking him. Every move."

"There's something else, boss," says Jericho, catching my eye in the rearview mirror.

Something else? At the moment, all I want to think about is a soft bed and a warm shower. I can see that Jericho is nervous. He glances back at Maddy. "You want to tell him, or should I?"

Maddy leans forward until her chin almost touches the back of our seat. "The murderer at the World's Fair," she says. "I found him the other night. I almost had him."

I feel myself flushing with anger. "*Maddy!* For Christ's sake, what the hell were you doing there at the fair by yourself?"

"We *talked* about this!" says Margo. She's furious, too.

Maddy looks right at me. "I wasn't by myself. Which you know perfectly well. Because you're the one who told Jericho to tail me!" Her voice rises. "That's why the killer got away. If I'd been on my own, I would have nailed him."

I kick the back of Jericho's seat. "You saw him?"

Jericho looks back. "You want a description? Tall, strong, and ugly as shit."

Tapper hops onto the running board, then squeezes into the back with Maddy and Jessica. As soon as he shuts the door, Jericho hits Forward and heads for the airport exit. The heavy Humvee rattles and shakes. It's no cushy limo, that's for sure. More like riding in a tank.

Suddenly, there's a huge blast behind us. The whole inside of the vehicle lights up. A concussion wave rocks us to the side. I jerk my head around to where the jet was sitting. All that's left is a column of flame, with shreds of metal raining back down through black smoke.

"Jesus!" says Jericho. He hits the power and cranks the Humvee onto the main road. In a few seconds, we're doing sixty. I look around for attack drones. But the sky is empty. What was it? Bomb? Missile? Lightning strike?

I look over at Margo. I can tell she's way ahead of me.

"That was a welcome," she says. "Your girlfriend's in town."

CHAPTER 80

AS WE PULL into the driveway, Bando runs out to meet the Humvee, wagging his tail like crazy and jumping up against the side panel. I can see Burbank waiting outside the front door of the house. When Margo slides out of the vehicle, she walks right up and gives him a big hug. He flinches. Awkward to watch.

"Thanks for keeping track of us," says Margo, squeezing him tight.

"You're welcome," says Burbank, his voice strained and anxious. He gives Margo a tentative pat on the back. "I'm glad you're both okay." His expression says, *Please let me go*.

We all gather in the front parlor for a crisis meeting. Except for Burbank. He skitters back upstairs to the privacy of his comms room. Enough close human contact for one morning, I guess. Maddy kneels on the floor to give Bando some attention. Everybody else is looking at me.

"What now, boss?" Tapper is still in his bright red jumpsuit, practically bouncing on his toes. After two hours in a cramped cockpit, he's clearly ready for action. I am, too. But the question is, which problem to attack first? Too many to choose from.

The Destroyer of Worlds is clearly in New York, and gunning for Margo. And somewhere, her scientists are working on some kind of super-weapon. The dictator of Chinasia is lurking nearby, too. If the Destroyer and Toor Bayani are planning an alliance, we're looking at a partnership made in hell. These two are bad enough operating separately. Who knows what horrors they could bring down on humanity if they team up?

And then there's the World's Fair killer. Not just a serial murderer, but an actual monster—a monster who almost took Maddy's life, even with the mighty Jericho Druke watching over her. Who knows how many more young people have been murdered in the past few days? The cops will never tell, that's for sure.

I decide to split my forces. I nod to Tapper and Hawkeye. "I need you two to find Bayani. Track him down and see what he's up to, who he's meeting with. Stay quiet and keep low. Remember, the Destroyer knows you're the ones who gave up her location."

"Right," says Hawkeye. "If she catches us, we're dead."

"Or worse," says Tapper.

I know what he means. I imagine the Destroyer would be very creative in her payback methods. I'm betting she could make a man *beg* to die.

"I don't suppose you can teach us how to turn invisible," says Hawkeye. He wiggles his fingers in front of his face, like performing a magic trick.

"Sorry. There's no crash course for that."

On the other side of the room, Jericho raises his hand. "I'll go. This Destroyer bitch doesn't know me from the hole in her ass. Never saw me."

I shake my head. "Sorry. I'm counting on you to guard the home front. I'm leaving Burbank and Jessica in your hands."

"And Bando," adds Jessica.

"Right," I say. "And Bando."

Maddy perks up at this. "Does that mean I won't have somebody following my every move?"

I give her a stern look. "Guess what? *I'm* your bodyguard now. You stick with me like glue. No more personal adventures, got it?"

"What about school?" Maddy asks. "I haven't been to class all week."

"School can wait."

Suddenly, I hear footsteps pounding down the back staircase, fast. Burbank rounds the corner into the parlor, breathing hard. He looks straight at me. "I've got a connection coming in upstairs on the secure video line."

"Who the hell is it?" It's not like our contact info is public. Somebody must've broken through Burbank's firewall.

"It's Lucian Diaz."

Terrific. We've been hacked by the president of the Americas.

CHAPTER 81

WE ALL RUSH up the back stairs and crowd into the comms closet. Sure enough, the handsome face of President Diaz fills the larges screen above the console. The image is grainy, but the audio is clear. Burbank sits down at the controls, trying to improve the video reception.

"Cranston? That you?" asks Diaz. The video must be muddy on his end, too.

"Present, Sir. The whole team is here."

"That's some setup you've got," he says. "It took my techies an hour to figure out how to connect."

"Home-grown equipment, Sir. It's a little patchy." Burbank looks up. I think I just offended him.

"Listen," says Diaz. "My spooks think they've located the Destroyer's build site."

"Okay. That's a start," I reply. "So what the hell is she building?"

A long pause, then, "What do you mean—*she*?"

Margo leans in toward the console. "The Destroyer is a female, sir." She looks over at me and adds, "A beautiful, clever, devious, spiteful, evil female."

"I'll be damned," says Diaz.

"Where's the target?" I ask.

"Mongolia," says Diaz. "The Kharkhorin region. Do you know it?"

Do I know it? Hell. I *lived* there. "Yes, sir. Very well." I neglect to mention that I haven't been back for ten thousand years.

"Hold on," says Margo. "If you know where the build site is, why don't you just blow it up?"

"Not that easy," says Diaz. "My people say it's powered by a nuclear plant. A missile strike would send a radiation cloud halfway across the continent. We need to be surgical on this. Cranston, I was told that this is what you do—get into places nobody else can without being seen. Am I wrong?"

"No, sir. You're not wrong. Not being seen is my specialty."

"Good. So when can you leave?"

I look at Margo, then at Maddy. "Tomorrow morning."

"Tomorrow?" asks Diaz, clearly irritated. "Why not now? I can have transport at your location in fifteen minutes."

"Sorry, Mr. President. I have a little problem at home I need to deal with first."

"What kind of problem? What could be bigger than this?"

"It's local, sir. But trust me, it needs to be handled. We'll be in touch."

I reach over and cut the feed. The screen goes dark. Burbank looks shocked.

"Did you just blow off the most powerful man in the western hemisphere?"

Maddy looks at me. "We're going back to the fair, right?"

"Correct," I say. "One killer at a time."

CHAPTER 82

I'M REALLY HOPING this is our last visit.

It's just after dark. I'm walking through the World's Fair entry gate again with Margo and Maddy. This time the buzzing crowd and bright lights are just background. I barely notice the magical Ferris wheel. All I know is that somewhere behind all these twinkling lights, a monster is lurking—a monster who killed Maddy's friend, then tried to kill her. This isn't just about protecting the city. It's about protecting my family.

"Tonight, we stay together, clear?" Margo slips her arm through mine. Maddy just nods. If I could get away with putting her on one of Bando's leashes, I would.

"I'll show you where it happened," she says, leading the way down the main concourse. We look like just another happy family in the crowd. On our way, we pass the hydroponics pavilion, the transplanted rain forest, and the dome where I took my asteroid ride—the exact spot where I first felt the killer's presence. As we walk, I hear the pounding of drums, getting louder with every step.

Maddy stops in front of a huge pavilion. The drum

sounds are coming from inside. "Right here," she says. "I chased him through this stadium. I thought it was Deva." She steps back and points to a dark passageway alongside the pavilion. "The fight happened back there."

From inside, the sound of the drumming intensifies. Margo makes a sour face and covers her ears. "Lamont, I can't stand that *din*!"

I glance up and down the concourse. "Let's keep moving. From the crime photos, it looks like the bastard never strikes twice in the same place. If Maddy saw him here, odds are he's hiding somewhere else."

"If he's a shape-shifter," says Margo, "he could be anywhere. Or anything."

She's right. Suddenly a pet dog licking spilled ice cream looks suspicious. So does a pigeon perched on a light pole. The monster we're looking for could be disguised as any person, any animal, any object.

Maddy heads across the concourse toward a structure that's designed to look like a giant high-tech cave. The surface seems to absorb light, creating a huge dark void in the middle of the fairgrounds. I hadn't noticed it before. Maddy stops at the entrance and waves us over.

"He likes the dark," she says. "This looks promising."

Margo and I follow her through the entryway into some kind of vacuum chamber. No light. No sound. After a few seconds, a door glides open to reveal a vast interior.

The walls and ceiling are flat black—and the space is filled with living, walking skeletons.

As soon as we step onto the floor, it happens to us, too. Some kind of wide-angle X-ray beam causes our clothing and flesh to disappear, leaving only our bones showing. Maddy does a slow spin, admiring her inner framework—arms, legs, hands, feet—all shining with some kind of phosphorescent glow.

Margo looks down and sees her pelvic bones and lower extremities. She gasps. "For God's sake, Lamont! This is *invasive*!"

Personally, I think it's fascinating. I've seen plenty of skeletons before, but mostly in bits and pieces. Watching the whole human architecture alive and in motion is something else. We're surrounded by pulsing rib cages, strutting femurs, and craniums of every shape and size.

Little kids are squealing and laughing, poking each other with their small, glowing phalanges. Anything metal is visible as a crisp white silhouette. Coins and belt buckles, jackknives and pacemakers. On some people, I can see pins and screws from orthopedic surgeries. One man has a plate in his skull. I hold up my left hand to admire the bright symmetry of my wedding band.

"Lamont, please!" says Margo, her jawbone moving up and down. "I can't stand this!"

I do another quick scan of the crowd, looking for any form that's abnormally large or misshapen. Does the monster even have bones? Can he mask them? All I see are fellow human beings, living images of the way we'll all end up—just a collection of hardened proteins and minerals. Whoever thought up this display was either a voyeur or a philosopher. Maybe both.

Margo grabs my arm. "Get me the hell out of here!"

I reach for Maddy on the other side. "Okay, let's go."

But she's not there.

CHAPTER 83

"MADDY!"

Margo is screaming at the top of her lungs as we push toward the exit. I'm thinking maybe Maddy turned invisible. Maybe she was embarrassed by her bones. Maybe she's waiting for us outside. Or maybe she went against my direct orders and set off on her own again.

"Dammit, Lamont!" Margo yells. "She promised to stay with us!"

Outside the pavilion, I turn to look in every direction. Margo is frantic, calling out Maddy's name again and again. From across the concourse, a small girl walks toward us, staring at me as she comes. Blond hair, blue eyes. In her right hand, she's holding a string with a black balloon attached. It bobs a few feet above her head. Margo turns around just as the girl hands me the string.

"Pop it," the girl says. Then she walks away, melting into the crowd like she was never there. Margo yanks a clip from her hair and stabs the balloon. The rubber implodes and shrivels. A small card falls to the ground.

Margo bends over to grab it. We read the message together.

DON'T JUST STAND THERE. SHE CAN'T BE FAR.

Margo looks up at me with terror in her eyes. "The Destroyer has her."

CHAPTER 84

MARGO AND I are running up the concourse, looking left and right, ducking into entryways, peeking into the dark alleys between the pavilions. I realize that if the Destroyer really wants to hurt Margo, this is how to do it—by taking Maddy. There's nothing crueler. For Margo, losing that girl would be worse than dying. I think the Destroyer knows it, too.

People are staring at us. We probably look like two crazed parents with a lost baby. Which is exactly how it feels. Two undercover cops start moving toward us. I can't tell if they want to help us or stop us. I don't have time for this.

Time!

I pull Margo to a halt. "Lamont! What are you doing?"

"I'm not sure, but I have to try."

I've never done this. I'm not even sure if it's possible. It's way beyond my training. Another one of the forbidden skills. But if I can stop Maddy from being taken away, I'll try. I bend forward at the waist and press my hands against my head. It feels like I have a storm raging inside my brain. Images are whipping around like tree limbs in a tornado. I see green-painted faces. Glowing skeletons. The killer's face.

Focus! Make it happen!

Suddenly, everything stops.

Actually *stops*.

When I look up, everything is frozen in place. Rides. People. Margo. I'm the only thing moving. The only one breathing.

I've suspended time.

I start moving up the main thoroughfare, past people as still as statues.

Suddenly, I feel a vibration, fast and loud—pounding against the ground.

I look into the distance. Thank God! It's *Maddy*!

She's the only other person moving—coming toward me from about fifty yards away. She's screaming, but I can't hear her. Her eyes are wide and her expression is pure horror. She raises her arm and points behind me.

Suddenly I feel it—a squirming weight on my shoulder and a sharp pain on the back of my neck, like I'm being pierced with knives. I whip around and see a fat, greasy rat drop to the ground, its tail curling like a long pink worm.

The image of the rodent imprints on my brain. I shudder as I feel the shift—totally out of my control. I have no choice. Now I'm on the ground in a four-footed stance. Small and compact. The world is a blur of blues and greens. Vibrations shoot through my body. My hairs stand on end. A cocktail of hormones fires me up for the fight of my life.

Rat on rat.

CHAPTER 85

FOR THE FIRST few seconds, I'm in shock. I suddenly realize that most of my brain is now devoted to smell. Food. Garbage. Sweat. And an overwhelming musk from a few feet away. Before the human remnant of my brain can react, the other rat is on me, banging into me broadside, then turning to attack with its back paws—fierce, punishing kicks that I feel against my ribs, rattling my internal organs.

My muscles tighten. But it's all defense. I'm not sure how to retaliate. My instincts are still recalibrating. My senses are overloaded. Then the other rat turns and rushes at me, ramming into me so hard I can feel the bones under its fur. Sharp claws rake across my face. Fangs dig into my neck again, shooting hot sparks of pain through my whole body. I'm twisting, writhing, trying to escape. Suddenly, I'm on my back, belly up. I squeeze my eyes shut to keep them from being gouged out. The odor of musk and greasy fur is overpowering. My ears are filled with high-pitched squeaks and hissing. I thrash to one side and throw the weight off me. And...

Pow! A loud thud and a sickening crunch.

I look up and see a human shape and a black work boot.

Maddy's boot.

In a blink, I rematerialize, still on all fours, staring at the body of a crushed wharf rat on the pavement. Its long yellow teeth are sticking out and blood is dribbling from its shattered skull.

The rest of the world slowly unfreezes. The rat is dead, but still twitching. The crowd backs away in disgust. A woman screams. A little boy spits up his milkshake. Maddy and Margo pull me up by my arms and hold on to me while I steady myself. I touch behind my neck. My fingers come back bloody. I'm breathing hard, feeling like I might collapse. I reach for Maddy.

"Where were you? Did she hurt you?"

"Who?" says Maddy.

"The Destroyer!"

Maddy shakes her head. "I saw the creature again," says Maddy. "I followed him. Then I turned around and saw him shape-shift into a rat behind you."

I'm starting to understand why time manipulation was a forbidden power. It sometimes allowed evil forces to slip through. I also realize that it's another way Maddy and I are connected. When the rest of the world stopped, the only ones moving were her and me. And a monster.

"Lamont, look!" It hurts to raise my head. Maddy's pointing toward the main pavilion, where the massive lighted crawl is running around the base of the structure. But instead of the usual news and fair announcements, there's a personal message.

It's for me.

...BONJOUR, LAMONT...THE KILLER WAS A SIMPLE DISTRACTION...EFFECTIVE, NO? ...AU REVOIR...

A message from the Destroyer, telling us that the World's Fair killer was just a decoy, under her control

258 · JAMES PATTERSON

the whole time. How is that possible? Unless her powers are beyond anything we've suspected. Beyond anything the world has ever seen.

I turn to Margo, confused and panting. *"Au revoir.* That means good-bye, right?"

"Not quite," she says. "It means *until we meet again.*"

I look at Margo and Maddy. I'm exhausted and in pain. But the night isn't over yet. Not by a long shot.

We've got a plane to catch.

CHAPTER 86

Orkhon Valley, Mongolia

I'M STILL SORE from the rat fight, and my neck is covered with a bandage. I'm pretty sure the antitoxins in my blood protect me against rabies. But I'm taking the HDCV vaccine to be safe. Margo gave me the first dose last night. I was still a bit woozy when we boarded the military cargo plane. It was about five times wider than Tapper's stealth jet, but just as uncomfortable. No matter. I slept the whole way.

Diaz provided the flight to an abandoned Chinese black site, but nothing else. No backup. No equipment. No supplies. The plane would return to pick us up in twenty-four hours. "Talk to the locals," Diaz told us, "and do what you do." I guess that gives him plausible deniability if we get captured—or set off a nuclear explosion.

Now we're on horseback—me, Margo, and Maddy—heading up a steep slope covered with stubby grass and loose rock. I haven't seen this kind of landscape for a long time. Not that it's changed much. In fact, it feels eternal.

I grew up riding Mongolian horses like this—short and sure-footed, with large heads and long manes. The last time Margo was in a saddle was probably at her country prep school. For Maddy, it's the first time riding an animal—*any* animal—and it shows. She's been complaining the whole way.

"How much farther?" she whines. "I'm getting blisters on my butt!"

"Over up there mountain," our guide calls back. Batuhan is about sixteen, riding in the lead. His English is iffy, but he knows the area. We found him yesterday feeding horses in a small corral about a mile from our landing zone. For more cash than his family probably makes in a year, he agreed to lead us to the site Diaz identified. It's been two hours since we started following him up an ancient goat trail. And I have no idea what we'll find at the end of it.

We're on our own here, and totally out of touch with the rest of the world. No biosensor is going to register from six thousand miles away. No sense even trying. I asked Batuhan if he had a set of walkie-talkies. He was not familiar with the concept.

The trail is getting more vertical. I'm clenching my thighs tight against my horse's sweaty flanks. Margo is riding ahead of me, right behind Batuhan. I turn around to check on Maddy. She's leaning forward and clutching her horse's thick mane for dear life. She looks miserable.

"Wouldn't it be easier if we just turned *into* horses?" she asks.

Margo looks back, eyes flashing. "Easy for you two," she says. "But some of us are stuck being human. So, no. I say we all suffer equally." Fair enough.

"Also," I add, "horses aren't that high on the intelligence chart. Right now, we need fully functioning homo sapiens brains." I pat my horse on the neck. "No offense."

I considered doing this mission myself and sparing Maddy and Margo the discomfort. But I figure the combination of our powers gives us a better chance at success. Three sets of eyes are better than one. And if the Destroyer is really in New York, I feel better about having Maddy and Margo with me on the opposite side of the globe.

The trail curls up and around a huge rock formation. Past the next turn, I can see smoke rising up against the afternoon sky. Batuhan turns around, smiling with bright teeth. "Camp!" he says. "Brothers!" He told us that we'd be meeting up with his three older siblings somewhere on the mountain. Fine with me. Couldn't hurt to have a little more local perspective. And maybe some extra muscle.

Batuhan uses his heels to nudge his horse into another gear. He looks up the trail and shouts out three words I don't understand. His brothers' names, I'm guessing.

"Batuhan!" Maddy yells. "For God's sake, slow down!" Margo hangs back to let her catch up. I move in front just as our guide disappears around a huge rock.

A second of silence. A sharp scream.

My adrenaline shoots up. I slide out of my saddle and pull Margo and Maddy to the ground. I motion for them to stay low. I creep forward toward the edge of the rock. I can hear Batuhan wailing from the other side.

I come around the rock face. I'm in a small dirt clearing with a campfire smoldering in the center. Batuhan is on his knees next to a large boulder. I step forward and look over it. I see three sturdy Mongolian horses lying on their sides, jaws hanging open, not moving. Behind the animals, three young men.

All dead.

CHAPTER 87

BATUHAN IS ROCKING back and forth on his knees, wailing his brothers' names. Margo kneels beside him and wraps her arm gently around his shoulders. He leans against her, sobbing. *"Yaagaad?!"* he moans. *Why?!*

I step slowly toward the bodies. When I hunted in these mountains, we were always told to watch for wolves. But wolves have been extinct for decades. Whatever killed these men didn't leave a single mark. Their faces are contorted in horrid death grimaces, eyes open, staring toward the sky. But no drool or foam from their mouths. No stippling or discoloration of the skin. No footprints from intruders or evidence of a fight. Somehow, they just dropped where they were standing.

"Lamont!" Maddy calls down in a loud whisper. She's on top of a huge rock overlooking the campsite, crouching to keep her profile low. I find a foothold at the base of the craggy formation and make my way up until I'm on my belly beside her. In a few seconds, Margo crawls up on my left.

Below us, hundreds of feet down, is a deep valley with a silvery river winding through it. On the far bank—totally out of place—is a huge three-story cement building with two large cones protruding from one side, belching steam. Nuclear exhaust stacks.

Looks like we just found the bomb factory.

Suddenly, I hear hooves pounding up the other side of the mountain. We all press our faces into the rock.

Sounds like somebody just found *us*.

CHAPTER 88

I LIFT MY head and look down as a lone horseman comes over the crest from the other side of the mountain. He's wearing a thick leather jacket and a fur hat. His right arm is crooked upward at a right angle. Fastened to his sleeve is a massive brown bird with a black hood over its head.

A falcon.

The man rides slowly across the clearing toward Batuhan. His horse skitters sideways at the sight of the dead animals. The raptor seems alert but calm. I can see its talons wrapped tight around the man's leather gauntlet.

Batuhan stands up slowly as the man approaches. It seems like they know each other. The three of us slide down the rock face and land feet-first on the dirt. I'm ready for anything. Batuhan confronts the rider in a wailing voice.

He's speaking Mongolian now. It's not the same dialect I was taught, but I can pick up the gist: *What happened here? What happened to my brothers?*

The falconer waves his left hand in a circle and points to the sky. His voice is rich and deep. It resonates in the still mountain air.

Maddy elbows me. "What's he saying?"

"He's talking about some kind of strange bird. Fat and fast."

I see Maddy's mind turning. "A drone."

I decide to step forward and try my hand at a language I haven't spoken in ten thousand years. Under its black hood, the falcon turns toward me. The falconer stiffens and sizes me up.

"Öglöönii mend," is my simple opening. *Good morning.* I'm holding my hands up to show I'm not armed. I see the rider ease back into his saddle. Then I ask about the building in the valley. It's like turning on a tap.

The falconer talks fast. I keep up the best I can. I know I'm missing a word or two here and there, but the basics are clear. The factory's only been there for a few months. It seemed to pop up out of nowhere. One day, the valley was empty. The next day, swarms of trucks and workers showed up. *"Shorgoolj shig."* *Like ants.* A few weeks later, the building was finished.

In my best Khalkha dialect, I ask what the hell they're making down there.

The falconer shrugs. *"Bi medekhgüi."* He has no clue. But he saw the fast, fat birds many times. His falcon wouldn't go anywhere near them.

Batuhan looks at me, hollow-eyed and drained. He tells me he needs to use our horses to carry his brothers back to the village. How can I say no? But that means I need a new plan, fast. I ask the falconer if he can take my wife back down the mountain with him. He looks Margo up and down, like he's calculating the weight of a feed sack. He gives a terse nod.

When I translate the arrangement for Margo, she looks incredulous. She comes at me with a hoarse whisper, close enough so Batuhan won't hear. "You want me to ride piggyback down a mountain with a man and a bird and three dead bodies? There's no way!"

"Margo, it's the *only* way. Maddy and I will meet you back in the village."

"Why? Where the hell are you two going?"

I nod toward the valley. "We're heading down to check out the factory."

"Why can't I come?" Margo asks. "I can hike as well as you two can."

I glance over at the hooded falcon. "We're not hiking. We're flying."

CHAPTER 89

MADDY AND I stand on the edge of the cliff watching the others start winding their way back toward the village. Then we turn toward the valley. The sun is high in the sky, causing reflections in the river.

I realize that Maddy and I have never shape-shifted together. It's risky, having two of us in nonhuman form at the same time. I hope Dache taught her well.

"Have you done birds?" I ask.

"Once," she says. "Red-tailed hawk."

"Okay. Then you know the drill. Ride the thermals for lift. Tuck in to dive. Watch out for wind shear."

"I know, I know," she says impatiently. "You go. I'll follow."

I close my eyes and focus my mind. I feel my body shudder and shrink. In an instant, the shift is complete. I sense the wind direction, raise my wings, and launch.

As a saker falcon.

My eyesight is incredible. I spot a rabbit in the grass a mile away. My bird brain pulls me toward the prey, but what's left of my human cortex overrules it. I feel Maddy behind me now, drafting on my current. Then she shoots past me like a bullet, wings tight to her sides, heading for the factory about a mile away.

She plummets toward the ground and pulls up about a hundred feet above the building. She starts flying in graceful circles. I swoop down and match her pattern. We're effortlessly in sync, communicating with twitches of our wingtips. Easier than talking.

I circle lower and lower, looking for an opening. But there are no windows, and all the vents are all gridded. As buildings go, this one is virtually bird-proof.

I touch down on the flat cement roof next to a maze of air-conditioning units.

Maddy flares her wings and lands beside me. I rematerialize and take a moment to adjust to my man-sized weight and piss-poor vision. In a second, Maddy is human, too.

She's breathless and excited.

"I could stay up there all day," she whispers. "The wind feels amazing."

I nod. "I'd rather be a bird than a rat, that's for sure."

We move toward a boxy structure with a metal door. The door looks thick and heavy. A fireball could probably get us through, but it would take me some time to work up the energy. Plus, I don't want the noise of the blast.

Maddy walks right up to the door and pulls it open. Unlocked. I guess they're not worried about intrusions from above. Or maybe somebody got sloppy.

We brace the door open in case we need a way out. A few seconds later, we're standing on a metal landing. I lean over and look down the staircase to the factory floor two stories below. I can hear isolated thuds echoing. It doesn't sound like machinery. More like somebody being punched.

I point down the stairs, then I disappear. A second later, Maddy vanishes, too.

I remind myself that when we're both invisible, Maddy can see me, but I can't see her. In that way, she's more evolved than I am. But it means I always have to take the lead. Otherwise, I'll keep bumping into her.

The air smells like paint and fresh cement. Standard new-building scents. At each turn of the staircase, I expect to find workers or guards, but so far, it's a clear path. Or maybe they're just waiting for us below.

My heart is pounding hard in my chest. I stop to look through a small port on the second-floor landing. All I see are catwalks and ductwork. Whatever they're making here, it must all be happening on the ground floor.

There are surveillance cameras at every corner, but that's one thing we don't need to worry about. All the cameras are seeing are empty stairs. If they were heat-sensing, we would have heard an alarm by now.

The punching sounds are getting louder, echoing in a large space.

I'm standing with my shoulder against the first-floor door. I feel Maddy pressing in behind me. I pull the door partway open, just enough for us to slip through. I swing to my left, and get hit hard in the gut.

By a soccer ball.

CHAPTER 90

GODDAMNIT!

The factory floor is as wide and long as an airline hangar. And it's totally empty, except for four kids in the middle—two boys and two girls in cheap athletic gear, kicking soccer balls back and forth. The kicks echo against the bare walls. Like punches. But the kids are oddly quiet.

They look about seven or eight. Maybe they're workers, or slave labor. But they're well fed, and they don't seem to have a care in the world. If they worked here, their bosses are long gone. Along with all the equipment.

I need to find out what the kids know. What they saw. Which means I have a choice to make.

Should I duck around a corner and rematerialize there? Or should I do it right in front of them? Sometimes the shock effect works wonders.

I whisper to Maddy. "Follow me."

I walk to the middle of the floor, right in the center of the quadrangle of kids. One of them kicks a ball waist-high across the space. I catch it in midair and hold it. Then I make myself visible. Maddy rematerializes right beside me.

I watch for the reaction—the kind I've seen a thousand times. Fear. Amazement. Disbelief.

But the kids don't look shocked at all. They just stand there, like nothing happened. Like seeing two people appear out of nowhere is no big deal. The tallest boy steps forward with a sneer on his face. He turns to the other kids. *"Suuder irlee,"* he calls out. I feel a chill in my belly.

"What did he say?" asks Maddy.

I give her the translation: "The Shadow has arrived."

One of the girls points toward the wall behind us. We turn around. My gut does a flip-flop. The wall is filled with a message in giant script. In the Destroyer's handwriting. No translation needed.

TOO LITTLE, TOO LATE, it says.

"Oh, shit!" Maddy grabs me. She's looking back over her shoulder. I spin around to see what she's seeing.

The kids are gone, soccer balls and all.

All that's left are four filthy, skittering rats.

CHAPTER 91

SOMETIMES FLIGHT IS smarter than fight. I've got no appetite for another rodent battle. Neither does Maddy.

In only took two seconds for us to shape-shift back into falcons, leaving the critters behind on the factory floor. Now we're soaring back over the mountain. From a few hundred feet up, I scan the ground for other factories or storage facilities—anywhere somebody could be building or storing weapons. With Maddy close on my tail, I do a slow loop across the valley. But all I can see are miles of Mongolian steppe, dotted with small huts and goat herds. It's no use. Time to get back to Margo.

As we swoop down back toward the village, I can see the falconer leading the way out of the foothills, with the bird on his arm and Margo in the saddle behind him.

Batuhan is leading the string of three horses—our horses—each one with a limp body draped over it. As they get closer, I can see villagers lay down their tools and baskets and move toward the procession. The village is tiny. No more than thirty or forty people. As they reach the horses carrying the bodies, I can hear wails rise up into the sky—like a collective banshee howl.

We land at the side of a small yurt and go inside to rematerialize. The second we step out, Margo spots us and runs over. She wraps us both up in a big hug, then pulls back. "Did you find it? What was in the factory?"

"Zip," says Maddy. That pretty much captures it.

"But the building," says Margo, "was *enormous*."

I nod. "Right. Enormous—and empty. There was nothing there. The Destroyer is one step ahead of us, just taunting us. Whatever weapon she was building is gone. Either she's hiding it somewhere else, or it's already out there in the world, ready to be used."

"Or it doesn't exist at all," says Margo. "Maybe this whole trip was a decoy."

"Like the World's Fair," says Maddy.

The cries of the crowd are getting louder. We all watch as the villagers untie the bodies of the three brothers from the saddles and carry them toward a small tin-roofed hut.

Batuhan walks slowly toward us, his back straight, his fists clenched at his sides.

His face is twisted with anguish and rage. He doesn't even attempt English. He speaks to me in Mongolian, practically spitting out the words. He wants to know if I found the people who did this—the ones who murdered his brothers. He wants to know if I killed them.

I hold him by the shoulders and look him straight in the eye. *"Ügüi. Gekhdee bi khiikh bolno,"* I tell him. Meaning, *No. But I will.* At the moment, it sounds like an empty promise, even to me.

Suddenly the sky begins to rumble and the ground starts to shake. The horses startle and the falcon cowers. I look up as the belly of a huge cargo plane passes overhead, not more than a few hundred feet up. The sound is deafening.

Our ride is here.

CHAPTER 92

New York City

IT'S 6:00 P.M. when the government SUV pulls through the gate and into our driveway. All these different time zones are starting to mess with my circadian rhythm, and putting me in a dark mood. Flying west from Mongolia, we technically gained an entire day, but in every other way, I feel like we're losing.

Diaz called the plane as soon as we took off. I was embarrassed to tell him that the trip was a bust. We were no closer to finding the super-weapon than we were before we left. At that point, the comms connection dropped. Either that, or Diaz hung up on me. Couldn't blame him. He hired somebody with mystical super powers and got nothing for it. He probably sees me as nothing but a waste of precious jet fuel.

Jessica and Bando rush out to greet us. Bando yips and wags his tail, begging for a head scratch. Maddy wraps her grandmother up in a tight hug. Jessica turns her head and pushes Maddy away.

"Good Lord!" she says. "You smell like a *horse*!"

"Very perceptive, Grandma," says Maddy. She steps

in again, opening her jacket to let the odor waft. "Which breed?"

Jessica holds her nose as Margo comes in behind us. "Take a shower, please! All of you!"

I ask Jessica where Burbank and Jericho are. She holds her breath and points upstairs. I head through the kitchen and up the back staircase. Hopefully, they've been checking in on Hawkeye and Tapper's attempt to track Toor Bayani. Maybe they're having better luck than I did on my mission. *Something* has to go right today.

When I walk into the comms room, Burbank and Jericho are huddled over the console. Jericho turns and gives me a quick wave. "Welcome home, boss," he says.

A pause. Then, "What's that *stench*?"

"One hundred percent pure Chinasian equine sweat," I tell him.

"What did you find over there?" asks Burbank.

"Nothing. Either the weapon has been moved, or it was a sham all along. Any trouble here while we were gone?"

"Quiet as a church," says Jericho. "I finally had time to plant some mines in the front yard."

"Speaking of Chinasia," says Burbank. He flips a switch. A speaker starts blasting static. He adjusts a dial and the sound clears, enough to hear a man's voice, talking in an Asian dialect. I can't understand a word.

"Tapper and Hawkeye managed to find Bayani's vehicle," says Burbank. "They bugged it." He points to the speaker. "That's him. That's Bayani talking right now." The voice sounds thin and reedy, not like a guy with his foot on the necks of billions of people.

I lean in. "*Dammit!* What's he saying?"

"Sorry," says Burbank. "I should've built in a translator."

"He's talking about the super-weapon." It's Maddy, from the doorway.

"You understand him?" I ask. She looks surprised, too.

"He's speaking Mandarin," she says. "I guess I absorbed it from Dache the night the commandos attacked us." Maddy steps up and leans over the console. "He's saying, no visible physical effects...no residue... clean kill."

"It's a biological agent," Jericho mutters.

Maddy nods. *"Bó wù."* She searches for the right word in English. "Mist."

I think back to Batuhan's brothers on the mountain. Not a single bruise on any of them. Clean kill.

"Where's he going?" I ask. "Where's the car headed?"

Burbank checks one of his screens. "Moving north along the Hudson River, out of the city."

"Wait! *Shhhh!*" Maddy holds her hands up and puts her ear closer to the speaker.

The transmission is breaking up. I can see her concentrating, trying to pick up whatever scraps she can get.

"It's for sale," she says.

This is driving me crazy. "*What* is?"

"The weapon. The formula. It's being sold to the highest bidder." She turns and looks straight at me. "Bayani's headed for an auction."

"When?" I ask.

"Jin wan," she says. "Tonight."

CHAPTER 93

IT'S ALREADY GETTING dark outside. I meet Burbank and Jericho in the basement supply room. I'm tense, but energized. Determined. Tapper and Hawkeye's sensors show them just outside Beacon, ninety minutes north of the city. Bayani's vehicle passed their location just before the bug stopped transmitting. With any luck, they've pinpointed his destination by now. The auction site. We need to get there fast. Before the deal goes down. Before the weapon gets sold. There are a lot of bad actors in the world who would be willing to pay top price for that kind of leverage.

Burbank is stuffing a case with electronic gear. Taps. Scramblers. Receivers. Jammers.

"Building yourself a robot?" asks Jericho.

"You never know what'll come in handy," says Burbank. Always diligent. Always overprepared. Just like his ancestor.

"As for me," says Jericho. "I like to travel light." He stuffs a sawed-off shotgun into a shoulder sling and jams a few extra cartridges into his pocket. Then he grabs a couple of small aerosol cannisters and hooks them on his belt. "Knockout gas," he says.

"Your house blend?" I ask.

He nods. "A little goes a long way."

Burbank is more hyper than I've ever seen him. I can tell that he's fed up with being stuck in the attic, just watching things happen. Sometimes even an introvert wants in on the action. I'm all for it. Compared to the rest of the team, he's not exactly in fighting shape, but we might be able to use skills on-site for surveillance and eavesdropping. Besides, he'll have plenty of protection. Tapper, Hawkeye, Jericho—and, of course, the Shadow. Although at the moment, I'm feeling like I might be the weakest link.

I grab a satchel of my own and throw in some smoke grenades, a pistol, and a few flares. Old-school stuff. But like Burbank says, you never know…

We haul our bags out through the lower exit to the Humvee. As soon as I step out, I see Maddy leaning on the vehicle, arms crossed, jaw set. I was expecting this. I walk over and set my bag down on the driveway.

"I'm coming with you," Maddy says.

"No, you're not," I tell her. For about the tenth time.

I've made up my mind. I have no doubts about her skills or her guts, but if there's even a slim chance that we'll be running into the Destroyer or more of her shape-shifters, I want Maddy and Margo back here, safe and sound—as far from danger as possible.

"Maddy. I'm not taking another chance on you getting killed. We're all wearing biosensors. You can track us the whole way from the comms room. If anything happens here, you can handle it. I know you can."

I'm not just blowing smoke. This is the girl who helped me defeat Khan in Times Square, not to mention tromping a shape-shifting rat to death. I trust her with my life.

"Don't forget," I tell her, "the Destroyer has it in for

Margo. I need you to keep her here with Jessica, and keep them both safe."

That argument seems to have some effect. Maddy steps away from the vehicle door. I pull it open. We start loading our gear. "Do you want me to get Dache here to back you up?" I ask.

"No," she says firmly. "I don't need him. I'm done with him." She grabs my arm and glares at me. "If I see one of your sensor needles in the black, I'm coming up there!" she says. "You won't be able to stop me."

"We'll be fine," I tell her.

I'm glad she can't read minds. Because if she could, she'd know that I'm not at all sure we'll be fine. I'm not really sure of anything. I lean in for a hug, but Maddy twists away. I know she's angry. But I also know it's for the best. I watch as she walks back into the house and slams the door. Jericho slides into the driver's seat.

"She's a tough girl, boss," he says. Big compliment, coming from him.

"I know. That's why I need her here."

I hop into the front passenger seat and give Jericho a nod. "Let's go."

As we pull out of the driveway, I look back to see Jessica, Maddy, and Margo looking out from an upstairs window. They've each protected me in more ways than they know. Now it's the Shadow's turn to protect them.

Along with the rest of the whole damn world.

CHAPTER 94

IT'S ALMOST 10:00 p.m. We've been driving for nearly an hour. Burbank is staring into a device on his lap, lit by the glow from the dashboard.

"Turn here!" he shouts, jerking his thumb to the west.

We all rock to one side as Jericho makes the hard left off the main road. Now we're heading down a rutted dirt lane directly toward the Hudson. Burbank is homing in on Trapper and Hawkeye. Closer and closer.

Jericho skids to a stop in a scrubby shorefront clearing. Water is lapping on the small, rocky beach. By the light of the moon, I can see an old concrete boat ramp and a sagging wooden dock sticking out about thirty yards into the river, with a few planks missing. At the end of the dock, Tapper and Hawkeye are waving at us, silhouetted against the water. They're standing next to some kind of low-slung boat. I hop out of the Humvee with Burbank and Jericho. We grab our gear and head down the dock.

"Welcome aboard, maties!" says Tapper as we get close. He waves his hand toward the boat. Now I can see what it is—some kind of speedboat, with a long, sliver-shaped front end and a small cockpit with a wrap-around bench in back.

"Twin two-fifties," says Hawkeye. I don't know much about twenty-first-century watercraft, but I assume he's talking about the engines.

"Where did this thing come from?" I ask.

"I promise the owner won't miss it until morning," says Tapper. Good enough for me. When it comes to Tapper and Hawkeye's methods, sometimes it's better not to ask too many questions. Just trust them to get the job done. Same as I did with their ancestors.

We stash our bags in the small cockpit and climb in. I can tell that Burbank is not happy with the tight fit. We're practically on top of one another on the narrow bench.

Tapper takes his seat behind the controls. Hawkeye unties the last line from the dock and steps in as Tapper fires up the engines. I feel the vibration from my toes to my head.

"Where to?" I ask.

"Bayani's vehicle is about ten miles upriver," says Hawkeye. "Water approach is better." That's the last thing I hear. Tapper shoves the throttle forward and the roar of the engines shuts out everything else.

As we speed up the Hudson, I feel the wind whipping my hair back, along with the skin on my cheeks. The river is choppy. With each hard bounce, cold spray flies up over the bow. Within a minute or two, we're all pretty much soaked. Burbank is crouching in the middle of the cockpit with his arms wrapped around his bag of electronic gear. He looks seasick. Probably sorry he came.

After a short ride up the dark river, Tapper cuts the engines and lets the boat drift forward. Hawkeye points to the cliff on the east shore. Set back from the edge, about a hundred feet up, is a huge mansion. Bigger than mine. It's glowing from inside.

"That's the place," says Hawkeye.

Burbank stares at the cliff rising out of the dark water. "How the hell are we supposed to get up there?"

Hawkeye pulls a canvas bag from under the console and unzips it. I can see ropes and grappling tools inside. "How else?" he says. "We climb."

Burbank looks at the bag, then at Hawkeye. "Maybe you," he says. "Definitely not me."

He's right. Burbank is in no condition to take on a nearly vertical rock face. Once again, time to split forces. "Fine," I tell him. "You stay in the boat with your bag of tricks. We'll come for you if we need you. Just monitor us, okay?"

Tapper lets the boat drift toward the cliff and then pulls out a massive paddle. He hands it to Jericho. "Okay, strongman," he says, "get us as close as you can to those rocks."

"Without sinking the ship," adds Hawkeye.

Jericho grabs the paddle and starts stroking through the water on the port side. I can see his muscles bulging under his shirt. Slowly, with a little help from the current, he brings us close enough for Hawkeye to jump onto a boulder at the bottom of the cliff. Tapper eases the boat anchor into the dark water. Then he and Jericho hop off.

From here, the cliff seems to be straight up. We're totally out of sight from above—at least for now.

"Coming, boss?" asks Tapper in a low voice.

"You three go ahead," I tell him. "I want to get a look from up top."

Hawkeye cocks his head. "Up top?"

I shape-shift right in front of them. Right there on the boat.

"Holy shit!" is Tapper's reaction. I'm sure he's speaking for everybody. Ten seconds later, I'm riding the updraft alongside the cliff. My first time in this particular form. But it was the best possible choice.

Great-horned owls have fantastic night vision.

CHAPTER 95

FROM UP HERE, I can see the layout of the whole property. The house is set back in a grove of evergreens. On the river side, there's a sloping lawn with thick hedges on two sides. A couple of limos and a few security vehicles are lined up around a circular driveway on the street side of the mansion. Strange. I expected more. Most of the guards are out front. Only a few are posted on the side facing the river, spread out on the far corners of the lawn.

Our black-hulled boat blends in with the water below, but I can clearly make out the top of Burbank's balding head in the back. I do a few slow circles while Jericho, Tapper, and Hawkeye make their way up the rocks. They're finding plenty of footholds. With their skills, they hardly even need the equipment. For them, it's pretty much a free climb.

I swoop lower as all three of them reach the lip of the cliff and start moving toward the house, using the hedges for cover. One by one, Jericho grabs the sentries and sprays them with knockout gas, then rolls them into the underbrush. Now I can see the team crouching against the stone foundation of the house. They're packed tight together, checking their weapons. Waiting for me.

Suddenly, I hear a high-pitched whir, like a very loud wasp. I feel an updraft under my wings. My heart rate explodes as I sense another predator. I turn my head.

Drone!

No time for human thought. Avian instinct takes over. I tuck in my wings and go into a dive, shooting down toward the river. I hear the whir of blades behind me. I bank right. My wingtip brushes the surface of the water. The drone stays tight behind me. I flap my wings hard to generate thrust. I hit a small thermal and ride it up. I look inland.

Maybe I can lose the drone in the trees. But as I start to head toward shore, it rises up in front of me, lights blinking. I make a move to get past, but the rotors almost clip my right wing.

I can't evade this thing.

I have to kill it.

I bank out over the water again, looking for room to maneuver. I glide, then dive. The drone follows, matching my every move. I can feel it trying to lock on to me. I can see dart-sized missiles bristling below the rotors. Probably programmed to seek a heat center. I need to keep moving! A stall means death.

I make another dive, heading straight for the water. The drone is as nimble as I am. Maybe even better. As I pull out of my dive, I bank hard to the right and gain altitude again until we're a hundred feet up. Me and the damned machine. I can see the lights from the mansion off to my left. I turn in a tight circle. The drone follows. For a second, its underside is tipped toward me.

Its belly.

I adjust my angle and head straight for it. I hit the underside hard with both talons. Hard enough to break an animal's spine. I feel a panel shake loose. The rotor blades tip toward me, barely missing my neck. The drone goes into a wobbly circle, trying to right itself. I attack again, heading straight for the loose panel. This time, my right talon hooks a small wire bundle. I rip downward and feel something give. The drone starts spiraling down. But I'm losing lift! I'm heading down, too.

I can see the water coming up fast. I tuck in right, almost into a ball. At the last second, I flare my wings to catch as much air as possible. I soar up again. The drone plunges in right below me, rotors churning the surface into froth. Then it flips and sinks.

Like a great dying bird.

CHAPTER 96

I LAND IN a tall pine tree near the back of the house, gripping a thick branch for dear life. My heart rate must be north of three hundred. I give myself a few seconds to settle. Then I glide to the ground and rematerialize.

Tapper, Hawkeye, and Jericho look over when they see me sneaking out of the trees. They've been so focused on the target, I doubt they even saw the fight. But I can tell that they're glad to see me human again.

Jericho points toward the great room above us. It projects out toward the lawn in a large semicircle, with floor-to-ceiling windows. But the curtains inside are drawn shut.

All we can pick up are vague silhouettes, and the low murmur of voices. *Dammit!* This is where Burbank's listening devices would have helped. Too late. No time to go back for him now.

I motion for the others to stay put. For a second, I feel like I'm about to pass out. I realize that it's too soon after my shape-shift to engage another power. My body needs time to adjust. But there is no time. I shake it off, take a deep breath—and turn invisible.

I'm still shaky as I climb up the steps to the side of the

porch. I hold on to the railing to steady myself. I see a
guard standing in front of the side door. A stair creaks
under my weight. The guard turns and looks in my
direction. I bend down and pick up a pebble. I throw it
hard against the wall at the far end of the porch. Old-
est trick in the book. I've been using it for ten thousand years. The guard whips around and starts moving
toward the sound. I slip through the door he's supposed
to be guarding.

The interior of the house is high-end, with custom
moldings and expensive hardwood floors. I pass the
entrance to the kitchen—marble counters and fancy
appliances. Ahead of me, I can see the arched entry to
the great room. The glow reflects out into the hallway.
There's only one person talking now. A woman.

A shiver shoots through me. I know that voice.

It's her.

The Destroyer of Worlds.

"You're weak. Incompetent!" she's saying. "You don't
deserve to lead!"

I come around a thick column at the entryway, and
there she is—hair pulled back from her face, wearing a
gold-embroidered floor-length robe. Like some kind of
ancient royalty. She has her back to a giant video monitor. Under the light from ceiling fixtures, she actually
glows.

I expected a roomful of people for a weapons auction
this important—a whole conclave of miscreants. But I
only see an audience of two, sitting in high-backed chairs
facing the screen. I work my way around to the side of
the room, treading softly. As soon as the profiles of the
two visitors come into view, I freeze.

Toor Bayani, I expected.

But not the man sitting next to him.

It's Lucian Diaz, the president of the Americas.

CHAPTER 97

THE DESTROYER IS talking to the two most powerful men in the world like they were schoolchildren. And they're both just sitting there and taking it.

"You ineffectual *posers*! I played you against each other and you both lost. Your emissaries bid top price for my technology, but neither of you will get it."

"Wait," says Diaz. "There must be some other deal we can make!" He sounds like he's trying to preserve some scrap of authority and dignity. But it's not working.

"The deal is done," says the Destroyer. "And the deal is this: now you both work for me."

Bayani takes a stab at English, heavily accented, but clear. "You cannot threaten me! I control an army of millions!"

"So you do, Minister Bayani," says the Destroyer. "Shall we take a look?"

She turns to the screen behind her. It lights up with a drone's-eye view of a huge Chinasian parade field. Soldiers are lined up in formation for some kind of ceremony or exercise. They're arranged in a dozen battalions of what looks like about a thousand soldiers each. An invasion-sized force.

"I'm sure you recognize the target, Mr. Minister. I believe it's one of your largest bases."

The drone dips lower until it's gliding over the formation at an altitude of about thirty feet. There is no sound accompanying the video. Suddenly, the soldiers start to collapse like rag dolls. Standing at attention one second, dead on the ground the next.

Bayani lets out a guttural growl and jumps up from his seat. Beside him, Diaz squirms.

"Sit down," says the Destroyer. "There's more."

The screen goes black for a second and then lights up again. This time the view shows the Wailing Wall in Jerusalem. Early morning there. But already a mass of pilgrims and visitors is crowding against the ancient structure, sixty feet tall and almost a third of a mile long. Again, the drone swoops low. Again, the bodies drop. Dead in an instant. In seconds, the holy plaza is a carpet of death. Innocent men, women, children.

By now, Bayani and Diaz are both pitched forward in their chairs, staring at the screen. Speechless and numb.

"It's as simple as that," says the Destroyer. "On my command, armies, workers, entire populations, *gone*. What do you think? Maybe it's better to start with a clean slate. Build the whole world up again from scratch. The way it should be. Just the three of us."

I feel sick to my stomach, but my rage is bursting, too. I've felt it a thousand times. Whenever I'm in the presence of total evil.

"And now," says the Destroyer, "something a little closer to home."

She turns and looks directly at me. As if I'm not invisible at all.

"So rude, Lamont," she says. "Don't you know it's impolite to eavesdrop?"

CHAPTER 98

"ENOUGH!" I SHOUT. I rematerialize at the side of the room. Diaz and Bayani both leap out of their chairs.

"Cranston!" Diaz shouts. Like a man grabbing at his last chance.

The Destroyer glares at me. "I knew you'd get here somehow, Lamont. Your friends are superior trackers. Or, *were*. Soon to be past tense, I'm afraid."

The screen shifts to a drone's eye view of the river. Night vision gives the scene a greenish glow, but the details are clear. The speed boat is now floating in the middle of the current. A small rubber Zodiac boat approaches. Inside are Tapper, Hawkeye, and Jericho, with guns to their heads! Their weapons are gone, their shirts ripped, their faces bruised. Guards force them onto the speedboat, crowding them in next to Burbank. The Zodiac speeds off.

"A more intimate demonstration," says the Destroyer. "But maybe more powerful. As you can see, I gathered your associates together one last time. More poetic that way, don't you think? Fight together, die together."

The drone starts to swoop toward the boat. I can see the faces of my team, looking up.

On the screen, the drone is dropping lower and lower. I'm trying to muster my strength, concentrate my powers. I can feel the blood pounding in my ears. I see the faces of my friends. But I can't do anything! In the tiny cockpit, Jericho, Hawkeye, and Tapper are standing strong, like soldiers. At the last second, Burbank drops to his knees, terrified.

I thrust my arm forward. A small fireball shoots across the room. But not fast enough. The Destroyer dodges it. The blast hits the monitor just as the drone makes its final pass. The screen explodes into a thousand pieces.

"Look what you've done!" the Destroyer shouts. "You've spoiled the show! Now they're dead, but you didn't get to watch them die! Have you no sense of *theater*?"

She waves her arms in a fury. Suddenly the room is engulfed in a furious whirlwind. Furniture spins. Light fixtures shatter. Floorboards splinter. A shaft of electricity circles the room. Bayani and Diaz drop to the floor. Diaz stretches his arm toward me. "Stop this!" he yells. The bolt passes through him, then Bayani, incinerating them both in an instant.

The force of the blast rocks me back against the wall. In the center of the carnage, I can see the Destroyer standing poised and calm. Her dark eyes are shining, looking straight at me. I try to stand, but the force of the wind pins me against the wall. I can't move. I can't shout. All I can think about is my friends. *Gone!* My fault!

Suddenly, the Destroyer's shape begins to change. The glow around her intensifies. For a second, it seems like she's dissolving. No! Shape-shifting! The light from her body is blinding, whiting out everything in the room.

A second later, the wind dies down and my vision clears. I can't believe what I'm seeing. The woman in gold is gone—transformed completely.

"Did you miss me, Lamont?"

Dear God! *It's Shiwan Khan!*

CHAPTER 99

THE ROOM IS filled with swirling smoke and the smell of burned flesh. Out on the river, my friends are dead. And now I'm facing my worst enemy. My worst nightmare.

Again!

"I'm glad you're here, Lamont," Khan says. "You and my other witnesses."

I hear footsteps and a struggle in the corridor. *"Leave me alone, you goddamn assholes!"* Maddy's voice! My heart drops. I look toward the entryway. Two guards walk in, shoving Maddy forward. Then four more guards—two holding Jessica, two holding Margo.

"Lamont!" Margo cries out. "I'm sorry! They said they'd kill you if we fought back!"

I start toward them, but suddenly Khan is blocking my way, his gold robe twirling. "See that, Lamont? See how vulnerable love makes you? How it paralyzes you? How it reduces great power to *nothing*?"

I'm crazed with fear and rage, but I try to keep my voice under control. "Let them go, Khan. You've already killed enough people for one day. Keep me, but let them go!"

Khan steps over to my family. "Which one do you think is your biggest weakness, Lamont?" He points to Jessica. "Not this one. Her time is almost up anyway. She's served her purpose, don't you think?" He rests his hand on Jessica's narrow shoulder. She bats it away. "You want to kill an old lady?" she says. "Go ahead. I'm ready. But let the others be!"

Khan ignores her and turns to Maddy. The guards hold her back as Khan runs his long fingers down her cheek. "Or this one. You wouldn't be here without her, would you, Lamont? She's the one who found you. Brought you back to life after your long sleep. She's your heir now." He pauses for a second. "With her skills, she really should be mine."

"Don't touch her!" I shout.

I can see Maddy trembling with fury, but afraid to act on it. She knows that the wrong move right now will get us all killed. So do I.

Khan steps up to Margo. She pulls her head back in disgust. He leans in as if he's about to kiss her, then stops and taps her forehead. "When are you going to stop trying to control my mind, Margo Lane?"

I can see my wife seething.

"Or should I say *Mrs. Cranston*?" says Khan. "The blushing bride. The truth is, I've been jealous of you for a long time—envious of your connection with Lamont. Once, Lamont and I were close. Best friends. Isn't that right, Lamont? Long before the Shadow existed."

I ball my hands into fists, biding my time, trying to gather my strength. "We were never friends. We were training partners—rivals for our teacher's approval. But that was ten thousand years ago!"

Khan takes a step back toward me. "Aren't you curious about why I wanted to try out a female form, Lamont?" He thrusts his finger toward Margo. "Because of *her*! Because I was curious. I wanted to feel what she felt toward you. Just once. It's powerful, isn't it? Love. Desire. But in the end, not stronger than hate. Hate is pure. No complications. Hate can survive on its own."

Suddenly, there's a blast of white light from the center of the room. Khan whips around to face it. The glow intensifies and a figure starts to take shape inside it.

"Dache!" Maddy shouts. "Thank God!"

The brightness dissipates and there he is. In the midst of the smoke and carnage, my old teacher looks as serene as ever, dressed in scarlet robes. I can feel energy radiating from him like a physical force.

"Dache!" Maddy shouts again. "Do something!"

But Dache just stands there. "Not my place, Madeline." He looks at Khan, then at me. "This is their moment, not mine. Everything has been leading to this. These two were once my most accomplished students, miles above the others. But now they are opposite poles in the same universe, with powers that keep escalating. You can see how destructive it is to life on earth—to the whole order of things. So now they must battle alone, as men. And only one can survive."

"That's insane!" Maddy shouts, straining against her guards.

"No, Madeline," says Dache. "It's fate. Not even I can control it."

Khan turns to face me. I see a shift in his eyes and feel the same change happening to me. My energy is draining. The Shadow is gone. I'm just a man with no weapons, terrified of losing my family—and my life.

For the first time in thousands of years, I feel totally powerless. I blink and sense a blur in the air.

The punch knocks me on my ass.

CHAPTER 100

FOR A SPLIT second, all I see is a shower of sparks. Then my vision goes black. I'm on my knees, gasping. My eyes are watering and I can taste blood in my mouth.

I lift my head as my eyesight clears. Khan sheds his robe. Over his gold sirwal pants, his bare torso is muscled like a prizefighter's. Nothing like mine. I should have known this day would come. I should have trained for it.

"Look how soft you are," says Khan. "You should be ashamed."

He's right. I've been leaning on my powers—and on other people. And now it's too late. What have I got now? *Nothing!* I struggle to my feet and raise my fists like a schoolboy. For a few seconds, Khan and I circle each other in the middle of the room.

I can see Dache out of the corner of my eye, arms folded, just watching.

I glance around for something I can grab. Some way to defend myself. Something to even the odds. But there's nothing in reach.

I lunge forward and take a swing. Khan darts away and my momentum throws me off-center. His leg whips around and catches me in the shoulder, knocking me down again. I flash back to our battles in the sand pit in Mongolia. Back then, whoever lost the fight had to go three days without food.

Now I could lose *everything*.

Khan moves forward and lands two quick punches to the side of my head. I back off, dazed. He just keeps coming. I spin around and land a hard kick in his solar plexus. For a second, his diaphragm is paralyzed. I see his eyes go wide as he gasps for breath. While he's reeling, I throw a jab to his jaw, but it's like hitting a brick. He rushes me and grabs me around the waist, flipping me onto my back. I hit the floor hard.

The pain spikes from my tailbone to my skull. I turn toward my family. I can see them shouting, but my brain is numb. All I hear is a loud hum.

I feel myself being lifted by my neck. My hearing clears. My eardrums throb. I feel Khan's hands around my throat. I kick against him, but he just shakes me and squeezes harder. I see Maddy wrest one hand loose and thrust it forward. I pray for a fireball or lightning bolt— even if it blasts Khan and me both.

"Do it!" I grunt.

But nothing comes. The guard pulls Maddy back again. And Dache still doesn't move.

Khan's face is an inch from mine, his teeth bared like a crazed animal. His thumbs are compressing my carotid arteries. I feel myself blacking out. In the fog, I hear Maddy scream. *"Why can't I help him?"*

"Not the time," says Dache firmly.

Time! That's it! My external powers are gone. But I have one last chance. One final forbidden skill. Nothing physical. Just my brain. With my last spark of consciousness—in a single instant—I throw myself into the past.

But this time I'm not just an observer, seeing through somebody else's eyes.

It's me. I'm physically here. Hundreds of years ago.

Along with the man who's trying to kill me.

CHAPTER 101

WE FALL TO the ground—on bare earth. The mansion is gone. Everybody else is gone. It's just the two of us, long before the mansion was built, or even thought of. We're near the top of the cliff, surrounded by raw dirt and boulders. Khan looks around. For a second, I see the confusion in his eyes—then the cold realization. He gets to his feet and regains his balance.

"I salute you, Lamont. You've learned to manipulate time."

I pick myself up slowly. "It's just you and me now. Do you miss the audience?"

"There's a reason this was a forbidden skill," says Khan. "You do realize that when you die here—and you will—everybody you love dies with you. Margo will never conceive your child. Your descendants will never be born. The girl will never exist." He moves in closer, eyes flashing. "Too bad. I think she showed real promise."

I shut him up with a punch to the gut. It doubles him over for a second. It's about all the strength I have left. Before I can reset, Khan launches himself into a spinning kick. I feel a crack in my ribs, like a stick snapping. The pain brings me to my knees.

"This is how I remember you, Lamont. On the ground. My foot on your neck."

I remember it, too. The taste of sand in my mouth. But that was before I had other people to fight for. "Times change," I gasp, holding my side.

Khan moves in and takes a hard swing. I duck, then ram my fist up under his jaw. He staggers back, grinning like a madman, his teeth coated in blood. I move in for another strike, then another, backing Khan toward the edge. He ducks into a crouch and whips around. My reflexes aren't fast enough. His foot catches me on the side of my leg and I hit the ground again, panting for air.

My leg feels numb, maybe broken. I watch as Khan picks up a boulder nearly as wide as his shoulders. He lifts it over his head and holds it there, sighting my skull, looking to crush it. There's one thing I've known about Shiwan Khan since the day we first met. Winning is never enough. He always goes for overkill.

This is my last chance. My *only* chance.

I have no powers left—just the strength in my one good leg. I lunge at Khan, forcing him off-balance. With a furious grunt, he heaves the rock. It grazes my back and lands in the dirt behind me. The cliff is only a few feet away now. With my final burst, I ram my shoulder into his chest. He grabs me as he topples backward. There's nothing I can do. His grip is too strong and the momentum is too much.

We go over the cliff together. A hundred-foot drop.

CHAPTER 102

I SEE THE ripples glitter for an instant before we hit. My head glances off something hard underwater. I'm dazed. Sinking. I try to kick, but I can't. Helpless. No fight left. The water is cold and black. All I can see is my pale arms suspended in front of my face, weak and useless. Then the darkness closes in from behind my eyes—a rapid fade. My breath is gone. My lungs are burning. My mouth opens. I suck in water, cold and gritty. My throat spasms, trying to keep the water out. But it doesn't work. I'm drowning and choking at the same time.

My bad leg hits the bottom and I barely feel it. I'm limp now...just suspended in the flow...drifting...

Suddenly, a shaft of moonlight pierces the water. Through cloudy green ripples, I see figures heading toward me. *Dozens* of them. Getting closer. I can see what they are now. Bloodsucking murderers! The Voodoo Master's mind slaves! The same ones I faced all those years ago. They're moving along the river bottom like a phantom army. Pale, expressionless faces. Scaly arms. They're coming for me! Reaching for me! Then, in an instant, they're gone—dissolving in a cloud of bloody bubbles.

Peace washes over me.

The monsters aren't real.

Nothing can hurt me now.

I'm dead already.

CHAPTER 103

"LAMONT!"

Bang! Bang! Bang!

The pain comes in shocking bursts. Someone is pounding on my chest—like hammer blows. My back arches. I feel water frothing out of my mouth.

I cough. I spit. I gasp.

"Lamont! Breathe, dammit!"

My eyes blink open. Maddy is leaning over me. She's soaking wet, her hair dripping onto my face. I feel hard ground underneath me, and see the cliff looming above. I'm lying on a narrow strip at the river's edge. I roll to my side and vomit on the sand. I can hear the water lapping against the rocks a few feet away. My guts convulse. I take in a gulp of air. Then another. I turn and look back at Maddy. My God! She's real! I grab her arm. "Where's Margo? Where's Jessica?"

"They're all right!" Maddy says. "They're alive. Margo and Grandma. They're safe. The guards took off the second you and Khan vanished. They just ran."

"But how did you . . . ?"

She lifts my head and rests it against her leg. "Dache told me where to find you."

I wipe the water and snot from my face. My memory starts to come back in small flashes. "Dache? He said he wouldn't interfere."

"He didn't," says Maddy. "Lamont—the fight's over. It's done."

I'm trying to make sense of what happened. I must look as confused as I feel.

"Wherever you went," says Maddy, "you're back."

The shock is wearing off and the pain starts shooting through every part of my body. My head. My ribs. My leg. I stare into Maddy's face and squeeze her hand. "If I'm alive, and *you're* alive...then Khan is..."

Maddy nods toward a shelf of granite peeking above the water near my feet. "He must've hit the rocks. Then the current carried him off."

ONLY ONE CAN SURVIVE, Dache said.

It was me.

It *is* me.

I pull Maddy close and feel her heart beating against my aching chest. My whole body is trembling. "Are you ready?" she says. "I'll help you up. Let's go home."

As soon as I put weight on my right leg, sparks shoot up my spine. I start to crumple. I reach for Maddy's shoulder for support. "Wait. Stop," she says. "You can't even walk!"

I ease myself back down to the ground and tip my head back to look at the beautiful night sky, open and welcoming. "No," I tell her, "but I bet I can fly."

CHAPTER 104

TWENTY-FOUR HOURS LATER, I'm feeling almost totally back to life.

My bad leg is stretched out under the dining room table in a homemade splint and I've got a bandage on my head. I'm sore and achy, but happy. It's one of those times when even the hurt feels good. For our celebration dinner, Jessica is serving up her famous lasagna, paired with a few special bottles of wine from the cellar.

Margo shifts her chair closer to mine and squeezes my hand under the table. "Just letting you know," she whispers, "I'm not letting go."

"Joined at the hip," I whisper back. "Forever." Maddy is sitting on my other side, with Bando on her lap. She looks more at peace than I've seen her in a long time. Our wise teacher is sitting at the opposite end. It's a rare honor to have Dache break bread with the family.

But that's not the most amazing part of the guest list tonight.

Because sitting across from me are four people I thought I'd never see again.

"Nice to be back—right, boss?" says Tapper.

Hawkeye stands up to propose a toast. "To the man of the hour!"

He doesn't mean me.

Everybody turns—to Burbank.

Hawkeye raises his glass. "Here's to the only man I know who could divert a killer drone at the very last second—with a jammer built from spare parts."

Burbank almost smiles. "I *told* you you never know what you'll need," he says.

Jericho raises his glass even higher. "I'll never knock you for overpacking again!"

I pick up my glass and stand up halfway. Best I can do. "To Burbank!" I call out.

Everybody clinks and drinks. I can tell that Burbank is still uncomfortable being the center of attention, even when he's more than earned it.

Jessica is at the other end of the table, spooning another helping of lasagna onto Dache's plate. "Eat up," she says. "I made it vegetarian just for you."

Jericho turns toward Maddy with a booming voice. He's already on his second glass of cabernet, or maybe his third. "So—Shadow Girl—how did all this craziness compare to the stories in your book collection?"

The table quiets down. Everybody waits for Maddy's reply. She probably remembers more about the Shadow's adventures than any of us, including me.

"It was right up there," she says. "Pretty satisfying ending." A little pause. "Except for one thing."

I see Dache raise an eyebrow.

Maddy leans forward in her seat. "I have a lingering question," she says. "And it's a big one—mind-blowing, in fact. I've been thinking about it since yesterday."

We all lean in.

Maddy rests her palms on the table and clears her throat. "Okay. The Shadow traveled back in time to kill

Shiwan Khan, right? Hundreds of years in the past." I shift my sore leg. I already know where this is headed. "So if Khan died back then," Maddy continues, "how the hell was he still alive, ready to kill all of us, just last night? Why didn't dying in his past negate his future? Is there some piece of the time–space continuum that I'm missing?"

Tapper thinks about it for a second, then goes back to his lasagna. "Way over my head," he says.

"If he's gone now, does it really matter?" asks Hawkeye.

"Actually, it's a very good question," says Margo. She looks down to the end of the table. "Maybe Dache can answer it for us."

We all look in his direction. Dache takes a slow sip of his wine.

"How about it, Dache?" asks Maddy. "Does it mean Khan isn't really gone? Is he lingering in some other dimension?"

Dache stays silent for a few seconds, as if he's thinking it over. Then he smiles.

"Sorry, Madeline," he says. "No lessons tonight. Only lasagna."

"Good enough for me!" booms Jericho.

And that's it. Everybody goes back to eating and drinking. Margo leans over to whisper in my ear. "I know what you're thinking."

She usually does.

What I'm thinking is that Dache knows the answer to Maddy's question. He just doesn't want to spoil the evening. Just like I know there's still a supply of deadly bioagent out there in the world, waiting to be found and unleashed. Not to mention a crop of evil schemers angling to fill the shoes of Toor Bayani and Lucian Diaz.

"Let it go for tonight," whispers Margo. "Enjoy this." She plants a kiss on my cheek.

My wife is right, as usual. I'll take a few sweet hours to celebrate life with my family and my friends, and give thanks that we've all survived this far. Tomorrow, it starts all over again.

Because if there's one thing I've learned, it's that when one evil dies, another rises up to replace it. It's been that way for as long as I've been alive—which is a very long time.

The Shadow's work is never done.

EPILOGUE

THE NEXT MORNING, Dan Rickter strokes his mottled gray beard as he motors slowly down the Hudson. He's relieved to have his high-powered speedboat back. A kayaker found it floating mid-river about ten miles north. There's no obvious damage, but Rickter is going easy until he can have his guy at the marina check things out.

As he purrs along the shoreline, he spots a piece of smooth driftwood floating about twenty feet out. He angles to avoid it. As he passes by, something makes him turn and look again. *What the hell…?*

Rickter cranks the wheel around, then shuts the engines down. As the boat drifts past the object, he peers over the stern and recoils.

He's staring at a dead man's back.

Rickter scans the river for help. Nobody in sight. He reaches out and pokes the body with his finger. It bobs lightly. Below the waterline, he can make out dangling gold pantlegs and a head with long, jet-black hair.

Stomach turning, he grabs a length of line and loops it around the torso. He grits his teeth and hauls the corpse aboard. The dead man flops onto the deck, faceup, eyes open and blank. The left side of his skull is caved in. A string of green weeds is wrapped around his bare muscular chest.

Rickter leans forward. Suddenly, he feels a blast inside his head, so sharp it makes his knees buckle. In his mind, he sees the same man—powerfully alive—dressed in a gold robe and surrounded by bolts of lightning. His eyes are flashing, his long black hair whipping in the wind, his name echoing like the howl of a hurricane.

Khaaaan!

Rickter stumbles back in shock, blinking as his vision clears. Suddenly, the corpse's gut begins to bulge, like it's boiling inside. Rickter is thrown against the steering wheel. He hears a sound like ripping canvas and sees the man's belly split open from ribs to waist.

He watches, trembling, as nine fat eels slither out of the cavity, leaving a trail of blood and mucus on the deck. They wriggle on the cockpit floor like snakes, two feet long and thick as the corpse's forearm, with gaping jaws and razor teeth.

Rickter kicks frantically. One of his shoes flies off. An eel wraps around his bare ankle like a wet fist. As he tries to twist away, he slips and lands on the slime-covered deck. In a second, the eels are on him, working their way into the legs of his shorts and up to his throat, digging in with sharp teeth—draining the life right out of him.

Rickter's shrieks are loud and horrible, but they don't last long.

Their work complete, the creatures slither overboard and move in relentless undulations toward Manhattan, like nerves of a single brain.

Khaaaan!

ABOUT THE AUTHORS

James Patterson is the most popular storyteller of our time. He is the creator of unforgettable characters and series, including Alex Cross, the Women's Murder Club, Jane Effing Smith, and Maximum Ride, and of breathtaking true stories about the Kennedys, John Lennon, and Princess Diana, as well as our military heroes, police officers, and ER nurses. He has coauthored #1 bestselling novels with Bill Clinton and Dolly Parton, told the story of his own life in *James Patterson by James Patterson*, and received an Edgar Award, nine Emmy Awards, the Literarian Award from the National Book Foundation, and the National Humanities Medal.

Brian Sitts is an award-winning advertising creative director and television writer. He has collaborated with James Patterson on books for adults and children. He and his wife, Jody, live in Peekskill, New York.

JAMES
PATTERSON
RECOMMENDS

JAMES PATTERSON
AND BRIAN SITTS
THE NEW YORK TIMES BESTSELLER
CRIME HAS A NEW ENEMY.
THE SHADOW
A THRILLER

THE SHADOW

Only two people know that 1930s society man Lamont Cranston has a secret identity as the Shadow, a crusader for justice—well, make that three if you include me, and it is my great honor to reimagine his story. But the other two are his greatest love, Margo Lane, and his fiercest enemy, Shiwan Khan. When Khan ambushes the couple, they must risk everything for the slimmest chance of survival...in the future.

A century and a half later, Lamont awakens in a world both unknown and disturbingly familiar. Most disturbing, Khan's power continues to be felt over the city and its people. No one in this new world understands the dangers of stopping him better than Lamont Cranston. And only the Shadow knows that he's the one person who might succeed before more innocent lives are lost.

THE PERFECT ASSASSIN

They never tell you how savage academic work really is. So, when Dr. Brandt Savage is on sabbatical from the University of Chicago he finds himself surprisingly enrolled in a school where he is the sole pupil. His professor, "Meed," is demanding. She's also his captor.

Savage emerges from their intensive training sessions physically and mentally transformed, but with no idea *why* he's been chosen. Then his first mission with Meed takes them back to her training ground, where Savage learns how deeply entwined their two lives have been. To prevent a new class of killers from escaping this harsh place where their ancestors first fought to make a better world, they must pledge anew: *Do right to all, and wrong to no one.*

DEATH OF THE BLACK WIDOW

A twenty-year-old woman murders her kidnapper with a competence so impeccable that Detroit PD Officer Walter O'Brien is taken aback. It's pretty rare for my detectives to be this shocked. But what Officer O'Brien doesn't know is that this young woman has a knack for ending the lives of her lovers—and getting away with it.

Time after time, she navigates her way out of police custody. Soon Walter becomes fixated on uncovering the truth. And when he discovers that he's not alone in his search, one thing is certain. This deadly string of secrets didn't begin in his home city…but he's going to make sure it ends there.

JAMES PATTERSON

AND

BILL CLINTON

#1
NEW YORK TIMES
BESTSELLER

THE
PRESIDENT'S
DAUGHTER

"PROPULSIVE, EXHILARATING, AND
UNNERVINGLY BELIEVABLE." —KARIN SLAUGHTER

THE PRESIDENT'S DAUGHTER

All presidents have nightmares. This one is about to come true.

Matthew Keating, a onetime Navy SEAL—*and a past president*—has always defended his family as staunchly as he has his country. Now those defenses are under attack.

A madman abducts Keating's teenage daughter, Melanie—turning every parent's deepest fear into a matter of national security. As the world watches in real time, Keating embarks on a one-man special-ops mission that tests his strengths: as a leader, warrior, and father.

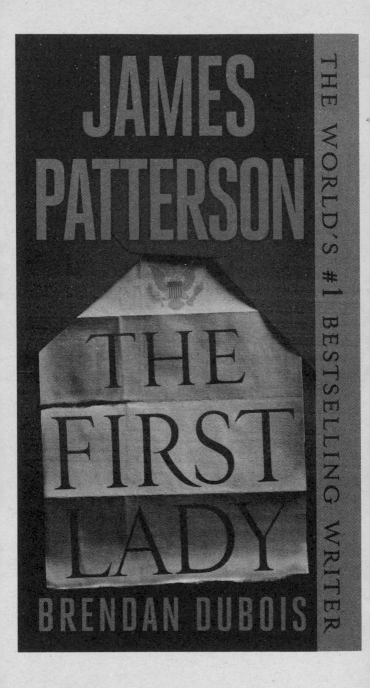

JAMES PATTERSON

THE FIRST LADY

BRENDAN DUBOIS

THE WORLD'S #1 BESTSELLING WRITER

THE FIRST LADY

The US government is at the forefront of everyone's mind these days and I've become fascinated by the idea that one secret can bring it all down. What if that secret is a US president's affair that results in a nightmarish outcome?

Sally Grissom, leader of the Presidential Protection Division, is summoned to a private meeting with the president and his chief of staff to discuss the disappearance of the first lady. What at first seemed an escape to a safe haven turns into a kidnapping when a ransom note arrives along with what could be the first lady's finger.

It's a race against the clock to collect the evidence that all leads to one troubling question: Could the kidnappers be from inside the White House?

For a complete list of books by
JAMES PATTERSON

VISIT
JamesPatterson.com

**Follow James Patterson on Facebook
@JamesPatterson**

**Follow James Patterson on X
𝕏 @JP_Books**

**Follow James Patterson on Instagram
@jamespattersonbooks**